Advance Praise for *It Started with a Whisper*

"Everyone wants to get their hands on this book."

—Z100 Elvis Duran

"What *Devil* did for the world of fashion, *Whisper* does for the world of gossip."

—*OK! Magazine*

"If Jackie Collins and Truman Capote had a child, it would be Rob Shuter."

—*Radar Online*

Also By Rob Shuter

The 4 Word Answer: Who Are You in 4 Words?

It Started with a Whisper

a novel—based on a thousand true stories

Rob Shuter

Post Hill Press

A POST HILL PRESS BOOK
ISBN: 979-8-89565-509-2
ISBN (eBook): 979-8-89565-510-8

It Started with a Whisper:
A Novel—Based on a Thousand True Stories

Cover design by Jim Villaflores

Post Hill Press
New York • Nashville
posthillpress.com

Published in the United States of America
1 2 3 4 5 6 7 8 9 10

To the leakers, the eavesdroppers, and
the "just between us" crowd—
You made this book possible.
And to anyone who ever said, "I probably
shouldn't be telling you this…"
Thank you for your service.

"Gossip is just news running ahead of itself in a red satin dress."
Liz Smith, The World Greatest Gossip Columnist!

Chapter 1

I was the first to hear the whispers. Not the loud, crashing kind that announces itself like an uninvited guest, but the soft, insidious kind that slips into the room, curling around your ankles.

Across the table, under the glare of the studio lights, sat Carol Ann. The show's token "hot girl." She had that lethal combination of Southern charm and Manhattan power, wrapped up in a package that could stop traffic—or reroute it entirely. Her drawl? Pure molasses, slow and sticky, but sharp enough to cut you if you didn't handle it with care.

She was sweet tea masquerading as Dom Pérignon, served in a Baccarat goblet with a sprig of mint—a detail as unnecessary as it was deliberate. Every inch of her was precision-engineered: the designer wardrobe tailored to perfection, the blonde waves cascading like liquid gold, and a body that could get away with murder.

But underneath all that polish, there was a story. Not a fairy tale, but rather a story as unpredictable and dangerous as the Mississippi River, just waiting for someone foolish enough to drive in.

Seated next to Carol Ann was Delores, radiating the kind of effortless majesty that could silence a room without so much as a glance. Her new silver wig wasn't just a style choice—it was a crown, a gleaming emblem of her authority in a world that often refused to see her. She wore it with the confidence of someone who'd long stopped asking for a seat at the table and simply brought her own throne.

But these days, Delores wasn't just Delores. Thanks to the show's Executive Producer, she was "Miss D." A non-threatening, endlessly loyal confidante designed to make the audience feel safe.

It wasn't a role she chose—it was one she mastered.

Her age? Oh, honey. That was as much a mystery as the love life of Shawn Mendes. All you needed to know was this: she looked *phenomenal.* A beauty so classic it wasn't just timeless—it was a personal affront to every expensive serum you've ever regretted buying. Her secret? A strict gym regimen and a taste for younger white men that she didn't just indulge, she celebrated.

Miss D wasn't aging gracefully; she was rewriting the damn script.

And then there was Mary—my best friend, my ride-or-die, bless her overachieving little heart. She had that bookish, slightly frazzled energy of someone who didn't just slog through *War and Peace* cover to cover, but somehow managed to come out the other side with insights so sharp they could double as stand-up material.

Her thick, oversized glasses? Gone. Banished from the show by some suit in a corner office who declared them "too lesbian" for daytime TV. So now there was Mary, squinting her way through each segment like a woman on a mission.

She wore a basic black blouse and skirt with the kind of no-nonsense determination that practically screamed, *I'm a serious journalist, thank you very much.* It was equal parts endearing and exasperating. And somehow, so perfectly Mary.

And then there was me—James. Dead center, presiding over a court of chaos, pretending I had everything under control. At 6'1", I had a presence that was impossible to ignore, whether I wanted the attention or not.

This wasn't my first stint in the splash zone of the spotlight. Years as a celebrity publicist—and as the youngest of five children, which, let's be real, might've been better training—had taught me how to navigate the glittering minefield of egos, scandals, and truly difficult people with a smile that screamed, *Everything's fine!*

It was a performance, sure, but one I'd mastered so completely that even I believed it most days.

But beneath the tailored trousers and the air of studied calm, my right hand stayed firmly tucked in my pocket. My "little arm," as I'd quietly named it. Damaged from birth, it was both my truth and my secret—the part of me that didn't fit the narrative I'd built. The part I wasn't ready to share with the world. If I'm being honest, I wasn't even sure I'd fully shared it with myself.

Together, we misfits—Mary, Carol Ann, Miss D, and I—helmed *The Gossip Gang,* the scrappy underdog of morning television. It wasn't glamorous, and it wasn't polished. In fact, it was the kind of budget-friendly production you'd expect from a struggling cable channel best known for washed-up comedians and reruns no one remembered watching the first time around.

No, it wasn't *The Today Show,* or *Good Morning America,* or even Gayle King's gig on CBS. But it was ours. And for better or worse, it had become the glue holding the four of us together.

Hovering at the edges of the set, four jittery production assistants darted around like caffeinated hummingbirds, clutching bottles of sparkling water and tins of mints as their eyes flicked anxiously to the door. We were all waiting—for *him.*

Then, as though conjured by some dark cosmic force, he appeared: the man we simply called *Producer.*

He didn't so much walk into the studio as *materialize,* bringing with him an aura that was equal parts boyish charm and divine authority. His thick, dark hair was in its perpetual state of artful disarray.

The second he arrived, it was like the air shifted, sharp and electric. I could never quite decide if he was the calm at the center of the storm or the storm itself. It didn't matter. Either way, when he walked in, Mary, Miss D, Carol Ann, and I snapped to attention.

Without a word, he made a beeline for the cue cards, his movements deliberate and precise. To anyone else, they were flimsy rectangles of cardstock. To him, they were the levers of control, the strings he used to guide the show—and us—with surgical precision.

The studio clock ticked closer to 9 a.m., its relentless hum filling the room with the tension of a bomb about to detonate.

Producer eyes darted across the room, scanning us with the precision of a sniper, each glance a silent critique. Flaws weren't just noticed; they were *cataloged.*

This wasn't his first rodeo—far from it. Producer had once been the golden boy of morning television, a star who could do no wrong. But that shine? Long gone, dulled to a muted sheen no amount of polish could ever bring back. The gleaming awards from a past life were no longer triumphs. They were tombstones, silent reminders of how far he'd fallen.

"Five, four, three, two..." His voice cut through the studio like a razor, each syllable sharp, deliberate, and unnervingly precise, as if conducting a masterpiece only he could hear.

Then, like clockwork, the red light blinked on. Showtime. We stepped into the spotlight, not as performers in a symphony, but as players in his perfectly *out-of-tune* orchestrated chaos.

The jib camera swooped in, its mechanical arm gliding with the precision of a graceful hawk. It swept over Miss D's wig and zeroed in on my dark brown, fur-like locks. For a moment, I froze, my gaze locking with Producer's sharp, unrelenting eyes.

And then, like flipping a switch, I came alive. Leaning forward, I let a playful smile spread across my face.

"Darlings," I began, my tone dripping with faux innocence, "has Reese treated herself to a facial...*down there*? Carol Ann will reveal *all* in a few minutes."

Below me, the chyron blazed to life, screaming in bold letters: Legally Bare!

The camera swirled away from me and landed squarely on Carol Ann. It lingered, utterly captivated by her every calculated wiggle, her sequins catching the light like a thousand tiny paparazzi flashbulbs. For a moment, it seemed the lens might never leave her, as if even the camera itself had fallen under her spell. But with what felt like genuine reluctance, it finally swung back to me.

"Prepare yourselves, poppets," I continued, letting a knowing glint flash in my eye. "Miss D is about to unveil the secrets behind Jada Pinkett Smith's stunning revenge body."

And then it happened. Disaster.

A shot of Kerry Washington—not Jada—flashed across the screen. My stomach dropped, but in live television, there's no time to panic. You don't fixate on problems; you simply pretend they never happened.

"And to top it all off," I pivoted, my voice as smooth as butter, "my best mate Mary is here to share a brilliant story of her evening with none other than... *OPRAH herself!*"

I leaned forward and unleashed my best larger-than-life Oprah impression:

"You get an Oprah. You get an Oprah. *Everyone gets an Oprah!*"

Mary blushed, caught between mortification and delight.

"So, my dears, don't go anywhere," I declared. "Because after a short break, we're about to dive headfirst into..."

"*THE GOSSIP GANG!*" we chimed together, almost harmonious, though Carol Ann's lilt lingered just a beat longer, like the final note of a country ballad.

We were officially in our four-minute break. The live feed had been replaced with a cringeworthy medley of 1-800 ads, the kind that hawked everything from memory foam pillows to "miracle" weight-loss teas. You could practically hear the desperation: *We couldn't sell this slot to a real advertiser.*

I blew my Roman nose, the sound ricocheting through the room like a misplaced cymbal crash in an already chaotic symphony. It didn't just cut through the tension—it practically slashed it.

Miss D, unbothered, was hunched over her ancient flip phone, scrolling with laser focus. It was the kind of intensity usually reserved for a breaking news alert—or a particularly scandalous text thread.

Carol Ann, meanwhile, was delicately plucking a handful of stray brunette hairs from her lap. Each one was scrutinized with an intensity that suggested it might unlock some secret, before being flicked away like an unwanted souvenir from a trip best forgotten.

Mary sat stiffly, her discomfort palpable, practically radiating off her in waves. The regret over her secret pancake breakfast was scrawled across her face, syrup-soaked shame clinging to her like the memory of a poorly chosen one-night stand.

And then, like a storm rolling in, Producer marched toward the table, his every step deliberate, his presence looming like a thundercloud on legs.

"That was an absolute *disaster!*"

Carol Ann froze mid-hair pluck. Miss D's furious texting came to an abrupt halt. Even Mary found her regret momentarily eclipsed by a sharper, more immediate dread.

But Producer wasn't finished. His grievances poured out like drinks at a Bravo reunion.

"Do you know how many Emmys I have?" he demanded. "*Four!*" he continued, holding up his fingers for emphasis. "One, two, three, *four!*"

Mary's ever-curious mind imagined the exact whereabouts of Producer's prized possessions. Surely, they occupied a shrine-like spot in his undoubtedly opulent Upper East Side apartment. A gleaming, glass-fronted display case, illuminated to perfection, sitting proudly in the corner of a tastefully curated living room.

Her lips parted, a question hovering on the edge of her tongue, but she quickly shut her mouth, snapping back to reality as her eyes landed on the looming countdown clock.

"*Thirty seconds!*" Producer barked, his voice slicing through the tension with the accuracy of a whip crack.

"Five, Carol Ann, hit Witherspoon *hard*," he commanded like a general rallying troops in the face of a losing battle. "Four,

Mary, go *soft* on Oprah. Three, Miss D, imply Jada slaps harder than her husband. Two, James, a little less...*gay.*"

And just like that, we slipped back into delivering celebrity gossip, mixing drama and humor with the finesse of seasoned performers.

But beneath the scoops and the soundbites, something far more interesting simmered: our own secrets. Bubbling just below the surface, waiting to escape.

We, of all people, should have known better. The thing about secrets? They never stayed buried forever. No matter how carefully you hid them, no matter how tightly you sealed the lid, they always clawed their way toward the light.

And when, *not if,* Mary, Carol Ann, Miss D, and my secrets finally surfaced, they wouldn't just rival the Hollywood scandals we dissected for the cameras.

They would *eclipse* them.

And, as always, I knew it would start with a whisper.

Chapter 2

Six months earlier, I stood at the top of the red carpet, the world around me a blur of flashing cameras and murmured conversations, the cold evening sharp against my skin.

As I waited for my client to arrive at her premiere, I slid my little arm into my pant pocket, as I always did.

My practiced eyes performed a final sweep over the meticulously arranged settings. I knew her tastes, her preferences, her aversions—better than I knew my own. The lighting had to be a soft, rosy pink, casting a warm, dreamy glow that was flattering but never obvious. The temperature must remain at a perfect seventy-six degrees, comfortable enough to feel like a gentle embrace but cool enough to ensure not a single bead of sweat would betray her. And carnations? Heaven forbid. If one of those audacious flowers dared to make an appearance, it would be the end of my career as I knew it.

Members of the media stood at their carefully assigned positions, ready to shout questions as celebrity guests arrived. Among them, I spotted one of my favorite reporters: Delores. Her talent was undeniable. And yet, despite this, she was still stationed well behind Billy Bush and almost everyone else on the carpet.

To the assembled crowd, it was dazzling, thrilling, intoxicating.

To me, amidst the glittering backdrop, I felt invisible.

First came Hoda Kotb, her bright, infectious smile cutting through the camera flashes like a beacon.

Next was the newly crowned *People* magazine's "Sexiest Man Alive," Josh Ellis, who had transitioned seamlessly from world-class athlete to America's favorite new morning show anchor.

Then, navigating the scene with less success, came Keegan Kelly, a host from a struggling cable channel trying to claw her way back into relevance. She arrived with her usual plus-one, the fame-thirsty psychic Johnny Futura.

But it was a figure further down the press line that truly caught my attention. A handsome producer with thick dark hair whose face still bore the faint traces of his former Emmy award–winning triumphs.

Somewhere concealed within the media maelstrom, I knew my best friend, Mary, was to be found. Mary—always the observer rather than the observed—wielded her journalistic prowess with a nuanced finesse that few could match.

I had never envisioned I would end up in New York, the center of the universe, but then again, I had never imagined I'd end up with someone as extraordinary as my American husband, Ari, at the center of my life either.

Ari—a silver-haired, majestic fox of a man with eyes as blue and dreamy as a Sinatra tune—strode into my world like the opening notes of an overture. Fifteen years my senior, fate brought my Brooklyn-born Jewish songwriter to Edinburgh where I was studying. He was there testing out his new musical before it headed to London's West End. I was working part time at the theater, selling ice cream to pay for school.

Our worlds collided over a chocolate cornetto, and in that moment, something melted between us—something far sweeter and more enduring.

"What do you recommend?" Ari asked, a cadence that carried more charm than any line I'd heard before.

"Depends. Are you feeling adventurous, or shall we stick to the classics?" I teased, hoping the sexy American would choose me!

Ari laughed, a rich, warm sound that wrapped around me like a perfectly tailored coat on a chilly Edinburgh evening. "Surprise me," he said, and surprise him I did.

Over the next few weeks, our connection deepened in ways I hadn't thought possible. He made me feel seen as we spent evening after evening wandering the romantic cobblestone streets, their quiet magic weaving seamlessly into the fabric of our growing bond.

From the outside, I knew what the straight world might assume about us. Whispers about financial motivations and green cards thinly veiled in polite curiosity, the casual cruelty of people trying to make sense of what they didn't understand.

But for me, it had never been about the money or America.

The truth—the fabulous gay truth—was that it had always been about something deeper with him, something only the heart, not the head, could comprehend.

Soon, the rhythm of newfound love carried me across the ocean, landing with my love in the heart of New York City.

Fresh off the plane, wide-eyed and dazzled by the neon glow of possibility, I got a job as a receptionist at a big-time publicist firm from Los Angeles that had just opened a sleek new office on the East coast.

Back then, I assumed famous folks were born under some enchanted celestial alignment.

I was about to learn the truth.

Stars weren't born—they were meticulously crafted. Their edges were smoothed, their flaws seemingly polished away until they gleamed with an otherworldly perfection. And I was about to discover that the transformation wasn't just for them.

Faster than a Kardashian marriage, I climbed the ranks. From receptionist, I ascended to junior publicist. And now, here I was, standing at the top of the red carpet, waiting for my A-list client to arrive.

"Hey, James," came a familiar voice. I turned to see Kevin, a wiry photographer with a camera slung over his shoulder, like an extension of himself.

"What's it like to be the King of New York? Everyone kissing your ass?"

With a cheeky British wink, I replied, "I prefer the word *bottom.*"

Kevin, ever persistent, finally got to what I knew he really wanted—*her,* not me.

"I'll kiss whatever you want if you set up a solo full-length shot when she arrives," he said. Then, with a devilish wink, he added, "How about I give you $400 cash—or something even better?"

"Keep your money and your kisses," I replied with a smile that managed to be both polite and firm. "I shall see what I can do."

Before Kevin could utter another word, I spotted the unmistakable silhouette of her silver Phantom Rolls Royce as it glided to a halt at the top of the carpet.

I quickly ran over and opened her car door. A long, impossibly elegant leg emerged first. It was as if a curtain had risen, signaling to the universe that the real star of the evening had arrived.

The assembled press screamed their demands. "To the left!" "To the right!" "Over the shoulder!" "Up here!" "Down below!"

Of course, I obliged when not forgetting the special favor for wiry Kevin.

This was the circle of celebrity life in its purest form. Stars needed the press, while the press needed the stars. And none of it worked without the fans across the street.

"Maybe a little nod to the folks across the street?" I suggested. "Some of them have been waiting overnight."

My plea was met with impassive nonchalance.

Undeterred, I pivoted seamlessly.

"Stick to the talking points," I encouraged, placing her in front of the flamboyant *Entertainment Tonight* reporter like a dog with a bone.

"We're hearing Oscar buzz," the gay host said with a straight face.

"And that is why you always secure the top position." I giggled to myself, knowing he had said exactly the same thing to Taylor Swift at the premiere of *Cats*. Meow!

As the media line wore on and on, I made a subtle gesture—a wave of my left hand, meant to signal the press to pick up the pace.

But instead, without so much as breaking stride, she spat out her gum directly into my outstretched palm.

I guess it was the only benefit of being invisible. I didn't feel embarrassed, I didn't feel ashamed. I felt numb.

Before I could find somewhere discreet to deposit the sticky gum—a voice sliced through the crowd.

My gaze fell on a beautiful blonde unfamiliar face, microphone in hand, with CNN's unmistakable logo emblazoned across it.

"One question," I announced, preoccupied with the mess at hand.

I didn't catch the question, but my client's response caught me like a lightning bolt.

"I think Putin should have been *People*'s sexiest," she replied, as if she were discussing her favorite brand of coffee.

I froze, a thousand thoughts racing through my mind. Damage control. Spin. Headlines. Social media.

"No more questions!" I barked as I placed a firm hand on her back and quickly guided her toward the press-free sanctuary of the theater.

Once safe inside, my fingers darted to my phone as I dialed CNN's assignment desk. If I could strike a quick quid pro quo deal, maybe—just maybe—I could ensure her answer would never see the light of day.

"I need to speak to someone about the red-carpet premiere this evening," I began, my voice as steady as I could manage under the circumstances.

"We didn't send a crew to a premiere tonight," the voice replied, blunt and matter of fact. "Budget cuts. We don't cover entertainment or, honestly, much of anything else anymore."

The words hung in the air, stark and unceremonious, like the sound of a door slamming shut.

I refused to give up. If CNN wasn't behind the rogue question, then who could it be? This was where the real *most trusted name in news* could help—my best pal, Mary.

She picked up on the second ring, her voice muffled, her mouth unmistakably full.

"Sorry, I can't talk for long," she said, mid-chew. "I'm at a restaurant waiting for a source."

"This is important. I will be quick," I pressed on. "Did you notice the young reporter holding a CNN microphone at the premiere tonight?"

There was a pause. "I stopped caring about CNN the day they replaced Don Lemon with Kaitlan Collins," Mary declared. "Call you in the morning. Gotta go. My source just arrived."

And just like that, Mary's attention was diverted, by the arrival of her favorite sauce: chocolate!

Lost in my problem, I barely noticed Kevin, sidling up to me with a sly grin and a mysterious gift in his hand.

"For the boss," he said, slipping the small package into my left trouser pocket.

As fast as he arrived, Kevin disappeared, back into the crowd of jostling photographers like a magician after a successful trick.

Before I could dwell on it further, my phone buzzed. Hoping for an update about the rogue reporter, I answered quickly.

"James here," I said, already preparing to juggle whatever new complication awaited me.

The voice on the other end stopped me cold. It belonged to someone I hadn't expected at all: the handsome producer with the thick dark hair.

I instinctively reverted to autopilot. "I'm sorry, she's not available for any more interviews."

"I'm not calling about her or any of your other clients. I am calling about *you*," he replied.

That never happened. And it immediately got my attention.

I straightened up. "Me?" I repeated, the word catching in my throat.

"The network wants to test out a new morning gossip show," he proudly continued. "And I want *you* to host it."

For a moment, the words didn't quite compute, like hearing a sentence in a language you didn't realize you understood. *Me? Hosting?*

"Why?" I asked, the word tumbling out before I could stop it.

"Because you know the ins and outs of the world of entertainment better than anyone else out there," he replied without missing a beat. "You've got the connections, the instincts, and let me be honest, that British charm. Plus, you've been recommended by someone I trust as much as my own dearly departed father."

That part caught me off guard. My mind immediately started scrolling through possibilities, but his tone didn't invite questions.

"Think about it," he added. "This could be the start of something big for the both of us."

Then the line went silent, leaving me standing there, suspended between exhilaration and fear. He wanted *me.* The notion was so foreign it bordered on intoxicating, like the dizzying first sip of champagne on an empty stomach.

In that instant, the suffocating numbness that had cocooned me for so long melted away.

For the first time in what felt like forever, I was seen. Not as the orchestrator, the fixer, the shadow pulling strings behind the stars, but as *me.*

And for the first time in an eternity, I felt alive.

An hour later, I found myself back in the haven of my chic apartment I shared with Ari. Its sleek lines, quiet modern elegance, and carefully curated decor were a sanctuary from the loud outside world. Tonight, though, tranquility was the last thing I felt.

With Ari at the recording studio, submerged in a world of music and passion, and Mary working late—no doubt elbow-deep in some scandalous tidbit she'd uncovered—I was left alone. Just me, and the steady hum of my insecurities filling the empty spaces.

As I slid my hand into my pocket, my fingers brushed against something unexpected. A jolt of surprise rippled through me.

I reached in and pulled it out—a small glass vial.

Kevin's "gift." The one he'd so nonchalantly slipped into my trouser pocket earlier, as if it were nothing more than a stick of gum. But it wasn't.

You see, Kevin wasn't just the photographer to the stars; he was their drug dealer too.

For a moment, I just stared at it, catching the dim light of the apartment. It sat in my hand like a cruel solution, daring me to react.

After a pause, I reached for my wallet, pulling out a crisp twenty-pound note tucked neatly inside.

A relic of home.

It wasn't just currency—it was a memory. A tangible reminder of who I used to be, back when my world was smaller, simpler, and infinitely happier.

Buoyed by the surge of confidence coursing through my veins, I felt a spark ignite deep within. It was thrilling, the kind of boldness that made the impossible feel possible, as if all the barriers I had built for myself had crumbled away.

I picked up my phone, fingers hovering over the screen before typing the words that would change my life.

I want to host the show.

Chapter 3

In lower Manhattan, where dreams were traded like stocks and ambition coursed through the air like electricity, Mary moved with the assuredness of someone who had not only mastered the professional urban jungle but thrived in it.

She entered the bustling newsroom in her comfortable jeans and her favorite cat sweater—a whimsical, almost defiant choice in a city that revered sharp suits and even sharper tongues. Yet somehow, it worked.

Inside, the newsroom keyboards clattered like machine guns, phones rang incessantly, and the hum of deadlines loomed over everything like a storm cloud. But within that chaos, Mary carved out a sanctuary.

Her cubicle, a bastion of order standing in stark contrast to everything around her. Each document was precisely labeled, color-coded with a meticulousness that could bring tears to a librarian's eyes. Even the surfaces gleamed, hinting at wipe-downs with the kind of devotion most people reserved for skincare routines.

As Mary settled into her chair, her gaze drifted to the chunky turquoise necklace draped over her desk lamp, a cherished piece from Joan Rivers's QVC collection. The necklace wasn't just an accessory; it was a memory, a keepsake from a whirlwind evening when Mary had interviewed her idol fresh off her *Celebrity Apprentice* victory.

But today, like every other day, there was no time to dwell on the memories. The past had no place here—not when the present was calling with its relentless demands.

Mary's phone rang. She adjusted her oversized black glasses and sighed, knowing exactly what lay on the other end.

"It never happened," the PR rep's voice oozed forced confidence, his spin sliding effortlessly from his lips like butter on hot toast.

Mary rolled her eyes, her patience already circling the drain. "It's not so bad," she replied dryly. "Who hasn't pooped their pants in public?"

The call ended with a resounding *click*, just as a large figure cast a shadow over her impeccably tidy desk.

"You've got a unique way of dealing with your comment calls," her editor mused, a glimmer of admiration flickering in his otherwise cynical eyes. "You should be on TV."

She delivered her retort without so much as pausing her furious typing. "Do you mind?" she snapped. "*TV* is for people too stupid to read. I'm a writer."

He chuckled, shaking his head in defeat. "Well, grab your pen, Shakespeare," he quipped. "You're late for the morning meeting."

For the past decade, this had been Mary's existence.

By day, she pounded away at her keyboard, her fingers flying across the keys as she unraveled stories with purpose. By night, she chased whispers, slipping into the shadows where secrets lived, piecing together the truth no one wanted told.

It wasn't just a job; it was her calling. Mary thrived on the thrill of discovery, the electric jolt of knowing she had something no one else did. Scandals didn't just land on her desk—she cornered them and wrangled them into something that could set the city ablaze.

As the evening descended, Mary meticulously cleaned the day's dirt off her desk. Each swipe felt almost ritualistic, as though she were washing away the scandal itself.

Tonight, she had something to look forward to—time with the only publicist who told her the truth—her best friend, me.

Nestled between 24th and 25th streets on Tenth Avenue in Chelsea, Bottino's wasn't just a neighborhood spot; it was *their* spot.

Mary burst through the door in a swirl of exasperation. "I'm wetter than Whitney Houston in a bathtub!"

With practiced correctness, she shrugged off her soaking coat and carefully placed her precious bag—her true priority—on an empty chair, shielding it from any splashes.

"Just think about it," she quipped. "If Whitney had taken a shower instead, she might still be alive."

I let out a reaction caught somewhere between genuine shock and absolute delight.

The waiter approached with the quiet efficiency of someone who'd seen it all. Without a word, he set our plates down.

Mary's usual vegetarian pasta sat before her, a pristine masterpiece she'd ordered countless times but almost never touched. By contrast, my plate was a hearty, well-done steak—an unapologetic British indulgence.

"What's new?" Mary asked, her tone light but her reporter's curiosity gleaming just beneath the surface.

"Oh, nothing much," I began, leaning back in my chair with deliberate nonchalance. "Just that a prominent producer wants to make a television show with me."

Mary froze mid-sip, her glass hovering just inches from her lips. Her eyes were sparkling behind her glasses.

"Talk about burying the lead, James!" she exclaimed. "Congratulations—you will get the show amazing press."

I shook my head, leaning forward with a giddy smile. "He doesn't want me to *do publicity* for it, Mary. He wants me to *host* it."

Her jaw dropped. "*Host it?*" she echoed, the words heavy with disbelief.

I nodded. "Apparently, he's got four Emmys," I added, as though that tidbit alone solidified my new path.

A surge of excitement swept over her, her face lighting up like a Christmas tree. "You're going to be *famous,*" she declared, as if my success were her own.

I couldn't help but grin, basking in the glow of her enthusiasm, but I wasn't done. There was more. "I want you to be a part of it with me," I said.

Mary blinked, the statement hitting her like an unexpected curveball. "James, I'm a *writer,* not a TV host," she protested, her hands instinctively diving into her beloved Chloé bag. Out came her trusty notebook, its pages overflowing with half-finished jokes and snippets of ideas she was clearly more comfortable hiding behind than performing.

She opened her mouth to argue, but I didn't give her the chance. "Nicole Wallace, Diane Sawyer—both of them started as publicists before television came knocking. They pivoted, Mary, and look where it got them."

Mary attempted a smile, but her effort was betrayed by the turmoil in her eyes.

"And Andy Cohen was a journalist before he was on television. Now he's a bestselling author. You could use the show to promote your writing too," I pressed, nudging her toward the possibility

Mary looked down, her gaze filled with vulnerability. "Nicole, Diane, and even Andy—they're all *cute,*" she murmured. "And I'm not."

My heart clenched. I wished, more than anything, that Mary could see herself the way I did—sharp, captivating, and uniquely beautiful in a way that transcended the shallow standards of TV. I opened my mouth to say as much, but before the words could escape, the door swung open with a sudden, forceful bang.

"He's here," I gasped, my voice tinged with a mix of nerves and anticipation.

"Who's here?" Mary asked, her brows knitting together as her eyes followed the man now striding toward our table.

Snapping his fingers at a passing server, he barked, "Macallan 18. Rocks."

"Dude, you said she was *hot!*" he blurted out, his bluntness landing with all the grace of a sledgehammer, "And what is she *wearing?*"

Mary's jaw dropped, her shock quickly morphing into indignation. "And who the hell are *you?*", she snapped.

"Producer!" I cut in quickly, as if trying to douse a fire I'd accidentally set. "This is the producer I was telling you about."

"Well, before you waste your time trying to convince me—*I'm not interested in being on TV,*" Mary replied, the words dripping with skepticism, as if the mere idea insulted her intelligence.

Producer let out an audible sigh of relief, his shoulders visibly relaxing. "Oh, thank *god!*" he exclaimed, extending a hand toward her. "In that case, it's good to meet you. And by the way, I have *four Emmys*," he added.

Mary didn't take his hand. Instead, her expression remained deadpan as she quipped, "And this chair has four legs."

The corner of my mouth betrayed me with a chuckle, but Mary wasn't laughing. Not even close.

She slung her Chloé bag carefully over her shoulder and stood up. "I'm outta here," she announced, her tone resolute and final.

"No, Mary, don't go," I pleaded, my voice softer, tinged with desperation. "Stay for one drink, please."

She hesitated, her sharp gaze softening just slightly as it landed on my face. I could see the wheels turning in her mind, torn between her instinct to flee and the recognition of how much this moment meant to me.

"Okay," she relented after a long pause. "Just one more," she added, setting Chloé back down in her rightful place. "But I can't stay for long. Ben Stiller is waiting for me."

Producer froze mid-sip of his Macallan, his eyes widening. "Ben Stiller?" he asked, his voice laced with disbelief.

Mary's eyes twinkled mischievously as she replied, "Yes, we live together."

After letting the statement hang in the air just long enough to pique his interest, I clarified with a Cheshire-like grin, "Ben Stiller is Mary's cat."

"She's *not* my cat," Mary interjected sharply, her playful demeanor giving way to mock seriousness. "She's my *daughter.*"

Producer laughed. Clearly, he'd underestimated Mary. Like so many before him, he'd judged her based solely on appearance.

As the evening wore on, the frost in Mary's demeanor began to thaw. The tension ebbed, replaced by a natural rhythm that felt familiar and comforting. Soon, the table wasn't a battleground—it was a stage, and Mary and I were performing our greatest hits.

"Want to hear about the time I wore a wire to catch him with hookers?" Mary teased, a mischievous sparkle lighting her eyes as she leaned slightly forward.

Producer's reaction was instantaneous, his face lighting up like a kid at a candy store. "Yes, *please!*" he exclaimed.

Not to be outdone, I prepared to unleash my own scandalous gem. "And get this," I began, "even though he was dating a supermodel, he couldn't climax unless he farted."

Mary didn't miss a beat, picking up the ball with effortless accuracy. "Oh, honey, *of course* he's gay. Do you know how many Bette Midler concerts he's been to?"

Producer doubled over in laughter, tears practically forming in the corners of his eyes. "These stories," he managed between fits of chuckles, "and the way you tell them—they're fantastic."

We had him hooked. And as usual, I knew it.

"Practice makes perfect," I admitted, thinking back to the countless evenings Mary and I had spent here, spinning our greatest hits like seasoned performers.

"It's because our material is top-notch," Mary declared, flipping her hair for dramatic effect.

"Maybe it's both," Producer suggested, his words slightly slurred as he snapped his fingers in a futile attempt to grab the server's attention—for what would undoubtedly be his fifth drink of the night.

The glint of a seasoned New Yorker lit up Mary's eyes. "The best way to get a waiter's attention in New York," she said with mock gravitas, pausing just long enough for effect, "is to call…"

"*Actor*," Mary and I chimed in unison, merging in perfect, practiced harmony.

Producer clapped his hands, beaming. "You two are *TV gold* together," he declared, practically glowing with enthusiasm. "It wasn't exactly what I had in mind a few hours ago, but this—it could work. Maybe morning TV is finally ready for a chubby girl and a disabled gay guy!"

Mary and I both froze, our smiles vanishing in an instant.

But Producer was on a roll, too wrapped up in his newfound talent's potential to notice the storm brewing at the table. "What we need," he continued, "is a Black girl."

Mary exchanged an uneasy glance with me. I was one of the few people in the world who knew her secret—that she was biracial but chose to pass as white.

Eager to redirect the conversation, I jumped in with a quick solution. "How about Delores?"

Mary nodded, visibly relieved that I had steered the conversation away from dangerously uncomfortable waters. "Is Delores still in the business?" she asked, tilting her head thoughtfully. "Last I heard, she was teaching spin classes uptown—way uptown."

"Yes," I replied confidently. "I just saw her at a premiere a few nights ago. She looked incredible and still had that sparkle. She'd be perfect."

"Perfect!" Producer declared, his face lighting up as if we'd just solved all his problems in one fell swoop. "Because next Wednesday, we're shooting a pilot. Now, all we need is someone *hot!*"

Thirty minutes later, Mary found herself perched on the edge of her bathtub in her tiny, walk-up studio apartment. The kind of place where neither the heat nor the Wi-Fi worked properly—a perfect metaphor for the precarious state of her personal life.

Blissfully unaware that she'd staggered home with her skirt still tucked into her knickers, Mary's gaze fell on the chipped bathroom door that never quite closed properly—a constant reminder of the things in her life that needed fixing.

Her eyes drifted to the framed picture of Joan Rivers perched proudly above her couch. It was a little crooked, like everything else in her tiny studio.

On her unmade bed, Ben Stiller lay curled up, snoring softly, her small frame rising and falling with each peaceful breath. At least someone in the apartment was at ease.

And then her eyes fell on it—the empty ice cream container sitting beside the fridge. The carton, smeared with traces of melted chocolate, seemed to mock her. A silent accuser, it was a tangible reminder of the weakness she despised and the compulsion she couldn't seem to shake.

With a weary sigh, Mary slid off the edge of the tub, her knees pressing into the cold, unforgiving tiles. Her trembling fingers hovered just above her lips, poised with practiced scrupulousness.

Mary had a secret eating disorder.

Chapter 4

Delores's gym was a relic from another era, with peeling paint, mismatched weights, and ancient treadmills that screeched when used. It looked like it had been plucked straight from the set of a classic underdog movie, the kind where grit and determination always trumped in the end.

In the aftermath of the snowstorm that had paralyzed the neighborhood, a sisterhood of local women gathered, brushing off the cold and embracing the warmth of community.

At the helm stood Delores. She was a vision in her vibrant ensemble—the perfect balance of style and sweat.

"All right, ladies, are you ready?" Delores roared, her voice a challenge and comfort.

"Remember, we've got every disadvantage we need if we're going to succeed," she declared, quoting one of her favorite Broadway musicals.

For over a decade, Delores had thrown herself into the relentless pursuit of becoming one of the top entertainment reporters in the industry. Not the top Black entertainment reporter, but simply the best. Period.

However, that dream had proven as elusive as it was cruel. A reminder that she was navigating a maze not built for her success.

Delores had tried for years to smile through it, played the game as best she could even when she felt like crying. But recently rejection had carved away too much of her resolve, until all that was left was a woman tired of fighting a battle she'd never been allowed to win. Now, she was all about one thing—making money.

And so, Delores found herself thriving in the one place that never shut her out—a dimly lit gym alive with her favorite Broadway showtunes and sweating bodies. Here, she wasn't just welcome; she was the captain of the ship, steering her own destiny without anyone else's permission.

Toward the back of the class, an older lady leaned toward her neighbor, whispering loud enough for Delores to catch. "She still ain't got no man."

"That's 'cause she got a thing for them white boys," another chimed in. "And there's no way her momma is going to approve of one of them."

Delores heard them, of course. She always heard them. But she didn't flinch. The chatter only reinforced what she already knew: her clients didn't just come to shed pounds, build strength, or gain endurance.

No, what they truly craved was connection—a space where they could gossip about love, fear, dreams, and heartbreaks. Delores gave them that.

She was more than an instructor; she was a confidante, a coach, and a therapist. Her sessions weren't just about the physical act—they were about listening. Delores knew that sometimes, what her clients truly needed wasn't to raise their heart rate but the chance for their heart to be heard.

As the last of her clients filtered out, Delores attention shifted to her phone, which buzzed persistently on the counter beside her. The aging device wasn't holding up nearly as well as she was.

Delores picked it up, tapping at the cracked screen with the efficiency of someone who didn't have a second to waste. Each message was a variation on a theme: a private client needing a time slot as soon as possible. She didn't enjoy the work, but it paid the bills.

Delores was halfway through composing one last response when her screen lit again up with a new notification. Her thumb hovered over the name, her heart skipping a beat as she read the message.

Hey, it's Mary. Not sure if this is still your number, but if it is, can you meet James and I tonight? And don't worry, James is paying.

Curiosity flickered like a candle in the dark—faint, but persistent. However, tonight wasn't exactly ideal. A packed schedule of private clients loomed large. The thought of rearranging her evening sent a pang of financial fear rippling through her chest.

But then there was Mary and me.

We were the only two people in the business who had ever gone out of our way to be kind to her, expecting nothing in return—until maybe now. That thought lingered, unspoken but undeniable, pulling at the edges of Delores's resolve.

Mary dear, can we meet at 8 p.m. in my neck of the woods?

Delores hit send before she could overthink it. Moments later, her phone buzzed with Mary's reply:

Sure, we can do that. See you at 8. Just let us know where.

Several hours later, Mary and I found ourselves uptown—*way* uptown—standing outside Delores's favorite bar. The neon sign above the entrance flickered faintly, casting uneven light onto the sidewalk. It was a nostalgic nod to another era, a time when places like this held stories in every creaky floorboard and stained barstool.

Mary tilted her head, taking in the scene with a mix of curiosity and skepticism. "This is *her* spot?" she asked, one eyebrow arched.

I shrugged, a small smile tugging at my lips. "Delores always did have a thing for hidden gems."

With that, we pushed open the heavy door, stepping into a tapestry of Harlem stitched together by regulars who greeted the bartender with first-name familiarity.

At the far end of the bar, Delores sat perched like royalty, her presence commanding yet approachable. Her attention was split between texting furiously and engaging in light banter with a tall, broad-shouldered young white guy standing behind the bar whose tight jeans revealed an even tighter posterior.

"Delores, is that you?" Mary called out, her voice carrying a mixture of disbelief and delight.

Delores turned toward us, one hand holding the edge of her slightly distressed wig in place. "My *lord,*" she exclaimed, her grin wide and infectious.

Mary's eyes immediately drifted to the bartender. "Let me guess why you picked this place," she said, her tone laced with mischief as her lips curled into a knowing smirk.

Not to be outdone, I decided to jump in with my own observation. "Delores, you look amazing," I said, tilting my head with exaggerated curiosity. "Seriously, what's your secret?"

"New hair," she shot back, her voice a mix of sass and triumph, giving a playful flick of her coiffed bob.

I couldn't hold it in any longer—the reason why we were all here.

"Delores, brace yourself," I blurted, my tone teetering between excitement and urgency, as if I were about to spill classified state secrets.

Her brow lifted, intrigued but cautious.

"Mary and I are working on a brand-new TV show," I continued, pausing just long enough for dramatic effect, "with a producer who has *four Emmys.*"

"James came up with this concept for a panel show," Mary explained. "Real-life entertainment insiders."

"People who've actually been in the trenches," I added with just a hint of pride.

Mary delivered the punchline with her signature flair. "Folks who can tell their Suris from their Shilohs!"

We fell silent, waiting for Delores's response. Her expression remained a mystery—carefully neutral, giving nothing away.

She sipped her drink slowly, finally setting it down with deliberate care. "I'll bite," she said at last, her voice firm. "What do you want from me?"

"We want you to join us. To be part of it," I replied with earnestness.

Delores didn't respond immediately. Her silence was deliberate, the kind that hung in the air just long enough to make you second-guess every word you'd just said. She swirled her drink slowly, before she finally looked up.

"So," she said, her tone calm but piercing, "what you're really looking for is a dark-skinned co-host, right?"

Mary froze, her stunned silence speaking louder than any words. For a moment, it felt as though the room itself had paused.

Delores leaned in, her voice softening to a near-whisper, brimming with warmth and compassion. "Child, don't you worry now. Your secret's safe with me."

Mary blinked, her expression shifting from startled to something softer, unexpectedly reassured. For someone who guarded her truths as fiercely as she guarded her columns, there was something profoundly disarming about being seen without feeling exposed.

"Thank you," Mary finally murmured, her voice threaded with genuine gratitude.

It was one of those rare glimpses when Mary's carefully crafted armor slipped away, and you could see the person behind the sharp quips and quick wit.

As the night stretched on, our conversation, mercifully, shifted to lighter territory—the kind of banter that felt as comforting as slipping into a pair of well-worn slippers.

"Want to hear about the time I wore a wire to catch him with hookers?" Mary asked, her tone impossibly casual, like she was offering a cup of tea instead of dropping a grenade.

Delores leaned back in her chair, a barely concealed smirk tugging at her lips as she watched the well-rehearsed *Mary and James Show* unfold like a Broadway production.

But her answer to our real question remained suspended in the air, unresolved. It was as if it were held hostage in the silence.

Finally, Delores glanced at the time, her face softening into a smile. "I'm afraid I've got to go," she declared, standing and adjusting her wig with the grace only she could muster. "I've had such a great time catching up, and let's be honest, you two still put on the best show in town."

Mary and I exchanged glances, silently acknowledging the truth of her words.

"But," Delores continued, smoothing her coat, "I've got to get back to work. I got paying clients waiting."

"Delores," I quickly replied, my voice tinged with urgency. "What about the show? Are you in?"

"I'm afraid it's a no," she said, her verdict landing with a flicker of sadness in her eyes—as though part of her almost regretted what she had to say. *Almost.*

Mary blinked, visibly thrown off balance. Her usual arsenal of quick comebacks and sharp quips abandoned her.

I swallowed hard, feeling the lump in my throat tighten as disappointment settled in, cold and sharp. Still, I forced myself to ask, "If you don't mind me asking…why?"

Delores tilted her head slightly, her expression as unreadable as ever. But when she spoke, her voice carried the weight of truths she'd only recently stopped sugarcoating.

"Because I've been hurt enough already by this business," she said, each word heavy with decades of unspoken pain. "You two have got to come up with something better than just needing a Black girl to get me to jump back into the rat race."

She didn't raise her voice—she didn't need to. The truth in her words carried more weight than any shout ever could.

And she wasn't wrong. Promises of a brighter future, no matter how earnestly made, couldn't erase the long shadow of challenges that never seemed to simply vanish.

I drew in a deep breath, summoning every ounce of determination I had left. This was my last chance, and I knew it. "Well," I began. "There is one other thing. The job pays two grand a week."

Delores paused mid-stride, her hand hovering on her wig.

She knew money wasn't a magic fix. It couldn't shield her from the bruises of rejection, the patronizing smiles, or the doors slammed in her face. But $2,000 a week? That wasn't just a paycheck—it was a *gamechanger.*

Finally, Delores straightened up, letting the moment stretch just long enough to remind me who was really in control.

"My fabulous Black ass will be there Wednesday," she declared.

Later that evening, Delores stepped into her small, rent-stabilized apartment, tucked even further uptown where the city's bright lights barely reached. The familiar creak of the floorboards greeted her as she kicked off her heels, letting them tumble haphazardly to the side. She sank into her well-worn armchair by the window, its frayed edges and faded fabric bearing the weight of countless late nights and hard decisions. It fit her perfectly—like an old friend that never judged.

Her phone buzzed on the side table, vibrating insistently against the wood. Delores glanced at it and sighed, her shoulders sinking under the weight of reality. It wasn't a friend, or family. No, it was a client, ready to start their evening session.

This was why she'd said *yes* to Mary and me. She wouldn't have to do this much longer once that TV money started pouring in.

Currently, by day, Delores made her living making Black women sweat in the gym. But by night?

By night, Delores paid her bills by making white men sweat over the phone.

Delores was a secret phone-sex operator!

Chapter 5

At CNN headquarters in Hudson Yards, Carol Ann's heels clicked against the marble floors. The walls were lined with glossy, oversized headshots—smiling faces of the network's precarious current roster of ever-rotating prime-time hosts. Carol Ann's gaze lingering on each photo—envisioning her own portrait up there one day.

It was a long way from where she'd started. Back in that one-stoplight Southern town, the only thing bigger than the church on Main Street was the sky that stretched endlessly overhead. From her bedroom window, she'd stare out at the stars for hours, willing herself to believe that somewhere, out there, was her escape.

Her first pageant crown had been a revelation, its cheap rhinestones sparkling like a beacon. From that moment on, every step, every victory, every sash pinned across her chest was one more rung on the ladder she was determined to climb. The pageants were never the dream, just the gateway.

Her journey to New York, like all great ascents, began with an unlikely twist of fate—a chance encounter that proved Carol

Ann's sharp instincts were her greatest asset. It was a random Tuesday night, the kind of evening that begged for reruns of *The Bachelor,* when she found herself logged into a free Zoom class. She didn't have much interest in the topic, but the class was hosted by a CNN legal analyst, and that alone was reason enough for her to tune in.

Maybe it was the late hour, or maybe it was the open bottle of wine that occasionally came into view just over the host's shoulder. Whatever the reason, when the class officially ended, the analyst, evidently assuming he was alone and unaware that Carol Ann had lingered in the virtual shadows, indulged in a personal, private moment pleasing himself.

A few weeks later, Carol Ann stepped through the sleek glass doors of Hudson Yards, a freshly minted CNN guest greeter. The position wasn't glamorous—corralling talking heads wasn't exactly hard-hitting journalism—but it was her foot in the door.

While she impatiently waited, Carol Ann took matters into her own impeccably manicured hands. Hidden in the depths of her Gucci purse, nestled between a lipstick case and a monogrammed planner, was her secret weapon: an old CNN microphone flag. It had somehow "fallen into her possession," though Carol Ann preferred not to dwell on the specifics.

And wield it she did, like a magician with a wand, slipping seamlessly onto glittering red carpets, star-studded premieres, and press-packed junkets. Security guards barely gave her a second glance, and the publicists—juggling a hundred moving pieces at once—didn't think to question the poised blonde wearing the CNN brand like a badge.

However, after six months of pushing, pulling, and plotting, with nothing big to show for it but a dubious on-air audition reel, Carol Ann knew it was time to make her next career move.

The moment the CNN elevator doors opened, Carol Ann's heart skipped—not from nerves, but from opportunity. There she was, standing like a statue of journalistic authority in a tailored navy pantsuit: Bunny Deadline. Sixty-two years of cutting through celebrity smoke and mirrors had solidified Bunny's status as a high priestess in the temple of gossip. Carol Ann didn't hesitate. She slipped in next to Bunny just as the doors slid shut, her smile wide and warm, her voice tinged with just the right amount of charm.

"It's good to see me...you," Carol Ann slipped, her drawl as smooth and deliberate as honey drizzled over a biscuit. "Miss Deadline, your segment went great. I had no idea Justin Bieber was sendin' a hidden message to Selena Gomez!"

It was a classic pageant trick: engage, dazzle, flatter.

But her magic seemed to be falling flat. Bunny Deadline didn't respond.

Calculating her next move, Carol Ann turned up the wattage, her smile widening to just shy of blinding.

"How does li'l old Meghan handle Harry's British uncircumcised penis?" she asked, her tone dripping with an innocence that belied the sheer bombshell nature of her question.

Bunny Deadline's seasoned ears practically twitched. The faintest glimmer of intrigue lit her eyes as she turned her head, finally giving Carol Ann her attention. "Now that's a headline," Bunny replied.

The validation sent a jolt of adrenaline coursing through Carol Ann's body. "Oh, I've got a million," she replied, her accent wrapping around the words like a velvet ribbon.

"This Meghan and Harry story," Bunny Deadline declared, her voice brimming with something close to triumph, "will get me booked on *Morning Joe, Entertainment Tonight,* and *Pornhub.*"

Carol Ann swallowed her excitement, forcing her voice steady despite the swarm of butterflies threatening to escape her chest. "I've always dreamed of being on TV, just like you," she said, knowing full well she only had a few more floors before the elevator doors would open—and this fleeting opportunity would vanish along with Bunny Deadline.

This was it.

She took a deep breath, her heart pounding so fiercely she wondered if Bunny could hear it. *Now or never,* she thought, summoning every ounce of confidence she could muster.

"Miss Deadline," Carol Ann began, her voice steady despite the tightness in her throat. "Can I work for you?"

The bold words hung in the air, echoing off the polished steel walls like a challenge to fate itself.

Bunny finally turned, her piercing gaze narrowing as if scanning Carol Ann's very soul. "You've got nerve," she said, her tone measured, carrying just enough edge to make it clear she didn't hand out compliments lightly. "This business is a battlefield unlike any other. Red carpets can be more treacherous than war zones. *Nerve* alone doesn't cut it here."

Carol Ann swallowed hard but didn't flinch. Instead, she squared her shoulders, letting a small, confident smile play at the edges of her lips. "Well," she said, holding Bunny's gaze without blinking, "I'm pretty too."

Bunny's lips curved into a sly smile, her eyes flicking over Carol Ann with renewed interest. "Yes, you are," she said, her voice deliberate. "Which is why I might have the perfect project for you."

The words exploded in the confined elevator like a firecracker. Nothing this thrilling had been uttered within CNN's walls since the time Wolf Blitzer accidentally borrowed Sanjay Gupta's makeup.

Before Carol Ann could respond, the elevator doors slid open with a soft *ding*.

Bunny stepped out, her heels clicking against the floor like punctuation marks. She paused briefly and turned back. "Well," she added, "welcome to my celebrity jungle."

And with that, the legend strode off, leaving her new apprentice behind to bask in the glow of her first successful elevator pitch.

The next morning, Carol Ann stepped into Bunny Deadline's office, her resolve as sharp as her stilettos. The place was everything she'd imagined and more—a magnetic hive of pop culture obsession that hummed with the urgency of breaking news, viral hashtags, and the ceaseless churn of celebrity drama.

Everywhere she turned, youthful staffers zipped between desks, their eyes glued to their screens, fingers tapping out headlines, captions, and cutting commentary. It was a sea of oversized headphones, half-empty coffee cups, and the faint glow of smartphones and gadgets—the unmistakable battlefield of the digital age.

Bunny's arrival was unusually delayed, the buzz of the office punctuated by curious glances at the clock. When she finally appeared, her typically commanding presence was offset by a noticeably stiff gait and a pained expression. Word spread like wildfire—an unfortunate incident with a Goop vaginal steamer.

"Traffic is down, down, *down,*" Bunny snapped as she strode—or rather, hobbled—into the office. Her entrance was punctuated by the toss of a tablet onto a nearby desk, its screen displaying a graph with numbers plunging like a freefalling rollercoaster. "I want it up, up, *up!*"

Her eyes swept over the sea of heads like a predator hunting for prey. "Where is my new hire from CNN?" she barked, her voice slicing through the hum of keyboards and hushed whispers.

"Here, Miss Deadline!" Carol Ann piped up from across the room. She added a quick wave for good measure, as if she hadn't just painted a target on her back.

All heads turned toward her.

Bunny, without missing a beat, reached into her flashy designer bag—a monstrosity dripping in logos and rhinestones—and pulled out a gaudy gold trophy. Oversized, ridiculous, and absolutely perfect for the theatrics of the moment.

"This," Bunny declared, holding the trophy aloft like a prize-fighter with a championship belt, "is awarded at the end of each day to the person who delivers the most eyeballs. However, today...well, today, your Prince Harry foreskin story is so far ahead, it's going to be impossible to beat."

With an exaggerated flourish, Bunny handed the trophy to Carol Ann. The presentation carried all the pomp and circumstance of a Pulitzer ceremony.

Carol Ann accepted it like she'd just been crowned Miss America. "Thank you, Miss Deadline," she said, her voice brimming with the implication that this wouldn't be the last time she'd earn such recognition.

Around her, the office quickly returned to its usual hum of activity, the brief spectacle fading into the background as if it hadn't even happened.

Meanwhile, Carol Ann, with the gaudy trophy still clutched tightly in her hands, made her way toward her newly assigned cubicle, catching the occasional curious glance from her coworkers.

Though her pace slowed as she passed Bunny Deadline's glass-walled office. A muffled voice—Bunny's, pitched low and almost conspiratorial—drifted through the air, snagging her curiosity like a fishhook.

Her eyes darted toward the queen of gossip, who sat uncomfortably at her desk, the phone pressed tightly to her ear.

Bunny's posture was tense, her free hand gesturing sharply as she spoke in hushed, clipped tones. Even from a distance, Carol Ann's knack for reading lips kicked in instinctively, her eyes narrowing as she focused on Bunny's every word.

"Never forget, I have the tape!" Bunny hissed, her lips forming the words with sharp clarity. "As long as he keeps chirping to me, the disk will never leave my cage."

The words sent a jolt through Carol Ann. This was big—*huge.* Whatever this tape was, it wasn't just a secret; it was leverage.

Before she could process further, Bunny's voice suddenly rang out, sharp and commanding. "*Carol Ann!*"

Carol Ann's heart lurched as Bunny's eyes locked onto her, a flicker of suspicion darting across her face. "Come in here *immediately.*"

Her stomach twisted, but she forced her expression into a mask of innocence, smoothing her skirt as she stepped forward. Whatever was happening, she'd just stepped directly into the middle of it.

"Remember I said I had the perfect project for you?" Bunny asked, her voice dripping with feigned benevolence. "Well, a very handsome TV producer with great hair and four Emmys is putting together a new gossip show and looking for someone hot."

For a moment, Carol Ann's brain refused to compute, the words swirling in her mind without forming meaning.

"Naturally, I should do it myself," Bunny added, a hand dramatically placed over her chest, "but you know how much I love helping others." Her tone convinced no one—not even herself.

Carol Ann's vision blurred as her heart raced. Her knees wobbled, and before she could steady herself, she sank to the floor.

When Carol Ann finally came to, blinking at the ceiling lights, Bunny's face hovered over her, equal parts amused and exasperated.

"Well," Bunny said, her voice sharp enough to cut through Carol Ann's daze. "Pull yourself together *immediately.* He's waiting for you in the conference room, along with some big-time publicist called James."

Carol Ann's heart slammed against her ribcage as she scrambled to her feet, the enormity of what Bunny had just said crashing over her. This wasn't just an opportunity—it was *the* opportunity. And it was waiting for her.

Later that evening, the atmosphere inside one of New York's most exclusive private members–only clubs was nothing short of electric. The space radiated privilege and prestige, its air heavy with the unspoken rules of power and discretion. Here, money wasn't the ticket—it was merely the baseline. True entry required influence, status, and the ability to keep secrets.

The staff moved like shadows, their presence invisible yet indispensable. Over time, they'd perfected the art of lip-reading to navigate the deafening cacophony of music and murmurs that filled the room.

In the heart of the club, under a soft spotlight, the star of the evening emerged: a mysterious woman with a cascade of impossibly lush brunette hair, each strand shimmering with an almost otherworldly glow.

She gripped the polished pole with an effortless grace, her movements a seamless fusion of strength and seduction. With each twirl and glide the laws of physics were merely suggestions she chose to ignore. Her performance wasn't just mesmerizing; it was transformative—a masterclass in commanding attention and vanishing into the very spotlight that illuminated her. Proving, once again, that stars weren't only discovered under the spotlight—they could disappear within it too.

There, hidden in plain sight, invisible in her own brilliance, was the club's most captivating performer: Carol Ann.

Chapter 6

I leaned back in my chair, the studio lights draping their relentless heat over me like the world's most unwelcome couture. My gaze shifted to Miss D, poised and ready to command the moment.

"It all began," she purred, her voice honeyed with just the right amount of edge, "with a tip about Jada showing up at the most exclusive gym in town."

Her tone carried just enough intrigue to hook the audience, leaving them leaning forward, craving more. But even as her words flowed effortlessly, I saw it—the flicker in her eyes, as she slipped back to what really happened last night.

"Thanks for the tip," Delores whispered as she sidled up to the trainer of the hour, a man whose roster included every Upper East Side lady with a titanium Amex and a restless marriage.

Once upon a time, he'd been just another eager face in Delores's uptown workout class, dragged along by his perpetually displeased mother. ("The music's too loud," she'd complain, every time.) Now? He was practically a walking *Forbes* profile, guiding his well-heeled clientele through overpriced squats and burpees.

Just as the clock threatened to strike again, the gym doors swung open.

Jada Pinkett Smith didn't just arrive; she *descended.* She moved with that effortless kind of confidence that doesn't need announcement or introduction.

Delores's lips twitched into a small smile as she transformed into Miss D.

The game was on.

"Jada, I'm Miss D from *The Gossip Gang!*" she called out, her voice dripping with charm. "Can I get a few quotes about your hot body?"

From out of nowhere, a linebacker of a security guard materialized, his broad shoulders forming an unrelenting wall between Miss D and her headline.

"Ma'am, you are going to have to leave," he grunted.

Before Miss D could even protest, she found herself being ushered—not escorted, no, *ushered*—out of the gym's eucalyptus-scented halls.

The air outside was sharp and cold, biting against her skin like the sting of rejection itself.

But then, a flicker of something unexpected pierced through the dark clouds. A voice, familiar and unmistakable.

"Wait!"

Delores turned, and there she was: Jada Pinkett Smith, radiant and commanding as ever.

"Girl, forgive my security," Jada said, flashing a smile so genuine it was surprising it hadn't sold more movie tickets. "After the Will incident, they're…extra protective."

Delores's heart swelled, the bruises to her ego instantly forgotten.

"Can I get a few sentences about your workout routine?" she asked, her voice carrying just the right mix of casual curiosity and polished professionalism.

"Of course, girl," Jada replied with the effortless grace of one Black goddess helping out another. "Us sisters have got to stick together."

The next ten minutes flew by as the two women chatted like old friends, the conversation flowing easily and punctuated by laughter.

When they finally wrapped, Delores thanked her, her gratitude genuine. With her fabulous exclusive story in hand, she slipped into the night, the sting of rejection replaced by the sweet taste of victory.

Back under the dazzling glare of the studio lights, Mary and I broke into enthusiastic applause. Miss D's segment had been nothing short of exceptional—a pitch-perfect blend of insider access and practical takeaway tips.

"Wow, Miss D, *fantastic* reporting," I said, my voice ringing with genuine admiration.

Producer, perched nearby with his ever-watchful eye, offered a vigorous nod, his usual poker face momentarily replaced with rare approval. He knew fitness exclusives always struck gold with the audience.

"Thank you," Miss D replied, ever gracious, her tone effortlessly humble as she basked in the moment.

I turned toward the next act. "Carol Ann," I announced. "Tell us all about your *unbelievable* Reese Witherspoon exclusive!"

As I spoke, I exchanged a quick, knowing eye roll with Mary. Her barely contained smirk hinted at the nonsense that was bound to follow. Whatever Carol Ann had cooked up, it was certain to be entertaining—even if it wasn't exactly *reporting.*

Just nine hours earlier, in the plush VIP room on the Upper East Side, Bunny Deadline lay in pain as the clock struck midnight.

"Tell me the truth," Bunny demanded, her voice sharp enough to cut through the awkward silence like a scalpel. "How does my vagina look?"

Carol Ann blinked, her brain momentarily short-circuiting. Pageant training had prepared her for a lot—but this? This was uncharted territory.

"Well..." Carol Ann began hesitantly, gingerly lifting the covers for a cautious look. "It's not exactly a peach pie."

Bunny narrowed her eyes, processing the words with the weight of someone who'd heard far worse. "God damn you, Gwyneth Paltrow and your Goop steaming," she muttered bitterly, her frustration dripping like venom.

Before Carol Ann could retreat, Bunny waved a hand dramatically toward a figure in the distance, strolling down the hallway with a small dog in tow.

"While I'm here, I'm relying on you to come up with great exclusives," Bunny declared.

Carol Ann tilted her head in genuine confusion. "I don't rightly understand," she admitted.

Bunny let out a small, pained sigh, shifting slightly in the bed. "There," she whispered, her hand motioning toward the woman in pink with the little dog trotting beside her. "See that woman? That could be Reese Witherspoon. It wouldn't surprise me at all if she wasn't thinking about getting a little tightening down there."

Understanding dawned on Carol Ann's face like a slow sunrise.

"Stories with just enough truth to make them plausible," Carol Ann echoed, the realization sinking in.

Bunny's lips curved into a faint, satisfied smile.

Now she got it.

For better or worse, Carol Ann had just received a master class in the art of scandal—the fine balance between fiction and fact, delivered with just enough truth to keep everyone hooked.

"Unbelievable," Mary huffed. The sharpness of her tone yanked everyone back to the present.

Producer's fingers twitched at his sides, a telltale sign that he was teetering on the edge of panic. Kathleen—known to Mary and I as "Kathlegal"—had just dropped a legal note into his earpiece that made his stomach churn.

With shaking hands, Producer snatched a blank cue card and scrawled a frantic note for me: *Allegedly!*

I caught it mid-breath. "Just to be clear," I said, my voice pitching slightly higher than usual, "Carol Ann's Reese story is *allegedly*."

Then I steered the conversation back to safer waters.

"Mary," I said, my tone deliberately light and inviting, "tell us about your mind-blowing night with Oprah."

Mary blinked and took a steadying breath. "Well, James," she began, her voice suddenly warm and shimmering, "it was a night I'll never forget."

Mary bid Ben Stiller a bittersweet goodnight, the ache of parting lingering as she trudged back toward the grind. Between her column and the show, a nagging thought gnawed at her: would she ever kiss anyone again—aside from her tabby cat?

The first raindrops kissed her head like a gentle warning. Determination flared in Mary's heart as she took off running, her budget-friendly black shoes clicking purposefully against the pavement. Within seconds, the polite drizzle exploded into a biblical downpour, a deluge so relentless it felt like Noah's Ark might soon appear on Tenth Avenue.

By the time Mary managed to secure a surge-priced Uber (because of course) and make her way to the white press tent outside the event, she was soaked to the bone.

She caught her reflection in the window of a parked town car. Her hair was plastered to her forehead, her makeup streaked, and her blouse clung like a bad second skin. Her worst fears were confirmed.

But Mary wasn't about to let a little rain—or a lot of it—stop her.

Squaring her shoulders, she scanned the tent. Her eyes darted past air-kissed greetings, searching for the press check-in table with the urgency of someone looking for a lifeboat on the Titanic.

Finally, Mary spotted a familiar figure. Lori Letmein. The event's publicist. Formidable. Legendary.

If anyone could help salvage the night, it was Lori.

"Name and outlet," Lori said, her voice clipped as her eyes scanned the clipboard in her hands.

"Lori, it's me. Let me in," Mary shot back, her voice cracking with equal parts exasperation and desperation as rain pelted the plastic canopy above them.

"Oh, it's you, Mary," Lori replied, her expression morphing into a perfect mask of pity and condescension. "You look awful."

"It's raining," Mary deadpanned, rolling her eyes so hard they nearly left her skull.

Lori's tone remained as dry as the expensive wine being poured inside. "You're not on the list."

The words hit Mary harder than the downpour ever could. "What do you mean I'm not on the list?" she snapped, her voice inching dangerously close to a yell.

Lori's expression was one of infuriating neutrality. "Could it be under another name?" she asked, as though this was all perfectly reasonable.

"Try Schindler," Mary shot back, holding up her phone as evidence. "Here," she said, jabbing at the screen for emphasis. "You invited me."

"Oh, that was before *Page Six* showed up," Lori finally admitted. "I'm sorry, Mary, their column is more important than yours."

Mary's jaw tightened, her frustration bubbling over as she opened her mouth, ready to unleash her own personal hurricane. But just as the first word formed, the air shifted.

"She's here!" a voice behind them shrieked, high-pitched and electric with excitement. "Oprah is here!"

In an instant, the unmistakable figure of Oprah Winfrey emerged, stepping into the white tent like an angel sent to rescue everyone. The crowd parted around her, their awe palpable.

"Oprah, can I ask a few questions?" Mary blurted out, seizing her chance like a lifeline.

"That's what I'm here for," the legend replied with a smile that could light up a thousand rainy nights.

Time seemed to suspend itself in the presence of greatness, the storm around them dimming into an irrelevant hum.

Then, all too quickly, Oprah disappeared into the event, her graceful stride leaving behind an air of wonder and finality.

The encounter replayed in Mary's mind like a scene from a movie she wasn't sure she'd ever truly been in, surreal and fleeting.

As she snapped back to reality, her eyes caught the flickering light of an approaching cab through the rain.

Without hesitation, Mary sprang into action, her legs propelling her forward like an Olympic sprinter chasing gold. She reached the curb, arms outstretched to flag it down, when fate—unpredictable and relentless—intervened.

The cheap heel of her shoe—already weakened by the rain—gave out with a dramatic crack. In an instant, Mary's athletic stride transformed into a flailing dive toward the cold, rain-slick pavement.

Then, just as her descent seemed inevitable, two strong arms caught her, halting the crash with a grip that was both firm and impossibly gentle.

Mary gasped, her breath catching as she looked up into the eyes of her savior—a modern-day knight in a perfectly tailored Tom Ford tuxedo. His umbrella, held high above them, stood like a noble sword fending off the stormy sky.

"Are you alright?" he asked, his voice carrying a kindness that softened the edges of the chaos around them, making the rain seem almost romantic.

His chiseled features bore an uncanny resemblance to ABC's Black Bachelor, and for a brief, dizzying moment, Mary wondered if she'd actually hit her head.

"Never felt better," she murmured, caught in the spell of the moment. "First Oprah and now you. All that's missing is Joan Rivers!"

The stranger blinked, his confusion giving way to a chuckle.

"Hang on a minute," he said, his tone playful as he studied her with a curiosity that sent her pulse racing. "Are you that funny girl from the new morning show?"

The surprising recognition made Mary's cheeks flush, a mix of embarrassment and pride swirling within her. "You watch that?" she asked, her voice soft, as if afraid to shatter the fragile magic of the moment.

"Your name is…Mary, right?" he said, his wide, unguarded smile breaking through the storm like sunlight. "I'm Ben."

"Hey, Ben," she replied softly, stepping into the cab he'd flagged for her, suddenly aware her heart felt lighter than it had in years.

As the car pulled away, Mary couldn't help but glance back. There Ben stood, umbrella in hand, his tuxedo dark against the rain, a beacon of possibility in a night that had started as anything but.

For the first time in a long time, Mary felt something stir—hope, excitement, maybe even the promise of kissing someone other than her cat.

Chapter 7

As the days blurred into weeks and the weeks stretched into months, *The Gossip Gang* defied expectations, transforming from a scrappy experiment into a very low-key hit—much to the dismay of Keegan Kelly, the network's other morning show host.

Naturally, Producer wasted no time seizing credit, though persuading the networks big-little boss to flood the city with an advertising blitz had undoubtedly helped.

Now, the cast's airbrushed faces were everywhere, as omnipresent as overpriced oat milk lattes. Billboards, buses, subways, taxis—no flat surface was spared. Even our dressing room on the 45th floor had been graced (or cursed, depending on who you asked) with a colossal poster of our collective likenesses.

Carol Ann, who had been explicitly instructed by Producer to arrive *at least* an hour early for her so-called "special artistry" requirements, swept into the room fashionably—though irritatingly—late.

"*Señorita*," Carol Ann said to Maria the makeup artist responsible for making all our faces ready for TV. "Tonight, I'll be needin' your presence at my apartment at 7 o'clock sharp. I have a *very* important 9 p.m. meeting. And I hate lateness!"

Despite Maria's deep reluctance to sacrifice another second of her life to Carol Ann's endless stream of self-absorbed chatter, the promise of an extra $250 in cash proved to be a seduction too tempting to resist.

"I promised not to spill the beans," Carol Ann continued. "But since ya asked.... Tonight, li'l ol' me has a rendezvous with none other than Josh Ellis. Yes, *Josh Ellis from TV!*"

Maria's brush froze mid-air. Josh Ellis—the former football star turned morning television personality—was a name that needed no introduction. Whether wrapped in an impeccably tailored suit or a jockstrap, he was the stuff of fantasy. His square jaw alone could break a thousand hearts, while his ego loomed even larger than his massive shoulders.

And yet, Maria said nothing, though her curiosity perked up when she noticed something curious: several long brunette hairs clinging to Carol Ann's blonde curls.

Unbothered and entirely oblivious, Carol Ann prattled on. "Alright, I *might've* sent Josh Ellis a DM or two," she admitted. "Just asking for advice on the TV business. The secret sauce."

Undeterred by the lack of response, Carol Ann pressed on. "Our meetin's set at The Tipsy Teapot, she announced. "It's undeniably the *fanciest* bar in all of New York City."

Maria nearly choked. The Tipsy Teapot? Fanciest? *More like the fakest.*

"Y'all know who else is a regular at The Tipsy Teapot?" Carol Ann drawled as she unfurled a copy of the *New York Post* from her Prada bag and jabbed her manicured nail at the front page.

"This cover boy."

The headline screamed in scandalized font: MOVIE PRODUCER HARRY STEINMAN GRABS ACTRESSES'S GOLDEN GLOBES.

A few blocks away, the cacophony of 42nd Street reached its usual fever pitch: honking taxis battling for dominance, herds of tourists armed with cameras, and a street performer delivering his impression of Celine Dion with all the fervor of a karaoke night gone horribly wrong. Through it all, an MTA bus trundled along, its exterior plastered with the unmistakable *Gossip Gang* poster.

Inside that very bus, the real Miss D was practically invisible, obscured by a rumpled copy of the *New York Post*. Only her gold sneakers and her silver commuter wig hinted at her presence. Next to her, a what appeared to be a scruffy Persian blue cat poked its head out of a plastic bag.

The irony of it all wasn't lost on her. There she was, blown up to billboard proportions on the side of the bus, and yet, not a single passenger had spared her a second glance.

When the bus screeched to a halt at her Times Square stop, Miss D rose and stepped off. She paused for a moment beneath a towering billboard bearing her own larger-than-life image smiling down at her, as if mocking the mundanity of her current situation.

She barely had time to enjoy the sight when a sleek black town car came hurtling past, screeching to a near-miss with both Miss D and the side of the bus that bore her likeness. Inside the car, Producer reclined, his exhausted face half-hidden behind the same issue of the *New York Post*. He had spent the night on a very important phone call.

Miss D straightened her shoulders and strode toward the imposing studio building, her gold sneakers bouncing against the marble tiles with every step. But her forward momentum was abruptly halted by the burly figure of a security guard. His expression was as impenetrable as the reinforced glass doors he guarded.

"ID, please," he barked.

Miss D hesitated, rifling through her glittering clutch for the requisite identification. The guard gave it a perfunctory glance before scrutinizing her face with equal suspicion. After what felt like an eternity, he nodded and stepped aside, granting her entry into the world where she was both a star and a stranger.

Mary stepped off the curb in Chelsea, her arm shooting into the air with the sharpness of someone running late. The yellow cab skidded to a halt, its tires narrowly missing a puddle. She climbed in completely oblivious to the giant poster atop the vehicle bearing her own face, alongside the title of her show.

The cab barely made it seven blocks before pulling over again at 24th and 10th. The door swung open, and I slid in with the casual elegance of someone who had mastered the art of synchronized transportation.

"Running on Carol Ann time today?" I teased, referencing Mary's legendary reputation for being early to everything.

She huffed, shifting her prized purse to make room. "Sorry," she muttered. "Emergency at the paper."

I stayed quiet, knowing she wasn't done. And I was right. With a flair that bordered on dramatic, Mary reached into her bag and pulled out a crumpled copy of the *New York Post*. She slapped it onto my lap, the headline practically screaming up at me.

"Have you *seen* this?" she demanded, her voice laced with the kind of frustration that only a woman who'd been fighting battles since sunrise could summon. "I've spent the last two hours battling Harry Steinman and my editor over this."

"You and Harry Steinman…talking directly?" I asked, unable to keep the mix of surprise and disdain from my tone.

"Yes," she snapped, tossing her damp hair over her shoulder. "I had the story yesterday and killed it in exchange for some gossip on that hot new pop star, Trevor Twinkle. Little did I know, those vultures at *The Post* would get it."

I leaned back, the former PR professional in me unable to resist doling out a golden rule. "The one who tells the story first always wins."

Mary nodded. "Exactly. That's why he wants to meet."

I froze. "Wait, you're meeting Harry Steinman?"

Before she could answer, the taxi's built-in television burst to life, blaring an ad for our show. In perfect synchronicity, Mary and I lunged forward, hands colliding as we silenced the offending noise.

"Oh my God. I buried the headline," Mary blurted, her hands flying to her face, excitement practically radiating off her. "Do you remember the guy who literally caught me in the rain a few months ago?"

I didn't even try to suppress the grin spreading across my face. "Of course I do," I said. "Two strangers, one umbrella, and not a single phone number exchanged. It's practically a Nora Ephron script."

Mary giggled, the sound light and infectious. "Well, I've got his digits now!" she declared.

I let out an exaggerated gasp, unable to contain my excitement. "Mary, that is the most brilliant news I've heard all week. How did you find him?"

With a mischievous glint in her eye, Mary leaned in. "I'm a great reporter," she said with a shrug. "And let's be honest, how many Black guys in tuxedos could Lori Letmein possibly know?"

I threw my head back, laughing, before throwing her a mock-serious look. "Tell me you're not planning to wait months again before you speak."

"Oh, we already talked," Mary replied, flashing a grin that could rival any winning racehorse. "For over an hour. Last night."

"And?" I asked.

"We're meeting tonight," Mary said, her voice tinged with a teenage giddiness that I hadn't heard from her in years. "Some tiny little spot on the Lower East Side. He said it's his favorite hidden gem."

"Hidden gem," I repeated, savoring the words. "That's code for romantic."

Mary's smile faltered, and a flicker of anxiety appeared as she glanced at the screen. "It's him," she said urgently. "I should answer, right?"

"Absolutely!" I nodded aggressively. "And tell him he better hand you a rose tonight!"

Mary groaned. "No, it's not Bachelor Ben. It's *Harry Steinman!*" she hissed, just as the taxi glided to a smooth stop outside the studio.

She grabbed her purse and quickly rummaged through her wallet. Mary handed the driver an extravagant tip—along with her phone number. "You know, just in case you end up chauffeuring Harry and Meghan," she quipped before answering her call.

Inside the studio lobby, the guard barely glanced at us before offering a nod of recognition. Mary ended the call, her expression unreadable but heavy with something unspoken.

"So," I said carefully, breaking the silence. "What did Harry Steinman say?"

Her shoulders sagged slightly. "He wants to meet me at that disgusting Tipsy Teapot bar. Tonight!"

I raised an eyebrow. "But you're meeting Ben this evening," I reminded her, watching her reaction closely.

Mary hesitated, her thoughts clearly tangled in the impossible choice before her.

As our elevator ascended toward the forty-fifth floor, Carol Ann slipped out of the solo makeup chair and made her way down the hallway toward the bathroom, leaving Maria and Miss D alone for a moment.

Miss D hesitated, then carefully reached into a plastic bag resting by her side. "Could you spare a moment to look at my dating wig?" she asked, her tone tinged with concern as she gently lifted the feline-like creation from its protective cocoon.

Maria, caught off guard, looked up from her brushes.

Lowering her voice, Miss D set down her old device. "I have a date," she admitted. She glanced at the wig beside her. "I guess we both need a little love."

Maria's expression softened as the excitement of the moment settled between them. "Let me see what I can do," she said, offering a nervous smile.

"Thanks, Maria," Miss D said, her gratitude carrying the fragile mix of hope and trepidation. "It's someone I've been talking to for a while, but we've never actually met."

"Where are you meeting?" Maria asked.

Miss D's lips curved into a small smile. "There's this new spot in the Chelsea Hotel," she said. "It's supposed to be really cool and romantic."

Maria paused, holding the wig up to the light, her artistic instincts already at work. "Well," she said with a reassuring nod, "let's make sure you walk in there looking like a dream."

Suddenly, Carol Ann burst back into the dressing room, her curiosity lighting up. "What y'all talkin' about?" she demanded.

"Oh, I was just telling Miss D about *your* date tonight," Maria replied smoothly, exchanging a wink with Miss D.

Carol Ann let out a playful giggle, the kind that made it clear she loved nothing more than talking about herself. "It ain't a date, silly. It's a *business rendezvous* between two esteemed television professionals."

Miss D raised a brow, but before she could fire off a retort, the door swung open again, and Mary and I swept in, like a gust of wind. "Did I hear someone mention a date?" I teased, leaning against the doorframe with a smirk.

Carol Ann didn't so much as blink, her drawl as polished and deliberate as the silk Hermès scarf she casually looped over one shoulder. She slid back into "her" spot in the makeup chair like it had been reserved for her since the dawn of time. "Just a lil' mix-up. Anyhow, Mary and I have far more pressing matters to discuss," she said with a practiced air of gravitas, holding up the *New York Post* like a trophy.

"He oughta be in a chain gang!" Carol Ann declared, her voice rising with the kind of conviction usually reserved for courtroom dramas or beauty pageant finales.

Mary didn't even flinch. Her response came swift and razor-sharp, slicing through the charged air with fineness. "I'll be sure to pass that along to him tonight if I decide to meet him," she deadpanned, like she'd just mentioned picking up her dry cleaning.

The room froze. Carol Ann, Miss D, Maria, and I—every one of us suspended in mid-thought, our gazes darting toward Mary like she'd just dropped a Birkin onto the floor!

But Mary, unbothered by the weight of our collective disbelief, slid on her headphones with an air of finality that shut the conversation down entirely. She understood the rules of this world better than anyone: the one who tells the story first always wins.

And Mary?

She wasn't just telling the story.

She *was* the story.

Chapter 8

I knew that if our show was going to be more than a fleeting success—more than just another flash in the pan of celebrity gossip—it couldn't rest on exclusive scoops alone. It had to mean something deeper. It was about the connections, those intangible, invisible threads tying Mary, Carol Ann, Miss D, and me not just to one another, but to every single person sitting on a couch with a remote in hand.

Our viewers didn't just crave stories. They craved connection. Companionship. We weren't just in the gossip business anymore; we were now in the friendship business.

"How about we spice things up with a personal headline?" I announced as I veered ever-so-slightly off-script. Producer, seated just off-camera, gave an approving nod.

"Someone's got a date tonight," I declared in the final minutes of the show.

Mary rolled her eyes, already wise to my antics. She shot me a reluctant grin that said she both resented and appreciated my meddling. "You're such a troublemaker," she said, her tone half-exasperated, half-amused. "Although, if Alec Baldwin can find love, I suppose I have no excuses."

But I wasn't about to stop there. "And that's not all," I continued, upping the stakes. "A little birdie tells me Miss D is meeting someone special tonight."

I glanced toward Maria, working her magic on Miss D's infamous blue wig. Her smirk, however, betrayed her complicity.

Miss D's eyes narrowed, locking onto me with a look that could stop traffic. "Miss D is all about dishing *other people's* gossip, not her own," she declared, her tone sharp enough to carve a line in the sand.

I knew better than to push further. After all, in the friendship business, some lines weren't meant to be crossed. "Fair enough," I said, offering a nod of truce.

Carol Ann, feeling left out, took a deep breath, and made it about herself. "James," she began, pausing for effect, "if either of my older sisters needs any courtin' help tonight, I'm more than happy to offer my expertise. In fact, why don't I lend y'all somethin' fabulous to wear?"

From behind the camera, Producer audibly gasped. This wasn't just TV gold—it was a full-blown nugget of glittering platinum.

"That's a *brilliant* idea," I said, my surprise genuine.

Miss D delivered her verdict with a dramatic shake of her wig, her disapproval radiating through every exaggerated movement.

I turned my attention toward Mary, who hesitated, caught in the crosshairs of Producer's pointed gaze. The weight of expectation was thick, and after a brief but telling pause, she offered a reluctant nod.

It was all I needed. "Perfect!" I said, clapping my hands together like a ringmaster pulling off a particularly tricky act.

"Join us tomorrow for the grand unveiling of Mary's makeover and all the juicy details about her date!"

As the final credits rolled and the crew began trickling out of the studio, Carol Ann sauntered over to Mary. "Can't wait to see you tonight, bestie!" she chirped.

For the briefest moment, Mary allowed herself to believe this could be genuine But the thought evaporated as quickly as it arrived.

"And don't you worry," Carol Ann added, "I've still got some of my *fat clothes* from before I discovered discipline!"

Back up on the forty-fifth floor, in our dressing room, Miss D and I stood side by side in front of the mirror, the glossy sheen of our TV personas slipping away.

"I've got to hand it to you," Miss D said, her reflection catching mine. "That whole Mary and Carol Ann stunt? Pure genius."

I offered her a half-smile, the kind meant to acknowledge the compliment but not dwell on it. "Thanks," I said, though the word felt hollow. "But I'm worried Mary's going to flake on Ben. You know how she is—always putting work first, no matter what."

Miss D nodded slowly. "I'll tell you one thing: there's no way I'd cancel my date tonight, not even if my entire career was on the line."

I leaned in closer, unable to hide the sparkle of curiosity in my eyes. "So, who's the lucky guy?"

Miss D reached for the vibrant blue wig Maria had so expertly revived. She held it up like a crown. Smoothing it down with practiced precision, she caught her reflection and nodded approvingly. "Actually, we've never met," she admitted. "That's why I'm wearing this," she added, gesturing toward the wig.

I couldn't help but chuckle, her excitement infectious. "I'm thrilled for you," I said. "How did this blind date come about?"

She hesitated, her lips parting and then closing again, like she wasn't sure if this was the right moment—or the right person—to tell.

The silence stretched, not uncomfortable but charged. Finally, Miss D spoke, her words deliberate. "It's complicated," she began.

Her eyes flicked to mine, searching for something unspoken. Trusting a white person wasn't something she handed out lightly. It was a gamble she'd lost more times than she cared to count.

But then again, this wasn't just anyone. This was me, James.

Maybe it was the way my right arm bore scars that whispered stories I rarely dared to tell, silent witnesses to a past I'd much rather leave behind. Or maybe it was the fact that I am, unapologetically and proudly, gay—a truth that both defines and defies me. Whatever it was, these unspoken markers of who I am forged a connection with Miss D. Fellow outsiders, carving our own paths in a world that didn't always know what to do with us.

Miss D exhaled, bracing herself for impact.

"We met on an adult phone line," she blurted, the words tumbling out in a rush, her voice laced with an unexpected hint of relief. "I've never seen that two grand a week you promised and needed the money."

My eyes widened, not with judgment, but with the shock of an unguarded truth breaking through the surface.

And in that moment, something shifted between us. The carefully curated facade of our TV friendship—the banter, the playful jabs, the on-screen chemistry—crumbled, leaving something far more genuine in its place.

We weren't just colleagues anymore, we were friends—real friends, discovering that genuine friendship wasn't in hiding the truth—it was in letting each other see it.

In a city where taxi drivers and lobby attendants moonlighted as the omniscient narrators of everyone else's lives, Mary had perfected the delicate art of cultivating sources. A casual smile here, a well-timed compliment there—it was all part of her arsenal, a skillset that allowed her to do her job well—really well.

But tonight, Mary lingered in the marble-clad lobby of a painfully trendy Soho high-rise for a very different reason. She wasn't there to charm her way into a useful connection or add another name to her arsenal of allies. No, tonight, her hesitation was purely strategic—she was avoiding the insufferable nemesis waiting for her in apartment 15C.

Eventually, fourteen floors up—thanks to the classic New York superstition of skipping the thirteenth—Mary knocked softly, hoping the sound would be swallowed by the plush carpeted hallway.

Maybe no one would hear. Maybe she could turn around and escape.

No such luck.

The door flung open with the kind of theatricality that could only belong to Carol Ann. And there she stood, framed by the doorway, wearing nothing but a pink lace bra and matching panties.

Mary blinked, stunned into silence. It wasn't just the distinct lack of clothing that caught her off guard—it was Carol Ann's *utterly* unbothered confidence.

"It's good to see me...you," Carol Ann said, striking a casual pose.

Mary opened her mouth to respond, but Carol Ann was already moving. "We're gonna get dressed together!" she declared. Before Mary could protest, she was being pulled inside, the door clicking shut behind her.

In that moment, Mary realized she had officially entered Carol Ann's world—and there was no escape.

For someone used to reporting on the glitz and glam of New York's most exclusive events, Mary was utterly unprepared for what awaited her inside Carol Ann's apartment. Her eyes widened as she took in the sprawling, impeccably decorated space. Floor-to-ceiling windows showcased the glittering city skyline, casting a warm glow over the sleek, impossibly expensive furnishings.

"Your apartment is beyond incredible," Mary said, unable to keep the astonishment from her voice.

Carol Ann beamed, clearly delighted by the reaction. "It's a fusion of Carrie Underwood and Carrie Bradshaw!" she declared with pride.

"Or Uday and Qusay Hussein," Mary replied.

Turning a corner, Carol Ann gestured toward a sprawling gourmet kitchen that looked plucked straight out of a magazine. "An exact replica of Paula Deen's," she announced, puffing her chest out with pride like a rooster greeting the dawn.

Carol Ann continued. "Let me show ya the *pièce de résistance,*" she declared, her Southern twang infusing the French phrase with an unexpected charm.

With a flourish, she reached for a set of pristine white, floor-to-ceiling curtains. In one dramatic sweep, she drew them open.

Mary's jaw dropped. "Oh my God," she breathed.

Before her stood the walk-in closet to end all walk-in closets. Rows of designer clothes, organized by color and season, stretched endlessly. Shelves displayed an array of shoes that could rival a boutique in SoHo. Sparkling accessories—glittering necklaces, statement earrings, and even a tiara or two—shone under the ambient lighting, giving the space an almost heavenly glow. Mary could only think, *Even Ross Matthews would stay hidden in here.*

Carol Ann then reappeared at her side, holding up two bottles of booze like trophies. "I snagged us a couple," she announced with a playful grin. "Don't worry, I got that Skinny Girl poison. The more ya drink, the skinnier ya get."

Mary snorted, shaking her head. "Why don't we tackle the shopping first and save the drinking for later?" she added, trying to steer them back toward the task at hand.

But Carol Ann had a better idea. "How 'bout we shop *and* drink at the same time?" she proposed.

Demonstrating a level of grace that seemed to defy the laws of physics, Carol Ann climbed a twelve-foot ladder and slid effortlessly along her closet's custom-built track. She paused mid-glide, plucking a sexy Tom Ford dress from its place.

"No," Mary declared firmly, rejecting Mr. Ford's creation even faster than Gucci had rejected him years ago.

Sliding back up the track, an undeterred Carol Ann continued, "You're Elphaba, and I'm Glinda. And tonight, we're gonna be *wicked!*"

Mary rolled her eyes, but before she could protest, Carol Ann let out a triumphant gasp, pulling a green Versace gown from the depths of her treasure trove. The dress shimmered like the Emerald City itself.

Carol Ann held it up against Mary, her eyes sparkling with excitement. "You," she said, twirling the dress for effect, "are going to stop traffic in this."

Mary raised an eyebrow, unimpressed. "And by traffic, you mean a line of furious nuns?"

Carol Ann ignored her, already imagining the grand entrance. "Oh, don't be so dramatic," she said, shoving the gown into Mary's arms. "It's time to defy gravity."

"I couldn't, could I?" Mary muttered, half to herself, half to the shimmering green temptation draped across her arms. She hesitated, biting her lip as her reflection in the mirror winked right back at her. "Maybe I could try it on," she conceded, her voice barely above a whisper.

With a deep breath and a sip of liquid courage, Mary slid into the gown. The fabric hugged her frame in all the right places, cool against her skin and whispering of elegance, rebellion, and possibilities she'd never dared consider. Her heart raced, and it wasn't just the alcohol. It was the sheer thrill of stepping outside her comfort zone, of trying on not just the dress, but a different version of herself.

"May I take a look in the mirror?" Mary asked, her voice betraying both curiosity and hesitation.

Carol Ann wagged a finger at her. "Not until I return with more booze," she added, disappearing toward the kitchen in a flurry of pink and confidence.

Left alone, Mary felt the temptation rise to sneak a peek at her reflection. Then stopped, her hand hovering in mid-air.

Instead, she redirected her energy to finding shoes—something that screamed *Emma Stone* rather than *Sharon Stone.*

She began to sift casually through the sprawling wardrobe.

But then, nestled deep in the back of the closet, her hand caught on something unexpected. Gently, she pushed the jackets aside, revealing a collection that made her breath hitch.

A brunette wig. Sky-high stripper heels and several shoeboxes, stacked neatly, filled to the brim with cash.

Mary had discovered the skeletons hiding in Carol Ann's closet.

Chapter 9

Bottino's provided the backdrop for my weekly meeting with Producer—a ritual that had evolved into a masterclass in watching my ideas be cherry-picked, rebranded, and passed off as his own. But tonight, I hadn't come armed with my usual arsenal of suggestions. Instead, I had a single, unshakable mission: securing a raise for Miss D.

Producer, of course, had his own agenda.

"The network is breathing down my neck to break more sensational stories," he complained, absently fingering the out-of-place red flower in his lapel. "Plus, television adds ten pounds, and Mary's the last person who needs extra weight."

A wave of frustration surged through me. "Mary is the best reporter ever," I said, my voice unwavering. "And she's my best friend."

Producer's eyes narrowed, undeterred. "Then she needs to start breaking bigger stories," he shot back. "Or her size will become a bigger issue."

His words were a punch to the gut. My mind raced, searching for a way to shift the conversation, to protect Mary. "Let's strike a deal," I said. "Carol Ann, Miss D, and I will handle the sensational stuff. Meanwhile, Mary can focus on genuine journalism—the stories that give us credibility. Her perfume covers our stench."

Producer leaned back, his skepticism as palpable as the overpriced whisky in his glass. "Give me examples," he demanded.

I seized the moment, forcing a smile that felt about as genuine as a reality star's apology tour. "Tonight, Mary's been invited for drinks with Harry Steinman—you know, the guy on the cover of the *Post,*" I explained.

Internally, I cringed. I'd been urging Mary to meet Ben all day, but here I was, pivoting for the sake of the show. "It's the kind of story that could land you a fifth Emmy."

Producer's expression softened. The mention of an Emmy had done its job. Now, all that was left was the hardest part: convincing Mary.

"Excuse me, I need a moment," I announced abruptly. Without waiting for a reply, I made my way to the restroom.

Dialing Mary's number, I pressed the device to my ear, only to be met with her voicemail.

"Hi, it's Mary. Leave a message and make it an exclusive."

I hung up and immediately started texting. *Mary, you need to meet Harry Steinman tonight.*

A few seconds later, my phone vibrated with her reply: *What's going on?*

I sighed, leaning against the cold tile wall. *Producer's talking about shaking things up if we don't break more sensational stories,* I typed back.

My phone rang, Mary's name flashing across the screen. I answered, bracing myself for what was coming.

"What else did he say?" she asked, her tone sharp.

I hesitated, the truth stuck in my throat like a thorn. "Mary…"

"Just tell me!" she snapped, her voice rising.

I swallowed hard, knowing there was no good way to deliver what she deserved to know. "He also made a comment about your weight."

There was a long silence on the other end. The kind that said everything words couldn't. "Well, screw him," Mary spat, each word landing like a slap. "Screw Harry Steinman. And screw you for not having my back."

Before I could respond, the call ended with a decisive snap.

Distraught and disheartened, I reached into my pocket. From its depths, I produced the only thing I thought could offer relief—a small glass container of magic white powder.

Mary inhaled deeply, trying to steady herself as she sat alone at a small table in a noisy bar. She pulled out her phone, not to distract herself, but to fix something more pressing. Something infinitely more important than Ben or Harry.

Her fingers hovered over the screen, trembling slightly as she began to type. *James, I'm so sorry. I was angry, and I took it out on you.*

My response came almost immediately: *"Love means never having to say you're sorry."*

Mary smiled faintly, knowing her best friend adored a good love story.

As she debated if she had made the right choice between Harry and Ben, Mary became acutely aware of a pair of eyes fixed on her from across the room. Without her glasses, the figure was nothing more than a blur. But as it drew closer, the shape sharpened into something unmistakably familiar.

It was Brett Bottom.

Brett Bottom was one of those quintessential New York characters who could only exist in this city. Mary had tangled with him more times than she cared to remember, always angling for a mention in her column.

His features had a boyish softness to them, the kind that wouldn't look out of place on the cover of a One Direction album. And yet romantically, Mary had always assumed he went in the other direction.

"Mary, is that you?" Brett exclaimed, clearly struggling to reconcile the Mary he knew with the one sitting before him, transformed by layers of makeup, clothing, and cascading extensions.

"I'm sorry, Brett," Mary replied, her tone polite but edged with finality. "I'm actually waiting for someone."

But Brett Bottom was not a man who took hints, no matter how overt. "I'm thinking about starting my own fashion line," he said. "And I'd *love* to see it featured in your column."

Mary resisted the urge to roll her eyes. "Tell me when you've got someone famous wearing it," she quipped, sensing Brett's short attention span waning.

Sure enough, his gaze shifted as someone—or something—caught his eye—like a lone poppy blooming in a field of gray.

It was Carol Ann.

She'd barely perched herself on a barstool when a ripple of whispers swept through the room, signaling the arrival of someone important. Heads turned, eyes widened, and conversations stuttered as *he* made his entrance.

Josh Ellis.

"Carol Lee," Josh said as he approached, his hand extended toward her, firm and ready, like a quarterback about to call the winning play.

Carol Ann tilted her head, her blonde hair falling just enough to cast a shadow of mystery across her face. "You can call me anything you want," she purred, each word dripping with suggestion.

"You sound like my kind of girl," he murmured, his voice so rich and velvety it practically dared her not to lean closer.

Carol Ann's lips curled into a slow, knowing smile as she lifted her drink, taking a deliberate sip. She let the anticipation linger. "So, Josh, tell me," she drawled, her voice like honey, "What's your secret sauce of success?"

Josh Ellis was used to admirers—people who craved his power, his money, his body, and sometimes all three. But Carol Ann was different. No, what Carol Ann wanted was his fame. The glittering currency of relevance that kept your name on everyone's lips.

Josh could feel his heart pounding as he wrestled with what she was asking. Fame wasn't something he shared. It was his armor, his sanctuary, and his weapon, and the thought of giving even a sliver of it away made his stomach turn.

Finally, he broke the silence, his voice edged with self-preservation. "This isn't going to work," Josh said, each word clipped, deliberate.

With a practiced flick of his wrist, he pulled out his Tom Ford sunglasses and slipped them on, as if they could shield him from her. Without another word, he stood up and moved swiftly toward a group of adoring young ladies further down the bar—fans who wanted to worship at the altar of his fame, not share in it.

While Josh Ellis made his swift, dramatic exit from Carol Ann, Mary quietly disentangled herself from Brett Bottom. She slipped away unnoticed as she sought the only haven she could think of—the ladies' room.

For the first time that evening, there was quiet. No meddling Carol Ann, no annoying Brett Bottom, no horrible Harry, or handsome Ben.

It was just Mary—or so she thought. She leaned into the mirror, her fingers gripping the edges of the sink for support as she let out a long, slow breath. But when her eyes flicked up, her breath caught in her throat.

The face looking back wasn't hers.

"Where are you?" Mary whispered.

The silence of the room pressed back, as if waiting for an answer.

Mary reached for a paper towel, the coarse texture biting against her fingertips, grounding her in the present. She began wiping away Carol Ann's expertly applied makeup, each stroke erasing layers of someone else's version of who she should be.

What began as a routine act of cleansing slowly transformed into something deeper. With every smudge of foundation removed, she felt lighter, as though she were peeling away all expectation and pretense. She reached up to unclip the expensive hair extensions, her fingers fumbling but determined. When the last piece fell, the cool air against her scalp sent a shiver down her spine. It was more than relief—it was liberation. She had unhooked herself from an invisible leash.

Mary leaned into the mirror, wiping away the final trace of lipstick. And there she was. Raw, unadorned, and real.

She drew a deep breath, her chest rising with an unfamiliar sense of clarity.

Mary was ready—ready to face what truly mattered.

No more waiting for Harry Steinman to show up with a story. It was time to find Ben—and write her own.

Twenty minutes later, Mary stepped into a cool East Village dive bar, the kind of place where neon signs buzzed quietly over sticky wooden tables and the scent of beer and fried food hung in the air like a familiar embrace.

As she entered, a burst of laughter caught Mary's attention, a sound so genuine it felt magnetic. Her eyes followed it to the far corner, where she spotted him—Ben. He was leaning casually against the wall, wearing a vintage Joan Rivers T-shirt, the kind that made you feel like you'd just uncovered a hidden gem at a thrift store.

"I like your style," Mary said, her voice laced with playful admiration as she approached him.

"Funny girls are my thing," Ben replied, thrilled to see her. "Although, I've got to say, I love Ben Stiller too."

"What!" Mary gasped, her laughter bubbling out as her guard lowered. "Ben Stiller is the name of my cat. She's a girl."

Ben chuckled, the kind of laugh that made you want to laugh along, even if you didn't catch the joke. "Of course, *she* is. Come on, tell my friends all about her," he said, his hand resting lightly on Mary's lower back as he guided her toward the pool table. The warmth of his touch sent an unexpected flutter through her, a mix of excitement and nerves.

As they approached the group, Ben leaned in, his voice low but brimming with enthusiasm. "You've got to meet my friend Peter. He works for that guy on the cover of today's *New York Post*."

Mary's steps faltered for a split second. She turned to Ben, her eyes widening with surprise. "Harry Steinman?" she asked, the name tumbling out before she could stop herself.

Ben grinned. "The one and only."

Mary's mind raced. It wasn't just the flutter of Ben's touch anymore—it was the sudden realization that the path she thought she'd left behind might not be entirely out of reach after all.

"And get this," Ben continued, his grin widening. "Peter's sister Ann works for that crazy pop princess in Vegas. You know, the one who married her backup dancer on a dare."

The conversation flowed easily after that, a blur of laughter, shared stories, and the kind of effortless connection Mary hadn't enjoyed with a straight guy in ages. Ben was charming, but not in a rehearsed, look-at-me way. He was attentive without hovering, confident without being overbearing. His friends matched his energy—a quirky, kindhearted mix who made her feel welcome instead of scrutinized.

The hours slipped by unnoticed, and by the time Mary and Ben stepped outside, the cool night air felt refreshing against her flushed cheeks. She and Ben lingered on the sidewalk, his arm draped casually around her shoulder as if it had always belonged there.

Mary left with an amazing Black man tucked under her arm, a red-hot story tucked away for the show, and a green borrowed dress—unbeknownst to her—tucked into her panties.

Chapter 10

Miss D pushed open the doors of Café Chelsea, her eyes widening at the unexpected scene before her. The place was shockingly alive with energy and the faint, upbeat jazz filtering through the speakers. She'd been here before, but never this packed. Not on a Wednesday night.

"Did you get a glowing *New York Times* review I somehow missed?" she asked, her voice teetering between curiosity and disbelief.

The nonbinary host, sharp and stylish in a way that seemed to define the café's effortlessly cool vibe, glanced up with a polished smile. "Even better," they replied smoothly. "Taylor Swift's Instagram."

"Good for you," Miss D said, offering a polite smile that didn't quite reach her eyes. "But not good for me. Can I get a table for two?" she asked, though her tone betrayed that she already knew the answer.

The host shook their head gently, their voice kind but firm. "I'm sorry, we're fully booked tonight."

Miss D's gaze drifted over the crowded tables, her shoulders slumping ever so slightly as her hope ebbed. She murmured almost to herself, "I never seem to be in the right place at the right time."

The host's expression softened, carrying a hint of sympathy. "You could try the bar," they offered, as if handing her a lifeline. "There's a chance something might open up later, but I can't guarantee when."

Miss D nodded, her attempt at a smile faltering before it could take shape. "Thanks," she murmured, though the host's words felt as distant as the idea of truly belonging.

She made her way to the bar, perching on the edge of a sleek stool and traced invisible patterns on it with her fingertips, as if searching for answers in the grain.

Then, cutting through the noise like a beacon of warmth, came a voice she knew well—welcoming and very British.

"Miss D, is that you?" I asked as I pointed Ari toward her. A wide grin spread across my face as I practically bounded over to where she sat. "The wig looks absolutely *bluetiful!*" I exclaimed, wrapping her in a hug so warm it felt like home.

"Oh. My. Goodness, you're meeting him here!" I suddenly realized, the puzzle pieces clicking together with a satisfying snap.

Miss D managed a nod. "I'm trying to," she admitted, her words tinged with frustration. "But apparently, you need a reservation thanks to Taylor."

Her tone carried more than irritation—it carried the weight of someone who had spent far too long being overlooked, sidelined, and unseen. But I wasn't about to let her night end like this, fading into the background of someone else's story.

Leaning toward Ari, I lowered my voice. "I've got an idea," I murmured, ensuring he was on board before I moved forward.

His quick nod was all the confirmation I needed; Ari's easygoing demeanor made him the perfect accomplice.

I scanned the room until my eyes landed on the host—an old friend who owed me a favor or two.

After a quick exchange of words—and a discreet $100 bill passed with the ease of long practice—the impossible became reality. Ari and I surrendered our table, and within moments, it had been seamlessly reset for Miss D and her mysterious date.

"You're all set," I said, my voice light with triumph. "Now go knock him dead."

Miss D looked at me, gratitude and warmth lighting her expression. "Thank you," she said quietly, the words carrying more weight than she likely intended.

With her table ready and her spirits lifted, I stepped back, catching Ari's proud grin. Miss D's evening had turned around.

Before we left, Ari's turned to Miss D, his curiosity sparkling. "So, who's the lucky guy?" he asked.

"He's a mystery date," she confessed, like she was balancing on the edge of a thrilling secret.

Ari tilted his head. "How will you know it's him?"

She paused, as if debating whether to share one last detail. "I'll recognize him by the red flower in his lapel."

My breath caught. The red flower wasn't an offhand detail; it was a ticking time bomb wrapped in delicate petals.

There was no time to waste, no room for hesitation. I had to stop Producer, and I had to do it *now.*

With that, I tugged Ari toward the door, my mind racing.

"I'll explain everything when I get back to the flat," I blurted to him as I launched myself into the chaos of 23rd street, weaving through the tangle of yellow taxis zipping by—their sides emblazoned with ads for *The Gossip Gang*.

Within minutes, I was back at Bottino's, though the familiar surroundings were tinged with a sense of foreboding that settled heavy in my chest.

My eyes darted from table to table, scanning the room, searching for any sign of Producer.

And then I saw it.

A single red petal, lying on the floor near the door, a silent and damning clue. My heart sank as the realization hit me: I was too late. Producer had left just moments before I arrived.

Producer pushed open the door at Café Chelsea, the inviting golden light spilling onto the sidewalk as he stepped inside. He paused briefly, adjusting his red flower, before striding toward the host with the confidence of someone who rarely heard the word *no*.

"Can I help you?" came a voice from behind the stand.

Producer didn't miss a beat. "No, I have four Emmys," he replied.

The host nodded. This wasn't their first encounter with difficult customers; just last week, they'd handled James Corden.

Producer's gaze darted nervously around the room as he scanned the faces. His eyes finally landed on the striking silhouette of a Black woman seated at the bar, her elegant figure adorned with a vibrant blue hat that caught the soft, ambient light just right.

With optimism, he stepped forward, and his hand hovered for a moment before he tapped her gently on the shoulder.

She turned as she slipped off the blue hat with a graceful motion. Beneath it, a magnificent black fro unfurled, crowning her head with natural beauty and undeniable presence.

Realization hit Producer like the light of dawn. She wasn't his mystery lady.

Disappointment flickered across his face, fleeting but undeniable. He nodded politely, mumbling an apology before stepping back.

With determination renewed, Producer continued his search. Somewhere in this maze, his lady in the blue wig was waiting.

And then, Producer spotted her.

She sat alone at a small table near the window, her back toward him. Her luscious blue curls cascaded down her neck like a waterfall of midnight silk. Time seemed to slow as he stared, the weight of his anticipation coiling tightly in his chest.

It had to be her—the lady who had haunted him over the phone for months, her voice weaving through his thoughts long after their conversations ended.

Producer took a tentative step forward, his throat tightening as he tried to summon the courage to speak. But just as the words began to form, a man—young, confident, and cute, swept past him and headed straight toward her.

"Miss D!" the young man exclaimed.

Producer's hand instinctively flew to his face, as if to shield himself—and the rose in his lapel. The truth crashed over him in a wave.

Without hesitation, he turned on his heels, weaving through the bustling crowd with an urgency that bordered on desperation. Each step quickened until he was practically running, the anonymity of the city streets offering the only solace he could find. In the blink of an eye, he disappeared, swallowed whole by the endless sprawl of Manhattan, as if he had never been there at all.

Back at Café Chelsea, the young bartender—his features so finely chiseled they seemed borrowed from a classical French painting—sat deep in conversation with Miss D. His skin was pale, his frame slender, and his crooked smile was utterly disarming.

"I love you on that show," he said, his voice carrying an earnest warmth that caught Miss D off guard. She blinked, momentarily stunned.

"James is a regular here," he continued, his confidence building with each word, "but you're my favorite on the show."

Miss D felt a flutter in her chest, a mix of surprise and something she couldn't quite name. "Wow," she said, her voice softening. "You watch our show?"

"My name's Jay," he added. "But my friends call me Baby J."

"Pleased to meet you, Jay—oh, sorry, Baby J!" Miss D said, her voice warm but her thoughts still tangled in the mystery man who hadn't shown up.

Miss D couldn't quite ignore the spark this sweet guy ignited, the way his presence seemed to cut through her disappointment. While her mind lingered on the unfulfilled promise of the night, her heart leapt quietly at the prospect of something new—something unplanned.

"Finally," she said. "I seem to be in the right place at the right time."

Chapter 11

I sat at the table under the right studio lights, uncharacteristically quiet, my thoughts tangled in the events of last night. What had truly transpired when Miss D discovered the identity of her mystery man? And when Producer learned the truth about the person behind the voice that had been "soothing" him?

Miss D, however, practically radiated happiness, her smile softer than the one she wielded on camera. The kind of grin that spoke of finding a long-lost treasure.

The door to the studio swung open with a force that made everyone flinch. Producer stumbled in, his bloodshot eyes wild, darting around the room, but very deliberately avoiding Miss D. Behind him trailed his usual army of assistants, clutching mints and bottles of water like shields.

"What did I do now?" Miss D asked, her tone shockingly innocent.

A rueful smile tugged at my lips. "I think we're both well aware of the answer to that," I replied, unable to resist.

Miss D arched an eyebrow, intrigued. "What do you mean?" she pressed.

Unable to contain myself any longer, I blurted out, "I know who you met last night!"

For a fleeting moment, Miss D appeared genuinely caught off guard, her confusion deepening into something unreadable. But then, just as quickly, her expression transformed. Bewilderment gave way to unrestrained delight, her eyes lighting up like fireworks.

"How do you know about Baby J?" she exclaimed, her words tumbling out in a rush of excitement.

I blinked, completely thrown off by her response. "Baby J?" I repeated, the name hanging in the air as I tried to reassemble the mental puzzle now in disarray.

Miss D nodded enthusiastically, practically bouncing in her seat. "Yes! His real name is Jay," she explained, her voice bubbling with pride and admiration. "He's bartending now, sure, but mark my words, James—that boy is destined for stardom as a singer."

I stared at her, speechless. This wasn't the reveal I'd been bracing for—it was something else entirely.

"My mystery date never showed up," Miss D clarified, her voice carrying a faint trace of melancholy. But even as she said the words, her expression betrayed her—her thoughts seemed to drift toward something far more satisfying, the glimmer of joy and Baby Jay.

"And know I'll never know who he is," she added. "Because I quit my other job. No more late-night private phone calls for Miss D."

My eyes widened in delight. "You quit your job?" I asked. "Because you met a new chap?"

Miss D shook her head. "No, silly," she said, her laugh light and carefree. "Because I don't need the extra money anymore."

I furrowed my brow, trying to piece it all together. "What do you mean?" I asked.

Miss D leaned in, her excitement practically radiating off her. "When I got home, there was an unexpected email from Producer. Miss D just got a big, fat raise," she said, her voice brimming with a newfound sense of liberation—the kind that only comes when a long-held burden is suddenly lifted.

I felt a rush of joy flood through me, mixed with a flurry of questions. "That's brilliant news. You deserve it," I said sincerely, though a loud voice in the back of my mind refused to let go of the nagging suspicion that this sudden windfall wasn't entirely coincidental.

"We must celebrate," I exclaimed. "What are your plans for this evening?"

"Well," Miss D began, her voice dripping with intrigue, "Baby J and I were planning to check out this new karaoke bar, but he got stuck covering a shift. So, count me in," she added with a wink. "And thanks to Producer, I'm payin' tonight."

My surprise must have been evident as I explained, "I've received a rather marvelous tip about Trevor Twinkle. Let's meet at Bottino's first, and then we'll track him down."

Before Miss D could respond, a loud, abrasive voice cut through the air. "The temperature of this bottled water is *unacceptable*!" Producer bellowed as he tore into one of his unfortunate assistants.

Miss D arched an eyebrow and nodded toward the commotion. "Looks like someone had a rough night," she observed.

Caught off guard, I let out a soft gasp. "You haven't the faintest idea," I murmured, my words laced with equal parts amusement and dread.

Across the studio, Mary and Carol Ann made their entrance, radiating the kind of chemistry that only two new best friends—one reluctantly so—could muster.

"How'd your little ol' date go?" Carol Ann asked, her tone drenched in genuine indifference, as if the answer were a chore she had to endure.

Mary's face lit up. "I absolutely made the right decision to follow my heart," she gushed. "Ben and I had a great night. No, scratch that—we had a *fantastic* night."

"Well, ain't that just precious," Carol Ann remarked, the boredom practically dripping from her voice as she inspected her nails with exaggerated disinterest.

Mary's cheeks flushed a delightful shade of pink, her smile growing wider with each passing second. "I know this sounds crazy," she said, her voice soft but resolute, "but I'm going to marry him."

The words spilled out with a certainty that seemed to startle even Mary.

Carol Ann's expression shifted immediately, morphing into a mask of suspicion. "You don't go hitchin' yourself to some fella you just met in the East Village." she drawled. "You marry fellas you meet at The Tipsy Teapot," she added, her tone brimming with unshakable confidence.

"And might I add," Carol Ann continued, her voice shifting into a register of exaggerated hurt, "it's quite self-centered of you not to inquire about *my* night, after *everything* I did for you, bless your heart."

Mary's smile faltered slightly, guilt nibbling at the edges of her joy as she remembered Carol Ann's earlier misguide efforts to help. "I'm sorry," Mary stammered, a genuine apology coloring her words. "How was your night?"

"Well," Carol Ann began, "Brett Bottom confided in me that he is bisexual. Which means," she said, pausing for emphasis, "he fancies me more than anyone else on God's green earth—be they man *or* woman. Now, darlin', that's what I call a real high compliment."

Mary bit back a laugh as they reached the table.

Producer strode toward the group. His bloodshot eyes betrayed exhaustion, but his energy was unmistakable—a man on a mission.

"Mary!" he called out, his voice threaded with a rare hint of genuine admiration. "That new reporting on Harry Steinman? Pure gold. I'm bumping you to the top of the show!" His grin spread wide, despite his hangover. "The only thing viewers love more than a scandal is a wedding."

At his words, a light bulb seemed to flicker on in Carol Ann's mind. "Mary, you sure are a sly fox," she drawled.

Mary blinked, caught completely off guard. "What?"

Carol Ann took a dramatic breath, like she was delivering the punchline of an especially juicy story. "Mary's fixin' to marry some scruffy fella she met down on skid row," she declared.

Producer paused, rubbing his chin thoughtfully. "It *would* be good for ratings," he mused aloud. "If only we could find a guy willing to marry Mary!"

Mary's hands shot up in exasperation. "I'm right here!" she protested, her voice rising with indignation.

Unperturbed, Producer shifted his focus to something he clearly deemed far more pressing. "Do not forget," he said, addressing the group with his usual authoritative air, "you've all got compulsory media training this afternoon with one of the best in the business."

As he walked away, Carol Ann couldn't resist the opportunity to stir the pot. "Is the special needs trainin' on account of Miss D?" she asked, her tone dripping with sweetness that only made it more sting.

Miss D didn't say a word, but her expression shifted, the flicker of hurt unmistakable.

I interjected quickly, determined to nip this in the bud before it spiraled further. "We could all use a bit of extra guidance, Carol Ann," I said, hoping to diffuse the tension.

"Not little ol' me!" Carol Ann shot back, her unshakable confidence radiating like a spotlight. "Brett Bottom insists I'm a star."

Miss D, still grappling with her thoughts, turned to me, her voice soft and unsure. "Should Miss D be worried?" she asked, her anxiety barely concealed beneath her polished exterior. "I can't afford to lose this job now, not after I quit my other one."

I leaned in closer, offering her the calm assurance she needed. "Why would you be worried? You've just received a raise," I reminded her. "Plus, the network investing in us is a good sign. And besides," I added with a faint smile, "our trainer's name is Nancy Reagan. How serious can this be?"

Miss D's lips curved into a small, tentative smile, but before she could respond, Producer reappeared, his expression sheepish and his tone tinged with urgency.

"James, can I have a quick word?" he asked, glancing around as if ensuring no one else was paying attention.

I nodded cautiously and followed him to a secluded corner of the studio.

"How do you get all this gossip?" he asked, his tone a mix of curiosity and caution.

I took a deep breath, knowing this moment was inevitable. “Is Kathlegal having issues with Carol Ann’s ‘reporting’ again?” I asked.

Producer surprised me by shaking his head. “This isn’t about Carol Ann,” he confessed, his voice dropping an octave. “Quite the opposite, actually. I’m curious about how you, Mary, and Miss D manage to get the real reporting.”

Relief washed over me like a gentle tide. I straightened up, preparing to share the secrets I’d guarded for so long. “It’s all about building relationships and staying connected,” I began.

“Give me an example,” Producer urged, his voice cautious but undeniably eager.

I smirked slightly, leaning in as if letting him in on a well-kept secret. “Remember when Ashton had a dalliance with that young lady at the hotel while he was still married?” I started.

“Afterwards, he arranged for a limo to take her home. Quite a gentlemanly gesture, wouldn’t you agree?” I paused for effect, then continued. “But here’s the kicker: the moment the young lady got into the car, she started calling her friends to boast about her encounter. Who wouldn’t?”

Producer’s eyes narrowed, the gears in his mind turning as he absorbed every detail.

“Well,” I went on, “the driver overheard everything. By the time she got home, that chauffeur had shared the story with four close mates. And those four? Each shared it with another four. Within hours, the story had legs.”

Producer nodded thoughtfully, taking a deliberate sip of his water. “Like a ripple in a puddle,” he murmured, his voice barely above a whisper.

A knowing smile tugged at my lips. “At all the awards ceremonies, you know those lovely folks who spend the entire night going up and down in lifts. They're all spies," I said with a touch of amusement. "Mary also stations people in the bathrooms. And do you know what's most surprising? The gentlemen's bathroom yields far juicier gossip."

Producer chuckled softly, but his smile faded as the weight of something more significant crept back into his expression.

"James," he began carefully, his tone like someone trying to navigate a field of landmines, "what if someone…if someone had been engaged in phone sex? How might that kind of thing get out?"

I froze for a split second, the realization hitting me like a jolt of electricity. I had been right about him and Miss D all along.

"Has this individual disclosed this to anyone?" I asked, my voice calm and steady, giving nothing away.

"Absolutely not," Producer replied with total certainty, his tone like the slam of a vault door, locking away secrets he clearly didn't intend to share.

"However," I continued, my words cutting through his confidence like a knife, "just because it shan't leak from *his* side doesn't mean it cannot slip out from the person on the other end of the telephone."

"Impossible," Producer replied, far too quickly. "She doesn't know it's me," he added, and with that, the last card in his hand slipped.

Inadvertently, he'd confirmed everything.

Chapter 12

Mary's eyes swept across the room, landing on the woman lounging with practiced ease on the dressing room's couch, a vision of timeless poise and calculated glamour. *The* Nancy Reagan. Media whisperer, star-maker, and a walking institution.

She was draped in a crimson tunic that fell in fluid waves over sharply tailored black palazzo pants, her silhouette a masterclass in effortless authority. Around her neck, layers of delicate gold chains caught the light with every tilt of her head, their sparkle somehow managing to feel both gaudy and utterly chic—like Mr. T reborn as a Met Gala centerpiece.

Nancy's voice broke the quiet, a smooth contralto honed by years of commanding rooms far larger and more intimidating than this one.

"It's borderline negligence to put you on live television without proper preparation," she intoned, each word dripping gravitas that could silence Meryl Streep. "Pavarotti had training. Marilyn studied technique. And Brando…well, he trained me how to kiss."

Mary's head jerked up, her composure cracking for the briefest second. *This woman name-dropped like confetti at a New Year parade*—sparkling, endless, and impossible to ignore. "Wait—did you just say you kissed Marlon Brando?"

Nancy allowed a theatrical pause, her perfectly arched brow lifting just enough to draw the suspense taut. "Do you use condoms?"

"Excuse me?" Mary stammered, her voice tinged with shock and a hint of amusement.

Nancy repeated herself, her perfectly lined lips forming each letter with deliberate, theatrical precision. "C-o-n-d-o-m-s," she drawled, her tone dripping with bemused patience. "Think of me as the world's most glamorous, colossal condom. Here to protect you."

Mary blinked, momentarily thrown off-kilter by the quirky metaphor. Odd as it was, Nancy's approach carried a certain charm. "Thank you," Mary managed. "I think."

Nancy leaned back with a knowing smile. "Relax," she said, her voice softening, as if the next words were a gift wrapped in silk. "I'm not here to pry into your love life. No, I'm interested in your *whole* life. Tell me—what led you here?"

The question was tender, disarming, and completely unexpected. Mary took a deep, steadying breath and smiled—a real one this time—ready to let a little more of herself slip into the room.

As she spoke, Mary realized that Nancy didn't just listen; she absorbed. Her head tilted ever so slightly, her eyes narrowing with a razor-sharp focus that bordered on unnerving. It was as if she were peeling back layers, not with judgment but with the precision of a master tailor, fitting together fragments of Mary's story into something whole.

After an hour of this unexpected excavation of Mary's soul, Nancy leaned forward, her elbows resting lightly on her knees. The movement was casual, but her words were anything but. "My friend owns a comedy club downtown," she announced. "You're performing there in two weeks."

Mary's jaw dropped, her mind spinning as her heart ricocheted between disbelief and outright panic. "Me?" she croaked, her voice so faint it barely registered. "I couldn't—I mean, I can't—" The words tangled in her throat.

Nancy didn't flinch. "Why not?" she challenged, her tone clipped but not unkind. "Do you have to stay home and scrub floors? Or are you afraid the neighbors will talk?"

The words hit their mark with laser-like accuracy. This wasn't just about Mary's fear of the standing on a stage—it was about finding the courage her mother never had.

In that instant, Mary realized something profound: Nancy Reagan might not have been the real First Lady, but she was the first woman to make Mary believe she could be more. And that, Mary decided, didn't just make Nancy presidential—it made her extraordinary.

Miss D stepped into the dressing room, and for a fleeting moment, the world around her seemed to pause. The view from forty-five floors above Times Square stretched out before her, a dazzling tapestry of lights that glittered like stardust scattered across the city. But tonight, the skyline wasn't what made her heart race.

It was the woman by the makeup chair.

Nancy Reagan. Alone, yet utterly complete.

"I hear you're a big fan of Cynthia Erivo," Nancy began, each word landing with exactness. Her gaze was steady, almost measuring. "You remind me of her."

Miss D blinked, the words hitting her like an unexpected melody. "Really?" she managed, her tone wavering between disbelief and curiosity.

"And I hear you can sing, too," Nancy added, a glimmer of something—encouragement? challenge?—dancing in her eyes.

Miss D took a breath, her lips parting as she let the first notes escape. Soft at first, then stronger, she began to hum *Ease on Down the Road.* With each note, Miss D felt a little braver, a little lighter, as if the city below and the woman before her were cheering her on.

Nancy joined in effortlessly, her voice intertwining with Miss D's so seamlessly it felt like they'd been singing together for years.

When the song ended, Nancy clapped her hands together lightly, her eyes alight with genuine excitement. "*This,*" she exclaimed, gesturing toward Miss D with a flourish, "*this* is the version of you the world needs to hear and see! Where has she been hiding?"

Miss D's smile flickered, then faded, replaced by a wistful look. "I've been too busy just trying to blend in," she admitted softly. "It's not easy navigating a world that doesn't always appreciate uniqueness."

Nancy nodded, her expression thoughtful. She didn't speak right away, but her silence felt intentional, a quiet acknowledgment that, as much as she might want to, she would never fully grasp Miss D's reality.

Finally, she asked, her voice as gentle as a breeze, "Tell me—how did all this start?"

Miss D's mind flashed back, vivid and clear as a photograph. Her parents, her church, the sound of gospel ringing out on Sunday mornings, and the first copy of *Us Weekly* she'd ever held, hidden between the pages of her Bible. It had been a world of contradictions—faith and ambition, tradition and rebellion, black and white, all wound up in a girl who dreamed of something more.

"Thankfully, things are changing," Miss D whispered, her words carrying both hope and a trace of exhaustion. "Slowly."

"But we've still got a long way to go," Nancy replied, her voice touched by the weight of decades of watching history ebb and flow. "Which is exactly why you need to grab this moment standing on the shoulders of those who came before you, while holding open the door of those who came after you."

Miss D's voice cracked slightly as she admitted, "I just wish my pappa were here to see his daughter—me—on TV."

Nancy's expression softened with the kind of warmth that could melt stone. "He's watching," she said, as if sharing a sacred truth. "So, stop trying to blend in and start standing out."

The words hung in the air, heavy and light all at once. They felt like permission, like a nudge from the universe—or maybe, Miss D thought, from her dad—for her story to truly begin. And for the first time, she let herself believe she was ready.

Moments later, I found myself face-to-face with the one and only Nancy Reagan.

"Finally," she exclaimed, her voice warm yet sharp, like a perfectly brewed cup of tea. "I get to meet the man with all the ideas!"

The compliment landed squarely in my chest, and for a moment, I let myself bask in it. "Cheers," I replied, my tone light. "For the record," I added, a mischievous glint in my eye, "it was *not* my idea to hire Carol Ann."

Nancy's laughter rang out, rich and full-bodied, before she shifted gears, her expression sharpening as she got down to business.

"I like to start all my sessions with a little getting to know you," she said like she was offering me a membership at a very exclusive club.

"Then let's start at the very beginning," I replied, channeling my best Julie Andrews.

Nancy's eyes lit up, her smile stretching wide as she caught the reference. "A very good place to start," she said, nodding approvingly.

I watched Nancy Reagan sigh as I spoke about my childhood, her eyes misting with memories of her own son's struggles.

"Your mommy was right," Nancy said. "Show me someone who never gossips, and I'll show you someone who's simply not interested in people," she quipped. Then, with a conspiratorial glint in her eye, she added, "Barbara Walters let me in on that secret."

I laughed, the sound bubbling up unexpectedly, like an overdue exhale. "Everyone has a story."

Nancy's lips curved into a knowing smile. "Give me just a minute to refill my tea," she said, her tone as casual as it was intriguing. "Then I'll tell you something surprising about my own son."

The door clicked shut behind her, and the silence wrapped around me like an unwelcome guest. Then the voices came. Cruel, unrelenting, and familiar.

You're not good enough. You don't belong here. You'll never be enough.

My hands moved instinctively, slipping into my pocket, searching for something to quiet the restless hum in my mind, to silence my lambs.

A few moments later, Nancy Reagan reentered the room, looking refreshed. I glanced up, feeling a similar surge of energy, but before I could say a word, the door flew open again.

Carol Ann swept in, her arms draped with bags overflowing with designer clothes, each one threatening to burst open.

"Let's make this quick because I need to return these clothes before 5 p.m., sugar," she said, her voice laced with the impatient tone of someone who always has something more important to do.

Sensing the storm brewing, I seized the moment to say "goodbye" and make my swift exit, slipping out with the same speed Carol Ann had burst in.

Nancy took a measured breath. "Typically, I prefer to chat with my new clients without letting them know they're being recorded," she said, gesturing toward a sleek, almost invisible camera perched inconspicuously in the corner. "But I think you've already shown me everything I needed to see."

With that, she slung her oversized bag over her shoulder, her expression betraying nothing, and exited the room.

"Being recorded," Carol Ann muttered to herself, the words barely audible as they slipped past her lips. Her pacing quickened, the small room suddenly feeling even smaller. "Without knowing they were being recorded," she repeated, her voice rising.

Then it hit her, sharp and clear, slicing through the fog of confusion. *Wait.* Mary, Miss D, and James—none of them had the faintest idea they were being recorded.

The realization sent a jolt of energy coursing through her. Moving with a speed born of adrenaline, Carol Ann snatched the remote control from the makeup counter and jabbed at the play button.

At first, the footage was a little dull. Mary rattling on about her overbearing mother, her noisy neighbors, and her compulsive need to turn everything into a joke to cover up her pain. Miss D lamenting her exhausting attempts to blend in. Then there was James—sharing details of a childhood marred by bullying, the taunts about his little arm.

But then, the footage shifted.

Her heart gave a startled jolt as the image came into focus. "James," Carol Ann said, caught red-handed with a rolled-up twenty-pound note.

Her lips curled into satisfied smile. At first, it was small, almost imperceptible, but it grew.

With careful precision, she leaned forward and eased the memory card from the camera. The weight of it in her hand felt heavier than it should, solid with promise and opportunity. Her mother's voice—sharp, relentless, and all too familiar—echoed in her mind: *Only first place counts.*

Now, Carol Ann knew she wasn't just *in* the game—she was about to win it all.

Chapter 13

Mary, Miss D, and I nursed our drinks at Bottino's with the kind of purpose that suggested our evening was only beginning.

"Where is that last round?" I asked, scanning the room like a hawk in Prada.

Miss D flashed a wicked grin. "Tonight, they're on me!" she announced.

"Cheers to that," I said, raising my glass to toast her generosity before hesitating for a moment. This was going to be the tricky part. "I, uh, invited Carol Ann to join us too."

The reaction was immediate and icy, as if I'd just announced we were splitting the bill. Mary shivered, her cocktail suddenly less interesting, while Miss D's eyes rolled so far back I half expected them to land in another time zone.

"Don't worry," I added quickly, smoothing the tension like a freshly pressed Hermès scarf. "She's not coming. I just thought it'd be nice to include her, but she's working late. Doing what, I have no idea."

"Probably making up stories," Miss D quipped.

"Well, we know who she's *not* doing. . . ." Mary let the words dangle like bait before adding with a sly smirk, "Brett Bottom."

"God bless America," Miss D laughed, placing a hand over her heart with exaggerated sincerity. "But seriously, what's the secret to a happy relationship?"

"Being gay?" Mary fired back, looking at me and thinking about Ari.

"Marry someone who's already happy," I replied, knowing the answer really was that simple.

We stepped outside; the cool air wrapped around us as we set out to hunt down Trevor Twinkle. On the cusp of another story, oblivious to the watchful eyes that had been following us all night from the moment we stepped into the bar.

Twenty minutes later, Mary, Miss D, and I walked into a downtown gentleman's club that felt like crossing into an alternate reality.

The star of the show had just finished her act—a striking brunette with a fierceness that was both magnetic and maddening. She moved with the kind of carefulness that left you guessing, always pulling back just before revealing too much—and quite literally, covering her ass.

Miss D's eyes darted across the room like a kid unleashed in FAO Schwarz, scanning every shadow for Trevor Twinkle. Mary, on the other hand, wore her disapproval like a designer trench—impeccable and impenetrable.

I stood somewhere in the middle, caught between Miss D's wide-eyed wonder and Mary's barely veiled disdain, feeling like an outsider trying to solve a riddle in a language I barely understood.

"Let's split up," I suggested, my voice rising just enough to cut through the music.

I turned to Miss D, my tone softening. "And tonight, this is yours—your exclusive. Consider it a gift," I added, letting a warm sincerity slip into my words.

Miss D's eyes widened, a flicker of surprise melting into gratitude. "Thank you," she said simply, but her voice carried layers beyond the words.

As Mary and Miss D disappeared into the shadowy depths of the club—one with purpose, the other with protest—I found myself lingering by the bar.

However, it wasn't the promise of a drink that pulled me in. My gaze snagged on a face that didn't belong here, an out-of-place expression in a room filled with practiced performances.

"Carol Ann, is that you?" I asked, my voice tinged with incredulity. Her signature blonde locks, usually coiffed to perfection, were tied back in a simple ponytail. "What are you doing here?"

She turned slowly. "Why, meetin' you, sweetie," she replied, the words tumbling out just a little too quickly, her drawl syrupy but strained.

A cold unease coiled in my stomach. This wasn't right. I had invited Carol Ann to Bottino's, not here. There was no way I'd let her anywhere near the Trevor Twinkle lead. She'd wrest it from Miss D faster than you could say "breaking news."

"Wait!" I called after her as she began to weave through the club's crowd.

Outside, under the hazy glow of a solitary streetlamp, I finally caught up to her.

"Carol Ann, what's going on?"

She twirled around the streetlamp, her movements practiced. She stopped abruptly. "For heaven's sake, James, I'm a stripper," she blurted out, the words cutting through the night air like a knife.

I froze, the revelation hitting me like a gust of wind that stole the breath from my lungs. My mind scrambled to catch up. She'd always been an enigma, a puzzle I'd worked hard to solve, but this—this was the piece that upended the whole picture.

"The only time my mama ever noticed me," she explained, "was when I was up on that stage. It's my drug, and let's not pretend you don't know a thing or two about that."

With a flourish, Carol Ann reached into her bag and pulled out a small memory card. She held it out to me, like an accusation.

My throat tightened, panic coursing through me like an electric current. "What's that?" I asked.

"We both know precisely what it is," Carol Ann replied. "Your 'media training' session was being recorded."

My pulse quickened with each word. *How could I have been so careless?*

But then, something shifted.

"Listen, thanks for inviting me to join you, Mary, and Miss D tonight," she said, with an unexpected warmth. "You didn't have to include me."

Her sincerity caught me off guard. I managed a smile, though my heart was still racing beneath the surface. "You're welcome," I replied.

Carol Ann drew in a deep, steadying breath—the kind you take before deciding to leap into the unknown.

She glanced at the memory card in her hand, her grip loosening slightly, as if weighing her options. She couldn't quite believe what she was about to do, but a fragile hope stirred within her—a hope that maybe, just maybe, she'd found something more valuable: a friend.

"Here, catch," she said, her tone casual, as she tossed the memory card to me.

I instinctively reached out, catching it in my left hand. The significance of the gesture wasn't lost on me. It wasn't just a memory card—it was a secret kept.

"Thank you," I managed to say, trying to process the moment under the streetlamp. It was quiet and tender moment, a stark contrast to the chaos about to explode inside the club behind us.

"Ben!" Mary gasped, looking across the room, her voice a mix of shock and disbelief. Her beloved purse slipped from her grasp, hitting the floor with a soft, defeated thud. "What is he doing here?"

Miss D's mouth fell open, her usually sharp wit rendered silent as she silently prayed for an answer to make sense of the moment.

"My dad left my mom for a stripper," Mary whispered, her voice breaking. "We need to get out of here. Now."

Miss D hesitated, standing at the edge of an invisible crossroads. Was she here for the exclusive, or was she here for her friend?

The answer came quickly. Miss D reached out and hooked her arm through Mary's, her touch firm but comforting. "Come on," she said, steering her away from the heartbreak and toward the front door.

As they stepped into the cool night air, they found themselves face-to-face with Carol Ann and James.

Miss D's eyes narrowed, suspicion flaring instantly as her gaze zeroed in on Carol Ann. "What is *she* doing here?" she snapped.

"I invited her," I said quickly, now trying to shield Carol Ann's secret. The soft glow of the streetlamp fell across Mary's face, illuminating her dark expression.

"Mary," I asked. "What happened?"

"We need to get her home," replied Miss D.

"Of course," I replied without hesitation, ready to spring into action. But before I could take a step, Mary shook her head.

"No," Mary said, her voice steady, each word deliberate. "Getting the story is more important than me."

"Nothing is more important than you," I shot back, my voice low but resolute.

Carol Ann turned toward me. "Listen," she drawled, "y'all get Mary home, and I'll handle gettin' the scoop. I know this place better than any of us," she admitted, lowering her voice.

"But you know this is a Miss D exclusive," I replied, my apprehension creeping in.

Carol Ann tilted her head and flashed a knowing smile. "That's just fine by little ol' me," she said. "After all, we are a team."

Back in her cozy Harlem apartment, Miss D stood in the tiny bathroom, her reflection glowing with the flush of the night's events, and then, as if compelled by a force deep inside her, she began to sing.

As she sang, pride welled up in her chest. Tonight, hadn't just been about finding her voice—it had been about *using* it for a friend.

Carol Ann twisted the faucet, listening to the soothing rush of water as her tub filled with luxurious, bubbly warmth. The scent of Jo Malone candles wrapped around her like a familiar embrace, the rising steam engulfing her.

Her eyes drifted to the large TV embedded in the mirror. With a casual flick of the remote, a copy of the tape she had handed to James earlier played, a quiet reminder of the lengths she'd go to ensure she always covered her ass.

Just when Mary felt like she couldn't cry anymore, something strange began to stir. Joan Rivers's words echoed in her mind: "Humor doesn't come out of the good times, it comes out of the anger, pain, and sorrow."

Mary scrambled around her tiny apartment, searching frantically for her beloved Chloé bag, the place she always kept her notebook. Losing a man was one thing—she could chalk that up to the universe's twisted sense of humor—but losing her beloved bag? That was like losing a piece of her soul.

The realization hit Mary like a punch to the gut.

Chloé was missing!

I found myself standing alone in my bathroom. The dim light above the mirror cast a harsh glow on my reflection, highlighting every line of exhaustion and regret etched into my face.

With steady hands, I reached into my pocket. The memory card Carol Ann had slipped me felt cold against my fingertips. Beside it was a small vial of white powder.

For a moment, I stood there, caught between two versions of myself. One wanted to hold on, to let the past and its comforts linger just a little longer. But the other—tired, worn, but not entirely defeated—was ready to let it go.

In one swift, decisive motion, I dropped both into the toilet.

It wasn't the kind of moment that changed everything all at once. But it was something—a small, hopeful step toward healing. And for tonight, that was enough.

Chapter 14

"Mary, these new jokes are actually funny," Producer said, looking surprised as the final credits rolled. He adjusted the sleeves of his jacket, a faint smirk curling his lips. "And I never thought I'd say this, but…I love the glasses."

Mary forced a smile, one that barely hid her exhaustion after days of tearing apart her apartment in search of her beloved Chloé bag and sidestepping Ben's increasingly concerned texts. "Thanks," she replied, her tone as drained as her patience.

"Miss D," Producer continued, his attention shifting like a spotlight. "The Trevor Twinkle exclusive is pulling in online views faster than a Taylor Swift concert. Stunning work, as always."

Miss D's face lit up. She glanced toward the rest of us at the table—a look brimming with unspoken gratitude.

"And," Producer said, as Carol Ann began to rise from her chair, ready to accept what she clearly assumed would be her moment. "Right after the show, we've got a post-tape in your dressing room."

Carol Ann froze, her smile tightening into something that looked more like a grimace.

"I hope it's quick," Mary muttered. "I have a column to get back to."

Producer ignored her. "Oh, and one more thing," he added, a wicked glint flashing in his eyes. "Expect an email from me later today. Very important. Life-changing, even. Be sure to respond immediately."

Five minutes later, the dressing room on the forty-fifth floor was packed with all of us, crammed together in front of the oversized mirror framed with glowing bulbs. The air hummed with a mix of curiosity and simmering unease as we exchanged furtive glances.

"What do you think the email is about?" Miss D asked, her voice betraying the nervous energy she'd been carrying ever since her recent raise.

I shrugged, leaning against the edge of the dressing table, where half-empty coffee cups and stacks of makeup cluttered the surface. "No idea," I said, the uncertainty in my voice mirroring hers.

Mary adjusted her glasses with an exaggerated huff, her irritation palpable. "Why can't men just say what they mean?" she snapped, the words more venomous than the situation required.

I raised an eyebrow, picking up on the fact that her frustration had less to do with Producer and everything to do with a certain someone else. "Maybe you should return Ben's calls," I suggested, my tone deliberately mild but pointed enough to make Mary shoot me a withering glance.

Miss D, ever the diplomat, nodded in agreement. "I'm with James on this," she said, her tone light but firm, as if delivering sage advice while trying not to escalate a brewing storm.

Carol Ann set down her lipstick with a flourish and joined the conversation. "Just 'cause you're in a strip club don't make you a monster," she quipped, her Southern lilt turning the phrase into something almost poetic. She threw me a playful wink. "After all, you were there workin' too."

I couldn't help smirking, while Mary sighed—a sound that carried the weight of grudging acknowledgment. "Let's talk about it after the post-tape," she muttered, her attention snagged by the sight of the camera crew striding past the open dressing room door, their equipment slung over their shoulders like battle gear.

"What exactly are we filming?" Miss D asked, her tone tinged with mild suspicion.

"We're fixin' to tape a 'special project' with that fabulous psychic Producer's been schmoozing with," Carol Ann chimed in, practically vibrating with excitement.

"So, let me guess," Miss D said, her brow arching with practiced precision. "Producer's using us to shoot a free pilot?"

Mary smirked, gesturing toward me. "He should just have you produce it—then it would be a hit."

I opened my mouth to retort, but the air in the room shifted like a scene change. Enter Johnny Futura, psychic to the stars, in all his electric, technicolor glory.

His jet-black toupee, slick and immaculate, was perched atop his head, perfectly juxtaposed against his impossibly thin mustache, which seemed sculpted with the care of an artisan crafting a Fabergé egg. Johnny Futura didn't just walk—he *arrived.* Each step was an event, each move radiating the kind of self-assuredness most people could only dream of.

The ensemble? Unforgettable. Electric-blue trousers clung unapologetically to his formidable thighs, paired with a hot pink silk shirt undone halfway down to reveal a chest that could double as a shrubbery. Over this masterpiece, he'd draped a sequined purple jacket that sparkled under the dressing room lights, throwing tiny rainbows onto the walls. And the pièce de résistance? Ruby-red patent leather shoes polished to a mirror finish, perfectly coordinated with lipstick so bold it could have stopped traffic.

"Hola, everyone!" Johnny Futura announced, his booming voice drenched in unapologetic drama. "I feel like we've all met before."

Mary exchanged an amused glance with me, a fleeting moment of silent acknowledgment that we were witnessing something truly *extraordinary*. Miss D's eyes widened, caught somewhere between disbelief and reluctant fascination, while Carol Ann flung her hand into a frantic wave, as if Johnny Futura needed confirmation that their lives had indeed intersected before.

"Oh, Johnny, you never fail to make an entrance!" Producer's voice sliced through the room, coated in enthusiasm. He practically stumbled over himself, trailing after his newest obsession, his eyes sparkling with the kind of joy usually reserved for winning an award. "Ladies and gentlemen," he declared, "this is my next star!"

Johnny Futura, never one to miss a moment to dazzle, swept into a deep, theatrical bow. "Thank you, my new dear friend," he purred at Producer.

Every single pair of eyes in the room was glued to Johnny Futura, utterly captivated by the kaleidoscopic figure soaking in their collective admiration. Well, almost every pair. Mary watched him with her signature blend of skepticism and detachment.

Carol Ann, on the other hand, was in her element. "Oh, Johnny Futura has done readings for *everyone*! Trevor Twinkle,

Anderson Cooper's dog, and, of course, little old *me*!" she gushed, clasping her hands.

Johnny Futura stood at the front of the room, poised like a magician ready to unveil his most dazzling illusion "Breathe in, breathe out," he instructed, his voice cascading over the room like a wave of silk.

"There's love for comedy within this room," he continued, his tone so smooth it practically left a trail of glitter in its wake.

Mary, perched stiffly in her chair, felt a smirk tugging at the corner of her lips. "Who doesn't like comedy?" she quipped, her sarcasm as sharp as the heels on Carol Ann's Louboutin's.

Johnny Futura could feel the resistance thickening in the air, like humidity before a summer storm. His eyes swept the room, before settling somewhere just past Mary. "I'm seeing a mother and her chubby daughter. They're cleaning," he declared.

Mary froze. Her smirk vanished in an instant, her knuckles gripping the arms of her chair as though bracing for impact.

But Johnny Futura wasn't done. Not yet.

"There are two figures," he continued, with the kind of drama that could make a Real Housewife blush. "They're sharing a kiss under the glow of a just-concluded, sold-out show."

Mary's breath hitched audibly.

"He's wearing a Ben Stiller T-shirt," Johnny finished, his eyes locking onto Mary with pinpoint accuracy.

A flush crept up Mary's neck, her skepticism momentarily abandoned. "That's…Ben," she murmured, her voice colored with equal parts shock and recognition.

Johnny's smile widened like a cat who had just cornered a particularly delicious-looking mouse. "…and you."

Without a moment's hesitation, Mary shot up from her chair with such force it wobbled precariously, threatening to tip over.

Her face flushed, her breath quickened, and the room seemed to shrink around her. "I've got to go," she blurted, the words tumbling out in a breathless, jumbled rush. "Back to the paper... deadlines."

Miss D, Carol Ann, and I exchanged a glance so heavy with unspoken understanding it might as well have been telepathy. It was clear: Mary wasn't rushing back to her column. No, Mary was headed straight for Ben.

Johnny Futura, emboldened by the seismic reaction to his previous revelation, turned his glittering gaze toward Miss D. "You know," he began, "things might have turned out differently for Jesus if he'd had better representation!"

Miss D froze mid-motion. The words hung in the air, electric and impossible to ignore. There was something about them—familiar, intimate, like a whisper from a dream she couldn't quite place.

She straightened her posture, her lips parting as if to speak, but no words came out.

"Dreams need time, patience, and sometimes...a little faith, Delores," he continued, using her real name with the kind of reverence that made it sound like a benediction. "But you're going to have to work twice as hard to do it."

Delores—Miss D—blinked, her eyes wide, her chest rising and falling as if she'd just surfaced from deep water, leaving her alone with Johnny's piercing gaze and the weight of his words.

Almost as an afterthought, but delivered with devastating accuracy, Johnny Futura leaned in for the final blow. "You won't just be the skinny boy's girlfriend; you'll be his manager too."

Delores froze for the briefest of moments, her face an unreadable mask. Then, she snapped into action.

She gathered her bag and an armful of wigs with a swiftness that suggested she'd just remembered an appointment so critical it couldn't wait another second.

In a flash, she was gone. Just like Mary, Miss D vanished—off to make the kind of private call that could change everything.

As the door clicked shut behind her, Johnny Futura exhaled a long sigh that seemed to pull the remaining air from the room. "I need a break," he declared, his voice heavy with the weight of his self-proclaimed genius.

Producer guided Johnny to his office, the two of them making a dramatic exit stage left. But Johnny wasn't just seeking solace or a moment to recharge. No, his ambitions reached far beyond the dressing room.

Johnny Futura had a bigger audience in mind—the one person in the building he truly cared about impressing. Producer.

In the now-empty dressing room, Carol Ann and I found ourselves alone. I couldn't keep my amazement contained any longer. "Your friend is a clairvoyant," I said. "How does he know all of that?"

Carol Ann's eyes sparkled with a secret she was too pleased with herself to keep. "Oh, honey, I might have given him a little somethin' to help."

My curiosity immediately piqued. "What do you mean?" I asked, leaning forward slightly, unable to resist being drawn into her web of intrigue.

"Well," she began, her voice dripping with theatrical suspense, "let's just say I stumbled upon some very intriguing information."

A mix of skepticism and curiosity danced across my face as I studied her, trying to decide if this was another one of her games. "Pray tell," I said, "how exactly did *you* stumble upon this 'intriguing' information?"

Carol Ann's her eyes were glinting with a mix of mischief and triumph. "Oh, I didn't," she admitted, her voice practically dripping with pride. "Nancy Reagan did."

My stomach dropped as the pieces clicked together in my mind, forming a sharp, jagged puzzle I hadn't wanted to solve. "Wait," I said, the realization hitting me like a slap. "You showed Johnny Futura the tape you gave me!"

Carol Ann's grin faltered, but only slightly. "I didn't think it'd matter," she started, her tone defensive, but I wasn't listening.

The truth settled between us, a palpable silence filling the room as the weight of her betrayal took root. Neither of us needed a shady physic to see what was painfully, glaringly obvious—our fledgling friendship, vibrant and messy and full of potential, was dead.

Chapter 15

Carol Ann stared at her computer screen in Bunny Deadline's office, the words blurring as the weight of what she'd done pressed down like a stone lodged deep in her gut. She had to fix things with James—there was no question about it—but *how*?

Her fingers hovered over the keyboard, hesitant, as if the gravity of the apology she needed to write was too much for the keys to bear. Just as she began to type, her computer pinged with an incoming email. The sender: *Producer.* The recipients: Mary, Miss D, Carol Ann, and me.

Her pulse quickened at the sight of the subject line: "Game Changer."

With a mix of excitement and unease, she clicked it open.

"I've got you booked at the prestigious 92nd Street Y. Malala Yousafzai canceled at the last minute. It's HUGE! Don't mess it up! —Producer."

Carol Ann blinked, rereading the email twice. Her stomach churned. She had never heard of the 92nd Street Y before, but the way Producer's words practically *screamed* with excitement made one thing clear: this was big. *Really* big.

Lost in her thoughts, she glanced over at the new intern, Eve, who was perched on the edge of her chair, typing furiously. The girl was like a younger version of Carol Ann—blonde, ambitious, and hungry for fame.

"Do you know what the 92nd Street Y is?" she asked her, her voice tinged with desperation.

Eve paused, blinking like a deer caught in headlights. "Um… no?" she said, her expression blank.

Carol Ann exhaled sharply, pivoting to plan B. She grabbed her sleek new phone and typed a quick message to Brett Bottom, her go-to source for all things hip and happening in New York.

Ever heard of the 92nd Street Y? she typed, her impatience leaking into every tap.

The reply came almost instantly, and Carol Ann's heart leapt—until she read it.

"The Village People song?"

Carol Ann frowned, irritation flickering across her face. There was no way Producer would lose his mind over a throwback disco reference. Determined to figure it out, she spun back to her computer and launched into her own research.

Within moments, the screen lit up with search results, and as Carol Ann clicked through, her irritation was replaced by growing awe. Line after line described the prestigious cultural institution that was the 92nd Street Y—a hub for world-class thinkers, performers, and trailblazers.

"Famed for its eclectic events, from thought-provoking lectures to captivating performances by prominent figures," she read aloud, her voice tinged with wonder. Each word painted a picture of a stage reserved for the best of the best, a spotlight that could illuminate not just talent, but destiny.

Her mind raced with possibilities. The perfect dress, the flawless delivery, the kind of performance that would have everyone talking about her for days, weeks, even months. She was ready to dive headfirst into planning—until Bunny Deadline's voice cut through her reverie like a fire alarm in a silent library.

"Carol Ann!" Bunny barked from her office, her tone sharp and unmistakable.

"Coming!" she called, scurrying toward Bunny's door, her mind already shifting gears. If she was going to conquer the 92nd Street Y, she had to survive Bunny Deadline first.

Inside Bunny's office, Carol Ann found her boss seated behind her oversized mahogany desk, her posture stiff and unyielding. Impatience radiated from her.

"Traffic is way down," Bunny began, her tone sharp enough to draw blood. "And I think it's because you're never around anymore. You always seem to be off at that little TV show."

Carol Ann opened her mouth to respond, but Bunny didn't give her the chance. Leaning forward, Bunny's expression remained a blank slate, her voice clipped and devoid of any warmth. "The solution is painfully obvious. You need to leave the show."

Carol Ann's heart plummeted, heavy and fast, like a stone tossed into a deep well. Her throat tightened as panic clawed its way up. "Nooooooo," she cried, her voice trembling with desperation. "I swear on the South. I will find a way to do both!"

Bunny's expression didn't change, but the lines around her mouth deepened. "It's not about promises, darling," she said with a frosty edge that could chill a summer day. "It's about results. And right now, the numbers are not good."

Carol Ann felt the weight of her carefully constructed dreams slipping through her fingers. The show wasn't just a job; it was her life, her redemption, her chance to prove to her mother that she *was* a winner, that she could make something of herself.

But now, Bunny's ultimatum hung over her like a guillotine, threatening to sever the fragile threads holding her world together.

"And before you think about leaving me and sticking with the show," Bunny added, her voice slicing through the air like a scalpel, "let me remind you—without me, you would never have met that handsome producer. And trust me, with what I know about him, I can make him disappear just as quickly."

The words hit Carol Ann like a slap, leaving her stunned and breathless. Bunny's calm delivery only made the threat more chilling.

Carol Ann took a deep breath, willing herself to stay calm, to keep the fear clawing at her insides from showing on her face. "I understand your concerns," she said. "I promise you, I can make this work."

"Prove it," Bunny replied, her words thick with skepticism. "I want a big exclusive by the end of the week. And it needs to be real. Now, back to work. You're going to be very busy."

Carol Ann nodded, her mind already racing as Bunny's ultimatum settled over her like a lead blanket. It felt impossible—like being tossed an anchor and told to swim.

Needing an escape, Carol Ann slipped out of Bunny Deadline's office and quickly made her way to the restroom. She pushed open the door with a little more force than necessary, craving a moment of solitude. Instead, she was greeted by the muffled sound of quiet sobs reverberating from one of the stalls.

Carol Ann wasn't the only one desperate for a reprieve from the unrelenting treats of Bunny Deadline.

"Ladies," Carol Ann announced, the unexpected steadiness in her voice surprising even herself. "We're all in this together, y'all."

For a moment, the restroom fell silent, save for the faint rhythm of uneven sniffles. Then, with an almost theatrical creak, one of the stall doors slowly swung open.

Eve, the wide-eyed intern, emerged first, her face blotchy and tear-streaked, her expression an open book of misery. "What do you mean?" she asked, her voice fragile, barely audible.

"Together, we can make a real difference," Carol Ann declared, each word a call to action as much for herself as for them.

It wasn't much. But it was enough.

One by one, the other young women stepped out of their stalls, their postures hesitant yet hopeful. The energy in the room shifted, the stagnant despair replaced by a faint but undeniable spark.

The restroom began to feel like a battlefield, a rallying point.

But nerves fluttered in Carol Ann's stomach. The words she'd been avoiding rose to her lips before she could stop them. "Here's the deal," she said. "I need a big real exclusive by Friday. Actual, genuine reporting."

The words hit the room like a record scratch. For a moment, no one moved. This wasn't just about them; it was about her.

"Even if we wanted to help you, why would you think we could?" asked a dark-haired designer, crossing her arms with a skeptical frown.

"I don't even know what *reporting* means," admitted another, her voice tinged with a kind of earnest defeat.

The flicker of rebellion Carol Ann had sparked began to dim, teetering on the edge of extinction. Her mind raced, knowing the next few seconds were critical. She needed to hold the room—no, *command* it.

Her mouth opened. "Flush if y'all with me."

Carol Ann held her breath, waiting for the rush of solidarity she hoped would echo like a chorus of Niagara Falls. Instead, a drip of water from the sink filled the awkward void.

As the women filed out one by one, the momentary charge in the room dissipated like steam on a mirror.

"Who might teach me to be a proper reporter?" Carol Ann whispered to the empty room, her voice barely carrying above the faint hum of the restroom's fluorescent lights. Her gaze fixed on her own reflection, she searched for reassurance, but for once, the beautiful woman staring back at her didn't deliver any comfort.

The silence stretched, heavy and unrelenting, until the groan of a stall door pierced it.

Eve emerged, making a hasty exit, entirely oblivious to the fact that her dress was tucked unceremoniously into her panties. Carol Ann opened her mouth to call out a warning but then stopped. Her eyes widened, as Eve's accidental misstep struck her with an epiphany.

"Mary can teach me!" Carol Ann's voice rang out, startling even herself. It was a declaration, a lifeline flung into the storm of her self-doubt.

Maybe Carol Ann didn't need a rebellion or a revolution. Maybe she didn't need to rally the troops. Maybe she just needed Mary.

Chapter 16

The *Sold-Out* sign above the entrance to the 92nd Street Y glinted in the soft evening light, catching on our shared look of disbelief. It was a scene straight out of an Annie Leibovitz spread—polished, perfect, and almost too good to be true.

"How did this even happen?" Mary said, gesturing toward the sign with a flourish.

I tilted my head, suppressing a smile. "Do you remember when I gave *The View* that reality star—the one mid-breakup with Nicholas Lee Shy?"

Mary's gasp was audible enough to turn a few heads. "Oh my *god,* yes!"

"Well," I said, allowing myself a hint of smugness, "Mabel Moses—the booker from *The View*—works here now."

Mary's jaw might as well have hit the sidewalk. "*Mabel Moses?* Big hair, lots of perfume?"

I laughed. "That's the one. We owe her a big thank you."

Mary tilted her head. "No, we owe *you* a big, fat thank you," she said, her voice firm. "Why do you let Producer take all the credit?"

Before I could conjure a response—truthful or deflective—we reached the dressing room door at the end of the hallway and pushed it open.

With matching strides, we entered, our footsteps soft against the carpeted floor. Inside, Miss D stood poised in front of a gilt-edged mirror, her posture regal as she adjusted a wig that radiated Upper East Side sophistication.

"Ari and I are heading to Joe Allen's afterward," I said, glancing between Mary and Miss D with a flicker of hope. "You two are more than welcome to join us."

Mary's shoulders sagged under the weight of her endless workload, her expression a portrait of invisible exhaustion. "I've got some jokes that need finishing," she murmured, almost to herself. "I haven't been able to stop writing since I became single. It's like all the punchlines were just waiting for him to leave."

Miss D tilted her head, the softest sigh escaping her, tinged with her own brand of regret. "I can't join either," she said. "Momma and Baby J are in the audience tonight. Not together, thank god."

"You're lucky," Mary said, her tone tinged with something raw. "I don't have anyone coming to see me."

Miss D's expression shifted. "Don't be so sure," she said with a sly grin. "Didn't Johnny Futura say he saw you and Ben kissing at that packed event? And guess what? We're *sold out* tonight."

I could feel my own expression darken, a storm brewing just beneath the surface. "Don't buy into anything he says," I snapped, the words coming out sharper than I intended. "He's a total fraud."

Mary nodded, her jaw tightening. After her reading, she'd swallowed her pride and called Ben. Then texted him. And called again. Radio silence. Maybe this was his way of teaching her a lesson—for all the times she'd left his calls unread and his texts unanswered.

"Tomorrow," Mary said, "I'm going to start digging into Johnny Futura myself."

Miss D and I barely had time to process her declaration before the door flew open with a gust of energy that could only mean one thing.

Carol Ann.

She barreled into the room, her cheeks glowing with the unmistakable evidence of Maria's expert touch. "It's good to see me…you!" she declared, her coat slipping off her shoulders with the flair of a curtain call. Her eyes avoided mine—a subtle, telling move.

And then it happened.

Mary's eyes widened to the size of dinner plates, her expression a mix of shock and disbelief. "You have *got* to be kidding me!" she screamed.

They were wearing the *exact same dress.*

Mary, whose relationship with fashion had always been one of reluctant coexistence, looked as though she might faint. Her eyes darted around the room, as though somewhere, hidden, lay an oversized, ill-fitting cat sweater waiting to save her.

Carol Ann, on the other hand, had entered full crisis mode. Her mind racing through scenarios more dramatic by the second: storming Saks Fifth Avenue, setting up an emergency stylist appointment, or marching onto the stage in nothing but her Spanx.

All eyes turned toward Producer.

His voice cut through the chaos like a blade, sharp and commanding.

"Ladies," he said, his tone brooking no argument, "the show must go on."

Mary and Carol Ann exchanged a murderous glance, but the room was silent.

For now.

"Does anyone have a question that doesn't involve fashion?" Producer continued, his tone teetering between exasperation and barely concealed amusement.

Mary slowly raised her hand. "Do we really need to revisit my Charlie Sheen tale again?" she asked, her voice laced with an undercurrent of humor and humiliation.

Producer's eyebrow arched in exaggerated mock surprise. "You mean the story where he insisted on you sending him a picture before agreeing to the interview?" he said, his words dripping with teasing glee. "Yes. And after you tell it, you can explain how you still managed to get him to talk!"

Mary rolled her eyes with the clarity of a seasoned pro. "Not funny," she shot back, though the corners of her lips betrayed a hint of a smile.

"This one is for you," Producer declared, lifting his gaze upward with a biblical flourish.

Mary, momentarily disarmed by the unexpected sweetness of the gesture, felt her usual armor slip just enough for her to murmur, "Don't worry. We'll make your father proud."

"Don't be ridiculous!" snapped Producer. "I'm not talking about my father; I'm talking about the president of the network. He's in the house tonight."

Seven days earlier, Producer stepped out of the exclusive confines of Zero Bond, the downtown club where Manhattan's elite sealed deals over Negronis and hushed whispers.

Just as he was about to get into his waiting car, he collided—quite literally—with the network's president. The man's modest stature belied the power he carried, a commanding presence akin to a general surveying the battlefield.

The president's eyes glinted, a sharp mix of authority and thinly veiled excitement. "I'm coming to see those gossip kids of yours next week at the Y," he announced. "That scrappy little show of yours is gaining traction. If the Y event goes well, I want to talk with you about taking over Keegan Kelly's show. *In addition* to *The Gossip Gang.*"

Producer's heart stuttered, then launched into a sprint. "Yes, sir!" he managed to reply, barely concealing the adrenaline coursing through his veins.

But the president wasn't finished. "Oh, and I want to throw a little after-party for the cast. Nothing fancy. $10,000 should cover it. I won't be attending, but I'll see you on 92nd Street."

The second the president disappeared inside, Producer's hand shot to his pocket, fumbling for his phone.

"We have an emergency," he barked as soon as Mabel Moses picked up. "How many tickets have we sold?"

She reached for the remote to mute *The Golden Bachelor.*

"Oh dear," she eventually replied, her tone heavy with dread. "We've only sold eleven tickets. Honestly, I think we should just cancel."

"Cancel?" Producer's voice cracked. "We *can't* cancel now! The president is coming!

He began pacing the sidewalk, his breath visible in the frosty air, muttering to himself like a man on the brink. *How are we going to sell 250 tickets in a week?*

Then, like a flickering lightbulb finally sparking to life, an idea struck him. He froze mid-step, his hand gripping his phone with newfound determination.

"Two hundred and fifty seats at forty dollars a ticket—that's $10,000," he calculated aloud, the math tumbling from his lips with an edge of hope. His eyes lit up, the wheels in his mind turning faster now. Maybe, just maybe, this wasn't impossible after all.

"We just need 250 warm bodies to fill those seats—for free," Producer declared.

There was a beat of silence, the kind where desperation teetered on the edge of inspiration.

"*The View*!" Mabel Moses suddenly blurted, her voice rising with excitement. "I'm still friendly with the audience coordinator. They give away free tickets all the time!"

Producer's eyes lit up, the pieces of the puzzle clicking into place.

This might just work.

Mary and I stepped onto the prestigious stage at the 92nd Street Y, following Carol Ann and Miss D's grand entrance, which had been met with a wave of modest applause. As we emerged into the spotlight, the sheer magnitude of the moment hit me.

Sensing my nerves creeping in, I decided to lean into humor, hoping to break the ice.

"Just imagine this," I said, my voice bouncing off the walls of the packed auditorium. "If Whitney Houston had taken a shower, she might still be alive!"

The silence that followed was so thick, you could almost reach out and grab it. My attempt at a joke hadn't just fallen flat—it had plummeted off a cliff and crashed into oblivion.

Thankfully, Mary swooped in like a seasoned pro. With a single, confident step forward, she turned to the audience, her timing as sharp as a scalpel.

"This," she declared, gesturing to her gown with a dramatic flourish, "is what Carol Ann's dress looks like in a *large*."

The audience erupted into laughter, the tension evaporating in an instant. Mary's wit was a lifeline, pulling the moment—and me—back from the brink.

From that moment on, the audience belonged to Mary. Every word she spoke, every glance she cast, drew them in further. It was as if she had them on invisible strings, eating out of the palm of her hand with every perfectly timed punchline and heartfelt moment.

After the show, the tiny-but-mighty president of the network wasted no time. He made a beeline for Mary, his eyes gleaming with genuine admiration.

"That story about Charlie Sheen was gold," he said, his laughter spilling out in a way that felt completely unguarded. "Absolute gold."

Not far away, Producer darted toward Mabel Moses. "I was worried no one would show up," he confessed shaking his head. "You can't trust people who watch *The View*."

"What are you talking about?" Mabel shot back. "There were almost a thousand people here tonight!"

Producer's jaw dropped. "A thousand?" he repeated. "That's impossible! We only bought and handed out 250 tickets."

Mabel raised an eyebrow, clearly perplexed. "Then why did I have to move the event to the Kaufmann Concert Hall?" she countered, her tone laced with a note of satisfaction as she referenced the grand, main auditorium.

Producer froze, the gears in his mind grinding to a halt. Slowly, as if piecing together an impossible puzzle, he whispered, almost to himself, "Wait...did these fools actually sell 750 tickets?"

Amidst the glittering swirl of the evening's success, Mary felt a hollow ache of loneliness settle deep in her chest. It was the kind of ache that no applause could cure.

As she stepped onto the street, a taxi approached, its headlights piercing through the misty night. With sudden urgency, she hurried toward it, her heels catching on the curb.

She slipped.

But instead of hitting the pavement, she found herself steadied by strong arms.

Mary looked up, her breath hitching. It was Ben.

"I wanted to see you in person," he said. "To give you this."

From beneath his coat, he revealed something instantly recognizable.

"*Chloé!*" Mary gasped, clutching it to her chest like a long-lost friend. "Do you have any idea how much I've missed you?" she whispered, the words directed at both her bag and Ben.

Ben tilted his head, a shadow of hesitation crossing his face. "I thought maybe..." He paused. "I thought maybe you had second thoughts about dating a Black guy."

A flicker of horror crossed Mary's face. "No," she said, her voice firm. "That wasn't it at all. When I get scared, I run."

Ben took a tentative step closer. "Let's make a deal," he murmured. "The next time one of us wants to run, we talk instead."

Mary nodded, tears brimming in her eyes. "Deal," she whispered.

"No more secrets," Ben added, his tone steady but kind.

Taking a deep, trembling breath, Mary looked into his eyes and spoke the words that had been locked away for too long.

"Ben, my father is Black."

Chapter 17

Summer Fridays in the city had their own peculiar rhythm, a seductive waltz between the pretense of office hustle and the magnetic pull of weekend getaways. By noon, the city's towers were ghostly quiet, their inhabitants already en route to various escapes. The masses crammed onto trains and jitneys, while the elite soared above it all in helicopters bound for the Hamptons.

Carol Ann leaned against the vanity in the dressing room, her manicured fingers toying with her pearl necklace. "Mary, thank you teaching me how to be a real reporter, hon," she drawled. "Brett and I are off to our summer house the second we're done here. We've got a share with some big names; otherwise, I'd have insisted you join us."

Mary's smile didn't falter. It was Instagram-worthy—filtered, flawless, and entirely fabricated. "I appreciate the offer," she replied evenly. "But Fridays are my busiest day. I've got Saturday, Sunday, and Monday's columns to file."

Carol Ann tilted her head, her expression flickering with confusion.

"Besides," Mary added, "I've been working on a little personal investigation." Her hand drifted to her Chloé bag she'd recently reclaimed. The edge of a manila envelope peeked out, almost daring to spill its secrets.

Before Carol Ann could respond, a shadow moved past the narrow crack in the dressing room door.

"Did you see that?" Mary asked. "I swear, that was Producer. But what's he doing here today? We pre-tape Friday's show on Thursdays."

Carol Ann barely glanced up, too preoccupied with taming a rogue curl that refused to fall into place. "Didn't see a blessed thing," she said with a dismissive shrug.

Mary's gaze hardened, her reporter instincts on high alert. "You need to notice *everything*," she admonished. "First rule: to be a great reporter, you've got to always keep your eyes open."

A heavy sigh escaped Carol Ann's lips as she slouched dramatically against the window. "This is hard work," she grumbled, her tone dripping with self-pity.

"That's why it's so rewarding," Mary replied, her voice carrying the calm authority of someone who had slogged through tougher days. "Trust me, you can learn a lot just by paying attention."

Carol Ann perked up slightly, a mischievous glint in her eye. "How about we watch Miss D on *The Sherri Shepherd Show* and James on *The Today Show*?" she suggested, her voice sharpening with jealousy. "I don't know how those two fools landed them instead of me. They must've been sleeping with someone!"

Mary winced, a flicker of frustration crossing her face. "There you go again," she said. "You can't just make stuff up. Maybe Miss D and James have actually got something worth reporting."

Carol Ann sniffed but didn't respond.

Mary, meanwhile, glanced at her watch. "I've got to get back to the office," she said, her movements brisk as she gathered her things with the efficiency of someone who had far too much on her plate and not enough time to carry it all.

She paused at the door, one hand on the frame, as if considering whether to let the moment pass. But Mary couldn't resist. "Remember what I told you," she said to Carol Ann. "Keep your eyes and ears open, and I promise eventually you will be inspired."

Outside the iconic 30 Rock complex in midtown Manhattan, a sleek black town car glided to a stop, its polished surface reflecting the sea of waving flags and eager tourists jockeying for a perfect shot. Just a stone's throw away, tucked discreetly on 48th Street, was the lesser-known entrance to *The Today Show*—a secret door that hummed with the quiet thrill of exclusivity.

I stepped through it, descending the spiral staircase to the greenroom, which, despite its name, was more beige than green. The anticipation in the air felt almost alive, coiling and uncoiling with the hum of morning show energy.

"Welcome to *The Today Show.* I'm Linda, your producer," came a voice that blended warmth and authority in a way only a seasoned professional could manage. Linda's blonde hair cascaded in effortless waves, as if she'd just stepped off the Von Trapp family estate, all grown up.

"We went over everything last night, and there are no changes or updates," Linda assured me with a polished smile, her tone so soothing it could've doubled as a lullaby. Even Julia Roberts, I reminded myself, had to endure the same meticulous pre-interview prep before going live.

"All right—let's do one more rehearsal," Linda suggested, her voice bubbling with the optimism that comes from knowing every second of airtime is choreographed to perfection. "On today's *Buzz,* we're excited to welcome a new face to our broadcast: James!" she announced, slipping into her best anchor impression.

I chuckled, unable to resist her charm. "You're brilliant at this!" I said, veering off script, my admiration genuine and unfiltered.

Linda's smile widened, tinged with an air of bittersweet nostalgia. "Why, thank you. But tomorrow's my last show," she revealed, her eyes shimmering with excitement. "I'm leaving to create a new show. Can you tell I'm thrilled?"

"That's amazing," I replied, my grin matching hers.

"By the way," she added, "who came up with the idea for your show? It's genius."

I shrugged modestly, though a flicker of pride warmed my chest. "I reckon it was me."

Linda's eyes lit up with genuine admiration. "Wow. You should produce more shows—you've got a real knack for this. The hardest part is coming up with a great idea," she mused, her gaze sweeping over the greenroom where the familiar trappings of daytime TV cluttered every surface. "But weddings, food, and—oh yes—psychics always work."

Her gaze flicked toward a passing *Real Housewife* in towering heels, who swept through the room leaving a trail of chaos and perfume.

"And remember," Linda added, her expression a mix of resignation and hard-won wisdom, "it's always the tricky ones that are TV gold."

Without thinking, I blurted out, "Like Carol Ann."

Linda's eyebrow arched, her interest clearly piqued. "I don't think I know her."

"Oh, don't worry," I replied with a knowing grin. "Soon enough, you won't be able to forget her. She's the worst."

A slightly battered car cruised down 26th Street, navigating the lively energy of Chelsea as it swerved past cyclists and delivery trucks, finally rolling to a stop in front of *The Sherri Shepherd Show.* The sidewalk was alive with excitement, as audience members dressed in their Sunday best chatted and snapped selfies beneath the marquee.

Inside, Miss D was ushered through a maze of hallways and taken up to the fourth-floor greenrooms—a dazzling blend of bright colors, bedazzled accents, and not a hint of actual green.

"Welcome to *The Sherri Shepherd Show,*" said a strikingly beautiful woman with a confident smile. Her natural hair framed her face like a halo, adding an air of celestial authority to her presence. "I'm Keesha, your producer."

Miss D immediately warmed to her, charmed by the blend of professionalism and warmth radiating from her every word.

Keesha handed Miss D a glossy printout. "Here's a rough list of topics Sherri wants to gossip about," she said, her grin widening. "We want it to feel real, not rehearsed." Her voice took on a playful lilt, the kind that promised juicy fun just around the corner.

Miss D laughed, instantly at ease. "You're so good at this!" she said, her voice infused with genuine admiration.

"Thank you," Keesha replied, her composure steady but tinged with excitement. "But I'm moving on up into management." Her face lit up, pride and anticipation sparkling in her eyes. "The real power in this business is behind the scenes."

"Congratulations!" Miss D exclaimed, her enthusiasm genuine. "I've always dreamed of being a manager, but what do I know about handling other people's business?"

Keesha stopped mid-step and turned, fixing Miss D with a thoughtful gaze. "More than you think," she said gently, her voice firm with conviction. "You're talent. That means you know exactly what people want in a manager. Use that to your advantage."

Miss D blinked, the words striking a chord she hadn't considered before.

"Start small," Keesha continued, her tone encouraging. "Find new talent and develop them. Sometimes, they're right under your nose."

Miss D's eyes lit up as a thought struck her, her tone lifting as if announcing a grand discovery. "Like Baby Jay!"

"Baby Jay?" Keesha repeated, her brow furrowing slightly in curiosity. "I don't think I know him."

Miss D's grin widened. "Oh, don't worry," she replied, her voice brimming with confidence and excitement. "You will. He's the best."

Across town, a soft, almost tentative knock echoed against the frosted glass of Keegan Kelly's dressing room door.

Keegan had burst onto the scene like a rogue wave a few years ago, her brazen and provocative questions aimed at D-list celebrities sparking endless debates online. It wasn't long before she'd ascended from viral sensation to the host of her own cable TV show, the prime slot right after *The Gossip Gang.*

"Come on in!" Keegan called, her tone relaxed as she assumed it was the familiar presence of her go-to psychic.

But when the door swung open, it wasn't Johnny Futura—it was Producer.

"Oh, it's *you,*" Keegan growled.

Producer lingered in the doorway. "I can come back later," he said, his tone almost too casual, betraying the weight of what he was about to drop.

"No, let's get whatever you want over with now before Johnny Futura arrives," Keegan snapped.

A flicker of curiosity danced in Producer's eyes. "You see Johnny Futura too?" he asked, tilting his head. "He just reconnected me with my father, may he rest in peace."

Keegan's patience wore thin, her eyes narrowing. "Can we cut to the chase? I'm leaving for the Hamptons soon," she said, urgency sharpening the edges of her voice.

Producer's posture straightened as he prepared to deliver his grand announcement. "In addition to my role on *The Gossip Gang,* I'm taking over your show too," he said.

Keegan's heart stuttered, a somersault of disbelief leaving her momentarily breathless. "Impossible!" she gasped.

"It's not only possible; it's happening. And it's happening fast," Producer replied, his tone sharp and unyielding. "Our first show together is on Monday."

With that, he turned and left.

Behind the closed door, the full force of Keegan Kelly's emotions erupted. A scream—a raw, primal sound—tore through the 45th floor, so loud it echoed down the hall.

Intrigued, Carol Ann hurried to her doorway just in time to witness Producer barreling down the hallway and colliding directly with Mary, who was stepping out of the bathroom.

"Watch where you're going," Producer snapped.

"You bumped into me," Mary retorted sharply, and turned to walk away.

"Wait," Producer murmured, his voice softening. "Maybe you could help me."

Mary stopped, folding her arms as she turned back to face him. Her gaze was skeptical. "With what?"

"I need to win over Keegan Kelly," Producer confessed. "At least until I can replace her. Maybe you could write something nice about her in your column? You know, just to buy me a little time."

Mary didn't miss a beat. "My readers don't care about Keegan Kelly," she replied. "Is there anyone else who can help you?"

Producer let out a heavy sigh, then suddenly, he exclaimed, "Johnny Futura!"

Mary raised an eyebrow, unimpressed. "Hold on," she said, her tone cool as she reached into her bag and pulled out a manila envelope. "Before you do anything, read this."

She extended her research toward him, her demeanor leaving no room for negotiation.

Across the hallway, Carol Ann's pulse quickened as she watched the exchange unfold. Her mind raced as she recalled Mary's advice: "Keep your eyes and ears open, and I promise eventually you will be inspired."

Mary was no longer just Carol Ann's teacher anymore; she was a guiding light, her hero, her inspiration.

"Mary is *blackmailing* Producer," she whispered to herself. The word tasted sharp on her tongue—both bitter and sweet, intoxicating yet dangerous. "That's what I need to do," she murmured, the seeds of her next move beginning to take root. "I need to blackmail Bunny Deadline."

Chapter 18

Inside the studio, the energy was electric—it was a milestone day. We were shooting our very first sponsored commercial. Artists in aprons meticulously turned tacos into edible masterpieces. Each fold of lettuce, every delicate sprinkle of cheese was a deliberate act of culinary perfection, designed to make even the pickiest eater's mouth water.

But my mind wasn't on the tacos or the commercial. It was elsewhere, preoccupied, replaying Linda's words from *The Today Show* over and over, like a song I couldn't shake. I'd been dodging this moment for weeks, but I couldn't avoid it any longer.

It was time to face it head-on.

I straightened my shoulders and walked over to Carol Ann.

"I wish to discuss an idea with you," I began, my voice coming out too formal, too rehearsed.

She turned quickly, her surprise hidden behind a well-practiced smile. "An idea for little ol' me?" she teased. "Well, bless your heart, James, I'm all ears."

The unspoken tension between us hovered in the air, like an invisible third person in the conversation.

"I know we've had our…challenges," I said carefully. "But I've been thinking about a business proposal."

A flicker of curiosity sparked in her expression. "A business proposal?" she repeated, her tone equal parts intrigued and cautious.

"I believe your life would make a brilliant reality show," I said. "And I'd like to produce it."

A slow, almost mischievous smile spread across her face. "A reality star," she mused, the words rolling off her tongue like a foreign but enticing flavor. "Well, I do declare, that is simply genius."

The possibilities hung in the air between us. For a fleeting second, we stood on the brink of something exciting and unpredictable, an unwritten future ripe with potential.

But then, as if to remind us that reality never waits for dreams, Producer's voice cut through the room like a whip. "Remember, there's nothing worse than disappointing a sponsor!"

The tension on set was palpable as the countdown began. The lights brightened, the cameras zoomed in, and the stage felt like a pressure cooker. "Five, four, three, two…"

The director's silent "one" was the cue, and I was the first to jump into action, my smile stretching a mile wide as I picked up my taco. "I always go for a classic taco," I said, biting into it with gusto, the savory blend of flavors hitting just right.

The camera panned to Miss D. "I like my taco spicy," she managed to say, though her words were muffled by a strand of synthetic hair that had inconveniently found its way into her mouth.

Next up was Mary, who leaned into the camera, her smile practiced but knowing. "I love my tacos meat-free," she announced confidently. But as she took her bite, her expression froze. Her hand shot to her mouth as she registered the taste of sausage. Grimacing, she spat it out into a napkin, her face a mix of disgust and disbelief.

Producer, perched behind the monitors, gestured wildly for the cameras to keep rolling, his mind already spinning through edits for post-production.

Then came Carol Ann's turn. "And I would rather have a taco in a bum!"

For a beat, the entire set went silent, then the room exploded into laughter.

"*Cut!*" Producer's exasperated voice rang out. "Carol Ann, the line is, 'I would rather have a taco *than* a bun!' It's a burger joke! Reset!"

Food stylists swooped in like surgeons, restoring every taco to its picture-perfect glory. Maria darted between cast members, reapplying lipstick here, adjusting a stray hair there, ensuring everything was camera-ready.

Mary, still holding her napkin, surveyed the bustling crew with a mix of irony and disbelief. "After months of being told I'm too fat to be on TV, I'm now getting paid to eat on TV?"

Miss D, ever pragmatic, didn't miss a beat. "Who said anything about getting paid?" she replied, expertly repositioning her wig. "All promotions are contractually obligated."

Before Mary could retort, their conversation was abruptly derailed by Carol Ann's distressed moans. Shifting uncomfortably in her seat, she grimaced, her twang drenched in exasperation. "Somethin' ain't right with my plumbing," she announced, just before unleashing a thunderous, taco-fueled fart that echoed through the room like an unholy trumpet.

Mary began fanning herself with her script, her expression teetering between frustration and amusement. “I can’t believe we’re not getting paid for this.”

Later that evening, Mary and Ben found themselves cocooned in the warmly fragrant, dimly lit ambiance of The Cookshop in Chelsea.

Mary’s eyes sparkled mischievously. “I’m not used to having a straight boyfriend,” she quipped, her tone playful yet tinged with tenderness.

Ben chuckled, the kind that made her feel as if she’d just told the funniest joke in the world. “Boyfriend,” he repeated, testing the word like it was something delicious and new. “I like the sound of that,” he added.

Mary’s heart skipped a beat, her usual defenses dissolving under the warmth of his sincerity. The connection between them felt almost palpable, like an invisible thread weaving their worlds closer together, tighter with every passing moment.

The air shifted as Ben took a deep breath feeling, his demeanor suddenly very serious. “Mary,” he began, “maybe it’s time we considered getting a place together.”

Her heart raced, her pulse thundering in her ears. It was like the ground beneath her had disappeared, leaving her free-falling into something she didn’t quite understand.

Sensing her hesitation, Ben reached across the table, his hand finding hers—a quiet reassurance that he wasn’t going anywhere. “I love you,” he said.

Mary’s breath hitched. She wanted to respond, wanted to tell him she felt the same, but the words refused to come.

A few hours later, Miss D found herself navigating the chaos of an African-American speed dating mixer in the heart of Harlem. The air smelled faintly of cologne and ambition, a heady mix that only served to heighten her discomfort.

She was here for her mamma, to show she was trying, that she wasn't wasting her life on men like Baby J, whose pale shadow loomed over her heart like an unwelcome guest.

But no matter how many dark, handsome strangers sat across from her, their eager smiles couldn't chase away the ghost of what she couldn't quite let go of.

Another man slid into the seat across from her, his grin wide and self-assured. "Well, what do we have here?" he asked, his voice dripping with expectation.

Miss D's lips pressed into a thin line. She couldn't even muster the energy for a polite smile. "Why don't you go first? It'll be faster," she snapped, her frustration bubbling to the surface.

The man didn't flinch. If anything, her bluntness seemed to amuse him. "I'm looking for a lady who wants to be a wife and a mother," he declared, his tone firm, as though he were listing job requirements.

Miss D's heart sank, weighed down by the familiar ache of disappointment.

After two hours and thirteen men, the answer seemed painfully clear: something had to change. If she was ever going to make her mamma happy, she'd have to become someone else, at least for tonight.

Miss D took a deep breath, steeling herself for the next round. She pasted on a bright smile, the kind that didn't quite reach her eyes, and decided to play a different role. "I'm an assistant at a fashion company, and I absolutely love babies," she trilled.

The stranger's eyes lit up. "You sound perfect," he said. "I'm a doctor."

Miss D's practiced smile widened into something closer to disbelief. "A doctor!" she exclaimed. "What has my mamma done to deserve you?"

The ambiance of Café Chelsea wrapped around Ari and me like a warm blanket, creating an intimate bubble at our table for two. The dim lighting, soft hum of conversation, and faint aroma of freshly brewed espresso made it feel like the rest of the world had faded away.

"I'm having trouble finding the right singer for my new project," Ari admitted, his voice tinged with quiet frustration.

Without hesitation, I reached across the table, letting my fingers rest gently over his—a small gesture, but one that carried both reassurance and affection. "If I can discover the next big reality star right under my nose," I said with a soft smile, "I have no doubt you'll find your singer."

His eyes sparkled with mischief. "Speaking of under my nose…are those new clothes?" he asked, his thoughts clearly already drifting toward taking them off once we got home.

"I haven't told Mary or the others yet," I replied, "but Producer insisted on hiring me a fabulous gay stylist."

Ari leaned in, pressing a soft kiss to my temple. "You always look amazing to me," he said. Then, with a wry smile, he added, "Just promise me they don't turn you into Brett Bottom."

The laugh that escaped me was genuine. "Oh, did I mention?" I said, my grin widening. "Brett Bottom is now styling Carol Ann. They're even talking about launching a fashion line together, which will be *great* for the reality show."

Ari's giggle followed, bright and infectious, lighting up the moment. "Great," he quipped, his eyes dancing with amusement. "So now both you and Carol Ann have gay stylists."

Hours later, Carol Ann and Brett stood cloaked in the heavy silence of the night, just outside Bunny Deadline's darkened office. Her stomach churned with a persistent, gnawing unease.

The memory of a *Dateline* episode looped in her mind—the one where the murderer, inevitably the spouse, had been tracked down through cell phone tower pings. It was a chilling thought, and one that had made her adamant about leaving their phones at home. Brett, dragging his feet like a sulky teenager told to clean his room, had protested. But in the end, he'd relented.

Carol Ann paused, the weight of what they were about to do pressing down on her shoulders. This was the moment to take control of her destiny—or lose everything.

Brett leaned in close, his voice barely more than a tremble. "What exactly are we looking for?" he whispered, his breath warm against her ear.

Carol Ann's jaw tightened as she shot him a withering look. "The disk," she hissed, her voice clipped.

Without waiting for a response, she set to work, her fingers flying across Bunny's desk drawers, opening them with haste.

"This is like finding a needle in a haystack," he moaned. "You're never going to find it."

Carol Ann spun around, her frustration boiling over. "Hush yourself!" she snapped. "If I don't find it, my TV career is over. Which means our reality show is dead too."

Brett froze, his face a mask of confusion. "Reality show?" he asked.

"Oh, did I forget to mention? James wants to produce a reality show about me getting married!"

"Marry who?" Brett asked, genuinely caught off guard.

Carol Ann flashed him a playful grin. "You, silly," she teased.

Brett visibly relaxed, reassured by her response, though a hint of skepticism still lingered on his furrowed brow. "Shouldn't we go with someone more experienced than James? Like Producer from your morning show?"

Carol Ann opened her mouth to reply, but her eyes suddenly locked onto something nestled in the shadows of Bunny Deadline's desk. Her breath caught in her throat. There it was—the disk. It seemed to radiate with an almost ethereal glow, as if it had been waiting for her all along.

Without hesitation, Carol Ann lunged forward, her fingers trembling with anticipation as she carefully plucked the disk from its hiding spot. In her hands, it felt almost sacred, as if she'd unearthed a relic capable of rewriting history—or at least salvaging her career. A triumphant smile spread across her face. The universe seemed to be aligning perfectly in her favor.

Then, everything took a sharp, unexpected turn.

A loud, jarring noise tore through the office, shattering Carol Ann's fleeting moment of triumph. An unmistakable, stomach-turning scent quickly followed.

Brett's eyes widened in pure horror as he staggered backward, his face a mask of disbelief. "You just took a dump in your boss's office!" he gasped.

Chapter 19

Carol Ann and Brett made sure they were the first to arrive at Producer's apartment, their eagerness palpable as they plotted to pitch James's idea for a reality show before the others could filter in.

She floated through the threshold, a vision of calculated glamour in a borrowed purple Gucci dress. Her matching handbag wasn't just an accessory—it was a vault, guarding a secret.

Brett followed close behind, his pale blue suit perfectly offsetting the sunflower yellow of his shirt—a bold piece from his latest collection. Together, they looked like a power couple curated for maximum effect.

The apartment was a study in monochrome, everything from the rugs and walls to the furniture, and even the people were blindingly white, making the place feel like an overexposed photograph.

"Shoes off," Producer commanded. He then gestured toward the striking woman standing beside him. She radiated a quiet, effortless beauty, the kind that didn't demand attention but captured it nonetheless. Her petite frame was perfectly poised, her naturally blonde hair falling just so, framing a face that seemed to hold a thousand untold stories in her piercing blue eyes.

"This is my wife, Jess," Producer casually added.

Carol Ann didn't bat an eyelash at the revelation. "And this here is my soon-to-be fiancé, Brett Bottom," she replied with the poise of someone unaccustomed to sharing the spotlight.

"We're getting married," Brett blurted out, skipping any preamble as he dove headfirst into the real purpose of their visit. "And we're hoping you'd produce a reality show about it."

Producer shook his head. "I'm already knee-deep in Johnny Futura's new show," he replied. "Plus, I'm working on a new cooking show with Chef Gilda Green. She's phenomenal—Johnny introduced us. And, of course, there's *The Gossip Gang,* along with another special project I'll be announcing tonight."

The rejection lingered uncomfortably as the front door swung open, and Miss D made her solo entrance. "Wow, this place is so fancy, even the doormen are white!"

Producer continued on, unfazed by her observation. "Shoes off, please," he said. "And this is my wife, Jess."

Miss D's jaw dropped, her eyes nearly doubling in size as she stared at the pair, trying to process what she'd just heard. "What? You're married?" she blurted.

"Of course I am," Producer replied, as though the very idea of him being anything but was absurd. "Successful people are never single."

Miss D shifted slightly, her gaze landing on Jess, who extended a hand, as toned and sculpted as Miss D's own.

"It's nice to meet you," Jess said warmly, her voice steady and inviting.

Miss D hesitated for a fraction of a second before taking Jess's hand. "You look like someone who knows their way around a gym," she observed.

Jess nodded. "I'm a personal trainer."

Miss D's eyebrows lifted in mild surprise. "No way. I used to be a personal trainer myself," she confessed. "But now I'm too busy with the show…and my new *boyfriend*."

She paused just long enough for the words *new boyfriend* to hang in the air, a calculated move to make sure they hit their mark—especially with Producer.

"He's a doctor, and—before you all start askin'—he's Black," Miss D added.

A sudden knock at the door shifted everyone's attention toward Mary, Ben, Ari, and me as we swept in.

Mary's focus landed immediately on the centerpiece of Producer's living room: four Emmy awards, proudly encased in a sleek, custom-designed glass cabinet.

But as she stepped closer, something unusual caught her eye.

One of the statues wasn't pristine like the others. Its right side was marred with large dents, as if it had taken a brutal tumble. The damage gave it a peculiar look, as though the statue had suffered a stroke and never quite recovered.

After Mary and I introduced our significant others and slipped off our shoes, the group drifted into the blindingly white dining room. The space was so pristine it made Mary's borderline obsession with cleanliness seem almost casual by comparison.

"White carpets in New York?" Mary chuckled, the absurdity of it tickling her far more than it should. "That's bold."

Jess responded with a slight, composed smile. "My husband's idea."

Mary's eyes widened as her brain scrambled to process what had just been said. "Your husband?" she gasped, the words almost too surreal to grasp.

"Darlin', labels don't mean a thing," Carol Ann declared. "Unless they're stitched into a dress, which you certainly are tonight."

"Thank you," Mary replied, her tone tinged with the need to explain herself. "Carol Ann was kind enough to explain that everyone on TV borrows clothes."

"Only those who can squeeze into a sample size, like you do now," Carol Ann replied, admiring Mary's borrowed white satin dress marred only by the conspicuous price tag dangling from the hem. A silent reminder of its temporary nature.

"And don't forget," Carol Ann added with a knowing smile, "whatever you do, don't spill anything on it, or they'll charge you full price."

The group chuckled as Mary's eyes caught sight of a lively little puppy, Darby, standing in the hallway. "So, watch those dirty paws," she mock growled.

He responded with an enthusiastic tail wag.

"Everyone, help yourselves to drinks," Producer announced, his arm sweeping dramatically toward the fully stocked bar in the corner.

Mary didn't hesitate. Lately, alcohol had become her quiet ally, blurring the edges of her constant hunger pangs that followed her everywhere.

But just as she picked up the bottle, something caught her eye. A manila envelope lay on the bar. She recognized it instantly—it was the one she'd handed to Producer days ago. Untouched. The seal remained unbroken.

Producer rose from his seat at the head of the table, his commanding presence silencing the room. He cast a glance toward the empty chair meant for his star guest but decided he couldn't wait any longer. "I was hoping Keegan Kelly would be here by now," he began, his tone tinged with impatience. "But since dinner waits for no one, I'll make my announcement: I am officially the Executive Producer of *The Keegan Kelly Show,* in addition to *The Gossip Gang.*"

Carol Ann leapt out of her seat, all charm and exuberance, to congratulate him. But in her enthusiasm, her elbow clipped her glass of red wine.

The glass wobbled precariously on the edge of the table, and suddenly, every eye in the room fixated on it as if hypnotized. The tension was palpable, the inevitable disaster unfolding in slow motion.

And then, in a moment of unexpected heroism, Darby sprang into action. The little Wire Fox Terrier, moving with the speed of a well-trained superhero, launched into motion.

In a miraculous display of canine athleticism, Darby redirected the wine's trajectory mid-air. The pristine white carpet was spared, its snowy perfection intact.

The red wine's new landing spot—Mary's lap.

"Noooooooo!" she wailed, the word drawn out like a melodramatic aria as she leapt to her feet and bolted towards the kitchen.

Ben and I immediately jumped up to help, but Jess was faster. She raised one hand to soothe us. "I've got this," she assured the room.

Once inside her pristine white kitchen, Jess moved with practiced efficiency, snatching a roll of paper towels and a bottle of club soda from the counter.

"Could it possibly have landed in a worse spot?" Mary groaned, casting a glance down at the offending stain, the placement so unfortunate it bordered on mockery. "I'm just grateful his white rug is safe," she added with a shiver.

Jess offered a faint smile, her hands still working on the wine. "You know," she said, almost as if thinking out loud, "he wasn't always like this."

Her voice tinged with empathy as she continued. "After his father's death, he felt so guilty. He looked for redemption in all the wrong places."

"Guilty?" asked Mary.

Jess paused, her expression darkened. "It's an ugly story," she said softly.

"And I look pretty right now?" Mary quipped, gesturing toward her wine-soaked crotch.

Jess took a deep breath. "His father," she began, "was killed in a freak accident. He was hit in the head by one of my husband's Emmys. The shelf broke."

Mary blinked, struggling to process what she'd just heard. "Killed by an Emmy?" she repeated, the absurdity and tragedy colliding in her mind like two clashing cymbals.

Jess nodded. "He hasn't forgiven himself," she admitted. "Until Johnny Futura arrived."

Mary's brow furrowed in disbelief. "Wait, Johnny Futura? The psychic?" she asked, her tone somewhere between astonishment and suspicion.

Jess nodded again, her eyes gleaming with a mix of gratitude and something almost reverent. "Yeah. Johnny helped him find closure with his father and saved our marriage."

Mary's heart began to race, a nervous flutter taking over her chest. She knew Johnny Futura wasn't the saint Jess seemed to think he was. In fact, she knew he was a complete fraud and had a file full of damning evidence sitting on the bar next door to prove it.

But even Mary had to admit that sometimes, bad people could do good things.

Slowly but surely, she knew what she had to do.

The envelope on the bar needed to be back in her hands before Jess or anyone else could uncover its contents.

Back in the dining room, Producer resumed the conversation as if there hadn't been an interruption. "Now, where was I?" he mused as Mary and Jess slipped quietly in. "Oh yes, sharing news about me."

No one noticed as Mary, with practiced nonchalance, poured herself another drink with one hand while smoothly sliding the Johnny Futura file into her Chloé bag with the other.

"Speakin' of sharing," Carol Ann interrupted with practiced ease. "Mary's been teaching me her impeccable reporting skills."

Mary instantly shook her head, a quick and unmistakable attempt to downplay the compliment. Beneath the table, Carol Ann foot tapped gently against her Gucci bag, where the incriminating disk lay hidden.

But she wasn't finished. "In fact," she continued. "Mary suggested I sneak into Bunny Deadline's office and steal her Trevor Twinkle disk!"

Before Mary could respond, the kitchen door swung open. Two waiters glided in, the gourmet dishes they carried offering a momentary distraction.

As one of the waiters stepped fully into view, Miss D froze mid-breath. There he was—her Black white knight from the speed-dating event, standing before her, looking as startled to see her as she was to see him.

"You said you were a doctor!" Miss D exclaimed, her voice ringing out with a volatile mix of shock and betrayal.

The waiter's face went pale, panic flashing in his eyes. In his flustered state, the plates of pasta, swathed in rich red sauce, slipped from his grasp. They tumbled to the floor in slow-motion chaos, crashing into a spectacular mess that splattered across the pristine white carpet like a crime scene.

For a moment, no one moved, the collective silence as loud as the sound of the plates shattering. And in that instant, the dinner party from hell reached its spectacularly dramatic—and utterly irrevocable—end.

Returning home in the back of an Uber, Carol Ann and Brett Bottom exchanged a glance laden with disappointment.

"Well, maybe James *should* be the one to produce our reality show, after all," Brett declared, his voice tinged with resigned acceptance, as if surrendering to the inevitable.

But in their haste to leave, neither noticed the Trevor Twinkle disk slip quietly from Carol Ann's Gucci bag. It tumbled unceremoniously into the gutter outside Producer's and Jess's apartment, swallowed by the shadows without fanfare.

A loss far greater than a white dress, a white rug, or a Black white knight.

Chapter 20

The moment Bunny Deadline pushed open the door to her office, a scream erupted, sharp and piercing, slicing through the air like a siren. It was enough to send the entire staff bolting from their desks and into her sanctuary, their eyes wide with fear and confusion.

As the chaos reached a fever pitch, Carol Ann, running late as usual, breezed off the elevator. She was mentally bracing herself for the fallout from the missing Trevor Twinkle disk—or so she thought.

But the moment the awful stench hit her like a wall, she realized, with dawning horror, that in her hurried escape the previous night, neither she nor Brett had erased the evidence of their smelly fiasco. Now, the lingering mess lay like breadcrumbs, leading straight to her—and her bottom.

Carol Ann's mind kicked into overdrive as she rushed to Bunny Deadline's side, her face a mask of calm professionalism. "I'm calling the cleanin' crew right this minute," she declared with practiced poise.

"Don't call anyone," Bunny snapped. "That's evidence," she added, her sharp gaze sweeping the room. "Carol Ann, get everyone lined up outside the bathroom. The intern can help."

For a split second, Carol Ann blinked, the unexpected command catching her off guard. Her eyes darted to intern Eve, whose stunned expression mirrored her own.

"Escort them in one at a time," Bunny barked, snapping on a pair of rubber gloves with the determination of a surgeon about to step into the operating room.

Carol Ann swallowed hard, her practiced calm slipping for just a moment as she nodded. "To do what?" she replied, her voice tight as she turned to Eve.

"To provide a DNA match," Bunny Deadline replied, pulling out a box of plastic cups as if it were the most normal thing in the world.

Inside the bathroom, Carol Ann and Eve worked with laser focus, ensuring each cup was filled with precision and every label applied with care. The room was filled with the faint hum of fluorescent lights, amplifying the tension that hung between them.

"What's the count now?" Carol Ann asked, as she paused to catch her breath.

"Forty-two," Eve responded, her tone clipped but steady.

"Just eight more to go," Carol Ann replied, pressing another label onto a sample with smooth efficiency.

Before they knew it, the task was complete. The samples were meticulously lined up on the counter, gleaming under the harsh light.

Carol Ann took a step back, surveying their work with a satisfied sigh. "Well, look at that," she said, a note of triumph threading through her voice. "We actually did it."

"Not quite," came Bunny Deadline's sharp voice from the doorway. Both women turned to find her standing there, her expression cool and calculated. Her eyes landed on Carol Ann and Eve like a laser. "Now," Bunny continued, her tone measured and firm, "I just need a sample from you two."

Carol Ann's eyes widened, panic flashing across her face. "Oh, shit," she gasped.

Mary burst into her office, her TV persona still shimmering with the post-show glow. Her appearance was meticulously polished, the borrowed DVF dress hugging her frame like it was made just for her. She barely had time to settle into her cubical when an intern from the web team skidded to a stop in front of her desk.

"The boss wants to see you ten minutes ago," he blurted out, his voice trembling with urgency.

Mary sighed, a thread of resignation threading through her tone. "What have I done now?"

"It's what you haven't done," the intern stammered, his hands shaking as he shoved his phone toward her face. The screen blazed with a headline from the *New York Post*: "Doing It Doggie Style!" accompanied by a picture of America's pop princess leading Mario Lopez on a leash.

Mary's heart sank like a stone, a realization settling in her chest. "How did they get that?" she murmured. But before she could process the image further, her British boss stormed up to her desk, his imposing beer belly arriving just before the rest of him.

"Darlin'," he began, his tone dripping with cockney condescension, "while you're busy pretendin' to be a star on the telly, you're missin' stories."

He jabbed a finger toward the incriminating headline. "Wot stories do you 'ave to compete with this?" he barked. "The gay bloke from Bravo gettin' married?"

A nervous laugh bubbled up inside Mary. "I thought my 'Andy Takes It Up the Aisle' headline was funny."

"I ain't laughing, love," her boss shot back. "Get me a follow-up story on that pop princess."

As he left, Mary took a deep breath and called Ben. She paused, biting her lip as she searched for the right words. "Do you remember that friend of yours I met at the dive bar on the Lower East Side? The one who used to work for Harry Steinman?"

"Peter," Ben answered, his voice thoughtful.

"Yes, Peter," Mary said, her tone sharpening with purpose. "Didn't you mention that his sister—Ann, I think—used to be the nanny for…?"

Ben interrupted, his tone shifting to mild amusement. "The pop princess who has a new puppy called Mario Lopez?"

Mary couldn't help but crack a small smile. "Wow, news really does travel fast," she replied. "Yes, I need to talk to her."

"Wait," Ben he, his voice suddenly sharper. "You want to talk with my friend's sister about her boss?"

"Her *former* boss," Mary corrected. "She's probably had a million nannies since Ann."

"Then why can't you speak with one of the other 9,999,999?" Ben countered. "This makes me very uncomfortable."

Her frustration surged, bubbling to the surface. Her voice rose, sharp and indignant. "Excuse me? *I* make you uncomfortable?"

"I didn't say that!" Ben's response was immediate, tinged with defensiveness. "I said—"

"I know exactly what you said," Mary interrupted, her tone cutting through his words. "Ben, this is my *job*. You've always known that."

He exhaled heavily, running a hand through his hair as frustration seeped into the already-tense air between them. "Well, it's a crappy job," he muttered, each word dripping with annoyance.

Mary's eyes narrowed, her voice rising in response. "Funny, you didn't say that when my *crappy job* got us a reservation at Nobu," she shot back, her words sharp with the sting of truth. "Or last week, when we had those VIP tickets to the movie premiere. And let's not forget the seats behind the dugout at Yankee Stadium."

Ben felt the weight of Mary's words press into him, each syllable hitting with the force of undeniable truth. She wasn't wrong—the perks were great, and he had benefitted from them more times than he cared to admit. He sighed, a long, weary sound that escaped like the last breath of resistance. "Okay," he said finally, his voice laced with reluctant surrender. "I'll ask Peter for her number."

Mary's posture straightened slightly, the tension in her shoulders loosening. "Thank you," she said, her tone softening.

"But," Ben added, his voice firm, "you have to promise me one thing."

She leaned forward, eager to secure his cooperation. "Absolutely," she agreed without hesitation.

"You must protect Ann," he insisted, the seriousness in his tone leaving no room for negotiation.

"I swear," Mary promised. "Everything will be 'off the record' from a close source. No one will ever know it's Ann."

The gravity of their agreement settled like a weight in the air. Then, almost sheepishly, Ben added, "Don't forget, we have dinner tonight at eight. I might have used your name to get the reservation."

A soft laugh escaped Mary's lips. "I've got to get back to work. Catch you later."

The second the call ended, Mary dialed Ann—again and again and again. Each failed attempt felt like trying to strike a match underwater: frustrating, futile, and draining.

Just as hope began to wear thin, her phone buzzed.

Mary glanced at the screen, her heart leaping as Ann's name lit up.

The message was short, but it carried the weight of a thousand words:

"I can meet tomorrow. Ann."

Relief swept over Mary. It wasn't much, but it was enough—a crack in the door she was determined to push open.

Outside a stall in Bunny Deadline's office bathroom, Carol Ann's voice slipped through the cracks, low and urgent. "Brett, are you positively certain no one caught sight of you when you arrived?" she asked, her tone laced with barely concealed worry.

"Is that why you told me to wear the long brunette wig from the back of your closet?" he replied, his voice carrying a faint note of exasperation.

"Let's save the chat for later," Carol Ann snapped, her patience thinning. "Right now, I need you to quickly fill up that plastic cup."

Inside the stall, a tense silence stretched as Brett fumbled through the task. After many agonizing minutes, he finally emerged, taking a deep breath and exhaling in palpable relief. He pushed open the stall door, carefully cradling the plastic cup labeled *Carol Ann* as if it were a precious artifact.

"Well done," Carol Ann said briskly, snatching it from his hands. "Now scoot on outta here and make sure no one sees you leaving."

Brett didn't hesitate. He darted out of the bathroom, eager to put the ordeal behind him. But as he slipped into the corridor, neither he nor Carol Ann noticed Eve lingering in the shadows.

Miss D and I nestled into the cozy corner of Bottino's summer garden as the day lazily dipped into dusk, the sky above painted with soft strokes of pink and orange.

"I've got an idea for a new show," I announced, my voice carrying a mix of nerves and pride. "And this time, I'm the producer."

Miss D's smile blossomed, warm and radiant, a true reflection of her delight. "That's wonderful," she said, her voice filled with genuine joy. "What's it about?"

"It's a reality show starring Carol Ann," I added, gauging her reaction.

Miss D's grin widened, her laugh bubbling up. "Love her or loathe her, there's no denying Carol Ann makes for great TV. Congratulations."

"Cheers," I replied, eager to shift the spotlight. "So, what's new with you?"

Miss D's eyes lit up, her grin spreading across her face like the first rays of morning sunshine. "Remember that swanky gym where I met Jada Pinkett Smith?" she began, her tone brimming with excitement. "Well, they saw me on TV, and guess what? They gave me a complimentary membership! And guess who I ran into there?"

I tilted my head, intrigued. "I don't know. Will Smith?"

"Even better," Miss D laughed. "Producer's wife, Jess. We hit it off, and guess what? We've got plans to grab drinks tomorrow night."

My brow furrowed. "Hold on a second," I said, the words tumbling out before I could stop them. "You're getting drinks with the wife of the guy you had phone sex with?"

"What?" Miss D gasped.

"Oh my god," I groaned, my hands flying up to cover my face. "I never told you, did I?"

"Told me what?" Miss D snapped, her confusion palpable, her voice rising with every word.

I took a deep breath, the weight of the truth sitting heavy on my tongue. "The guy you were supposed to meet the night you met Baby J was…it was Producer."

Miss D froze, her expression shifting from disbelief to a dawning realization, her mind racing to connect the dots. But before she could fully grasp the bombshell I'd just dropped, both of our phones erupted into a chaotic symphony of notifications.

"Celebrity Photographer Dead of Accidental Overdose."

I felt the ground shift beneath me, as though the world had tilted on its axis, leaving me unsteady and disoriented.

"I know him," I murmured, my voice barely audible, my eyes fixed on the image of Kevin that accompanied the heartbreaking headline.

"It says he died after taking a new designer drug called 'NAOMI,'" Miss D read aloud, the words sounding surreal as they left her lips.

My left hand trembled uncontrollably as I reached into my left pocket, fingers fumbling until they found the small, cold glass vial tucked away. Slowly, I pulled it out, holding it up to the light. Black letters stamped across the surface spelled it out clearly: N.A.O.M.I.

Chapter 21

The atmosphere inside Bunny Deadline's office was shockingly serene, considering the chaos that had unfolded the day before. But the calm shattered like glass under a hammer when Bunny's voice erupted.

"Nooooooooooooooooo!" she screamed, her anguish slicing through the air. "The disk…it's gone," she gasped, her chest heaving. "Gone…gone…gone."

Then, as if struck by divine inspiration, her eyes lit up, and the pieces of a puzzle seemed to click into place. "The person who took the dump also took the disk," she declared, her voice brimming with newfound certainty.

"Carol Ann!" she barked. "Get me those DNA results immediately."

Carol Ann quickly dialed the lab, her fingers expertly tapping the speakerphone button. The room was suddenly filled with the nostalgic strains of "Wind Beneath My Wings."

Bunny's voice cut through the music, uncharacteristically gentle. "I've never said this before," she began, her tone carrying a rare vulnerability. "But you've become my trusted right hand."

Carol Ann blinked, her mind struggling to process the unexpected praise. All her life, she had yearned for her mother's approval, only to find it forever just out of reach. Yet here she was, receiving it from the most significant maternal figure in her professional life.

"And you're terrific on that morning show," Bunny added, her voice tinged with a rare note of affection.

Carol Ann's legs gave way, her knees buckling as shock and confusion surged over her like a tidal wave. Before she knew it, she was on the floor, staring up at Bunny.

"But you demanded I quit the show!" she questioned, her voice thick with bewilderment as she scrambled to her feet.

Bunny didn't even glance at her, turning away with calm indifference. "I've reconsidered," she said, as if the previous conversation had never happened. "Now, get back to work while I wait for the results from the lab."

As Carol Ann left the glass-walled office, an unexpected warmth began to spread within her. It was faint, tentative, but undeniable. She slipped into the stairwell beside the elevator shaft, the cool concrete steps grounding her as she sat down, taking a deep breath to steady herself.

The melody of "Wind Beneath My Wings" still echoed faintly in her mind as she closed her eyes for a moment. When she opened them, her resolve had crystallized. She knew what she had to do.

"Brett," Carol Ann said, her voice echoing slightly in the narrow stairwell. "Go fetch the Trevor Twinkle disk out of my purple Gucci bag. I don't need it anymore."

She paused, taking a deep, calming breath. "It's time to put it back where it belongs."

A few moments later, Brett returned, sounding puzzled. "It's not in there," he said.

Carol Ann's frustration bubbled over, her patience wearing thin. "Take another look, sweetie!" she snapped.

Ten excruciating minutes crawled by. Finally, Brett reappeared, a faint glimmer of hope lighting up his eyes. "I found a tape…" he began, his voice carrying a tentative note of triumph.

"But it's not a tape of Trevor Twinkle," he continued, his tone hesitant. "It looks like a media training session with Mary, Miss D, and James."

Before she could process what was being said, a cold hand settled on her shoulder, sending a jolt through her body. Startled, she turned sharply to find Bunny Deadline standing behind her.

Bunny's expression mirrored Carol Ann's confusion. "The lab said there's no match," she reported. "Which means whoever took the disk—and a dump—is still out there, on the loose!"

The morning meeting in the basement of an old church in Hell's Kitchen was always packed. I paused at the threshold, my nerves jangling like the discordant notes of an out-of-tune piano. Just inside the door, I caught a hushed conversation.

"Legend has it, she got Liza through eight shows a week," a chorus boy murmured, as if recounting a tale of a mythical savior.

Taking a deep breath, I stepped inside. The idea of spilling my guts to a room full of strangers felt like jumping off a cliff with no safety net. But the alternative—doing nothing—felt like slowly sinking into quicksand. The fear of staying stuck outweighed the fear of the plunge.

"Come in and take a seat!" called the group leader, her voice warm and inviting, echoing through the room like a balm.

I halted mid-step and looked up. There she was—Nancy Reagan. It was like spotting your high school principal at the grocery store: completely out of context and more than a little jarring.

For a moment, I felt disoriented, but then Nancy's gaze met mine, and a flicker of understanding passed between us. In that instant, I knew that whatever I was about to share would not just be listened to but truly heard.

"Welcome, everyone, welcome," Nancy continued, her presence commanding yet comforting. "Now, who would like to begin?"

Instantly, a forest of jazz hands shot up, fingers wiggling with enthusiasm. But Nancy's gaze landed on me, her subtle nod directing me to start.

"I hail from the land of the stiff upper lip," I began, my voice quivering as I dipped my very English toe into this very American pond. "So, being here today is rather challenging for me. However, my name is James, and I believe I am an addict."

The words felt heavy, yet oddly freeing as they left my lips. I sank back into my chair, the weight of my confession both grounding and lightening me at once.

As the meeting continued, I found myself listening more intently than I'd anticipated. Each story resonated in ways that chipped away at the isolation I hadn't even realized I'd been carrying. This room, with its mismatched chairs and people, was becoming more than just a place to seek help. It was a space where past wounds could be examined under the soft glow of acceptance, where paths to healing didn't just seem possible—they felt attainable.

And as the session drew to a close, I realized I had taken the first step—not just in sharing my story, but in allowing myself to believe that maybe, just maybe, there was a way forward.

Mary sat across from Ann, the pop princess's former nanny, her excitement barely contained in the sterile conference room. The borrowed Diane von Furstenberg blouse Mary wore instantly caught Ann's eye. The luxurious fabric seemed slightly out of place against the muted tones of the office, but it made perfect sense on Mary, who had come straight from taping her show.

Mary placed her phone on the conference room's large table beside Ann's untouched black coffee. With a steadying breath, she pressed the record button.

"Would you mind taking notes instead of recording?" Ann asked, a trace of apprehension lingering in her tone.

Mary hesitated for a beat but then nodded with a small, understanding smile. "Of course," she said gently, turning off the recording. Reaching for a pen and notepad, she added, "Whatever makes you comfortable."

Ann's shoulders relaxed slightly, the fear in her eyes softening into a flicker of gratitude.

Mary sensed the shift, a subtle exchange of trust that seemed to open a door between them.

"My brother, Peter, mentioned you're engaged to Ben," Ann revealed, her words catching Mary off guard. "That's the only reason I agreed to meet with you."

Mary felt a hint of surprise, but kept her expression neutral. The journalist in her balked at the idea of perpetuating a lie, but she understood that sometimes, allowing people to believe what they needed to believe was a necessary part of the job. It made them feel safe, secure, and more willing to share. So, she decided to let Ann's assumption stand unchallenged.

"My name won't be on this?" Ann asked, her eyes searching Mary's face for reassurance.

"Absolutely not," Mary replied, her voice firm and reassuring, like a promise etched in stone.

The hours slipped by quickly as the afternoon sun casting its long shadow across the room, creating a quiet intimacy between them.

As they began wrapping up, Ann leaned back slightly, curiosity flickering in her eyes. "How did you become a journalist?" she asked.

Mary paused, her mind replaying memories of her journey, vivid and raw like scenes from an old film. "At the very bottom," she began, her voice tinged with both pride and exhaustion. "Answering phones, fetching coffee. Then, an opportunity arose on the crime desk as an assistant. I seized it. That's where I learned my craft—through a lot of late nights and long hours. There's little room for a personal life."

Ann remained undeterred, her expression resolute. "I'm not worried about that," she replied. "I've got time to find love, get married, and start a family."

Mary's gaze drifted to her own bare finger, the absence of a wedding band a silent reflection of the sacrifices she'd made for her career.

Feeling at ease in Mary's presence, Ann allowed herself a moment of hope. "If any assistant opportunities open up, would you consider me?" she asked.

Mary smiled, the sincerity in her answer immediate. "Of course," she said without hesitation.

In her enthusiasm, Ann jumped to her feet, inadvertently sending her black coffee splashing onto Mary's borrowed blouse.

Mary instinctively dabbed at the stain with a napkin, a soft laugh escaping her lips. "It's okay," she said lightly. "I'm not really sure it was my style anyway."

Miss D's heart fluttered like a butterfly trapped in a net as she awkwardly took her seat across from Jess and Darby at an outdoor table at The Bryant Park Grill. Her gaze lingered on the empty wine bottle at the center of the table, a glaring symbol of the unspoken troubles hanging in the air.

"Jess, are you okay?" Miss D asked gently, her voice softening as she leaned forward. "If you need to talk, I've got two good ears hiding under this wig."

"I'm fine," Jess slurred, her half-smile flickering like a fragile flame in the breeze, more performative than reassuring. "Just a bad day with a nightmare client that my boss won't let me fire," she added, waving her hand dismissively, as though trying to brush away the concern alongside the topic.

"Tell me about it," Miss D said with a wry smile. "Wouldn't it be lovely to own your own company? Be your own boss?"

Jess's cheeks flushed. "You know," she said, her words spilling out with surprising clarity despite her state, "we should open a gym together."

Miss D's eyes widened, sparkling with a sudden, intoxicating thrill. "I would love to," she replied, her voice electric with the charge of possibility. "All we need is half a million to get started."

The notion floated between them, buoyed more by the wine than by any real sense of feasibility, yet it felt alive, charged with the giddy energy of a shared dream.

"To no more awful jobs," Miss D declared, raising her glass with a flourish.

"Cheers to that," Jess replied, then added with a slur, "I'm too embarrassed to admit some of the jobs I've had."

Miss D, emboldened by the warm haze of their third—or was it their fourth?—bottle of wine, revealed a secret she'd never intended to share, especially not with Jess. "Please," she said, the words falling out before she could stop them. "I once worked as a phone sex operator."

Jess's jaw dropped, her eyes widening in disbelief. But instead of judgment, a surge of courage welled up within her. "I have a secret too," she confessed softly. "I wasn't drinking because of a difficult client," she admitted. "I was drinking because…I think my husband is having an affair with someone he works with."

Thirty minutes later, Jess tumbled out of the Uber Miss D had ordered for her, her feet hitting the pavement outside her apartment building with an unceremonious thud. Her ever-enthusiastic furry companion, Darby, tugged her toward the gutter, his nose leading the charge as though it had unearthed the secrets of the universe.

"What have you got there, Darby?" Jess asked, her voice slurring slightly from the wine and the weight of her troubles. She staggered, curiosity cutting through the haze as she bent down.

Darby held a small, shiny disk in his mouth.

With a gentle but firm tug, Jess managed to pry the object from his eager jaws. Her hands moved slowly, careful as though she were handling something fragile, something important.

"What on earth is this?" she murmured, turning the disk over in her hand.

Chapter 22

The studio buzzed with that warm, electric hum that lingers after a truly great show. Mary, Carol Ann, Miss D, and I exchanged a series of triumphant smiles—the kind that said more than words ever could. I leaned back in my chair, my grin spreading slowly, like the aftertaste of a really good wine.

"We're getting good," I said, pride threading through my voice. "Like, seriously good. Shame we're about to be on hiatus for a few weeks."

"I've got a plan to keep the momentum going!" Producer declared, bouncing over to the table like he was about to take flight. "Short online videos during the break."

Mary rolled her eyes, her expression a mix of amusement and annoyance. "Fantastic," she replied, her words dripping with sarcasm. "Just what I needed—another job."

"The future's all about online," I said, jumping in. "More people watch YouTube than TV these days."

Miss D, ever practical, perked up. "Sounds good to me," she chimed in.

No work meant no paycheck.

But Mary wasn't having it. "I think I'm gonna pass," she said firmly, her voice leaving no room for negotiation.

Producer's eyes flicked over to her with a flash of irritation before he pivoted on his heels, already moving on. "Suit yourself," he said dismissively.

I turned to Carol Ann, curiosity in my tone. "What about you? Are you going to do the videos?" I asked.

She hesitated. "Oh, I'm going to be in LA next week," she said, her words slow and deliberate, but her eyes betrayed her. They flicked over to Producer on the other side of the room with a sly look, like a secret trying to stay hidden in plain sight.

My eyebrows shot up in surprise. "Why?" I asked, the single word heavy with inquisitiveness.

Mary, never one to tiptoe around the truth, jumped in, her voice sharp and demanding. "What's going on, Carol Ann? And for once, tell the shocking truth!"

Carol Ann let out a resigned sigh, the weight of it all finally too much to bear. "Alright," she confessed. "Things between Producer and Keegan Kelly aren't working out, so he's meeting with a former boy band star to replace her." She hesitated, her cheeks flushing slightly before adding, "He wants me to do a chemistry test with him. I think it's Justin Timberlake?"

Miss D's eyes widened as her mind raced to process the unexpected twist. "There's no way it's Justin—not even after his DUI," she said, her voice tinged with disbelief. "Maybe Joey or Lance."

My expression shifted from irritation to understanding, my voice softening as I said, "You should have told us."

Mary and Miss D were already nodding in unison.

Mary's voice carried a note of sincerity that cut through the tension. "We get it. We know you're the one with the brightest future on TV."

I chimed in, my tone gentle. "We would have been happy for you."

Tears welled up in Carol Ann's eyes, blurring the edges of the room and making everything feel just a bit softer. She took a shaky breath, her voice trembling as she confessed, "I didn't say anything 'cause I got scared. I'm not used to having friends, and I surely don't want to lose y'all."

I reached across the table, my fingers brushing against hers in a silent, reassuring gesture. "You're not going to lose us," I said softly, my voice carrying the weight of a promise.

The fear that had clouded Carol Ann's eyes began to melt away, replaced by a flicker of tentative hope. A small, grateful smile tugged at her lips.

"Well," Miss D chimed in, her tone light, "with Carol Ann in LA and Mary not interested, that means more money for you and me, James." She giggled, rubbing her hands together like a mischievous villain, clearly enjoying the moment.

Mary's eyes widened, disbelief spreading across her face like a ripple in a pond. "Wait, we get paid to do them?" she asked, her voice a mixture of shock and curiosity.

Miss D nodded, her tone steady and matter of fact. "According to our contracts, the rate is $250 per video."

"No way!" Mary's voice shot up an octave, the surprise quickly giving way to outrage. "Why on earth didn't Producer mention that?"

A few days later, Miss D and I found ourselves standing in front of a vibrant green screen, crammed into a small closet-turned-video studio on the forty-fifth floor. The space was tight, the air thick with nerves and anticipation, each beat of our hearts a reminder that we were about to dive into uncharted waters. We exchanged a glance—a silent dialogue of *What on earth are we doing here?*—as we waited for Cliff, the new cameraman from Jamaica, to arrive.

When Cliff finally strolled in, he was everything we weren't prepared for: tall, dark, and impossibly handsome, with a smile so warm and effortless it felt like a reunion with an old flame. But it was his dreadlocks—thick, luscious, and flowing down his back—that added an extra layer of intrigue to his already magnetic presence.

"Ready to work some magic?" he asked, his voice carrying the rich, melodic cadence of his Caribbean roots.

I leaned toward Miss D, my eyes wide with disbelief. "The only thing tighter than this studio are his pants," I whispered.

Miss D's hand shot up to cover her mouth, her laugh barely stifled as she struggled to maintain composure.

Ever the professional, Cliff offered us a reassuring smile, his eyes twinkling with a blend of patience and humor. "Don't worry," he said, his tone soothing yet confident. "I might be the new guy around here, but I got this."

"That's good to hear," I replied, trying to match his ease. "Because we're new at this too."

Miss D stepped into full flirt mode. "Tell me exactly what to do," she said, her voice playful and laced with charm. "I'm a quick learner," she added.

Cliff's grin widened as he gently pointed to a spot on the floor marked with an *X*. "Just stand right here," he instructed. Then, with a nonchalant shrug that was almost too casual, he added, "I just wrapped up filming a porno in LA. Being in the right spot is everything."

Miss D froze for a beat, her flirtatious demeanor giving way to a stunned silence, while I choked on a laugh, half-shock and half-delight at his candor.

She took a deep breath, centering herself. "Hi, I'm Miss B from *The Gossip Gang,*" she began, her voice wavering slightly with the effort to nail it.

"Cut!" Cliff called out, his keen ear catching the slip. "You're Miss D, not Miss B," he corrected softly, his tone soothing and patient, as if he had all the time in the world to help her get it right.

Miss D's eyes widened, her face flushing with embarrassment. "Yes, I am?" she stammered, the question sounding more like an apology than a statement of fact.

Cliff's lips twitched into a small, reassuring smile. "No worries," he said. "Let's take it from the top."

"Hello, I'm Miss D from *The Gossip Gang,*" she announced again. But now, it was her feet that betrayed her, shifting nervously on the spot as if trying to escape.

"Cut!" Cliff interrupted once more, his tone still kind but firm. "You're swaying back and forth," he pointed out. "Think of yourself as a tree—rooted and steady," he suggested.

Miss D closed her eyes for a moment, as she let the metaphor sink in. She imagined roots unfurling from her feet, anchoring her to the ground below.

When she opened her eyes, there was a newfound steadiness in them, a quiet confidence that hadn't been there before. Taking a deep breath, she straightened her posture and smiled at the camera. "Hello, I'm Miss D from *The Gossip Gang,*" she declared, her voice clear and unwavering, not just addressing the camera, but claiming her place in the moment.

Cliff smiled broadly from behind the lens. "That's it," he said with genuine warmth. "Perfect take. You're exactly where you're meant to be."

Miss D grinned, her earlier jitters forgotten. In that moment, she knew he was right—she was in the right spot, and as Cliff had said, *that is everything.*

The next morning, we found ourselves back in the tiny studio, the lingering scent of fresh green paint mingling with the intoxicating promise of a new day. Miss D adjusted her sexy new wig with a flourish, her favorite green dress swirling around her as she moved with an unmistakable confidence.

"I know that look," I teased, a grin tugging at my lips. "Who are you trying to impress?"

It thrilled me to think that Miss D might like a guy her mother would approve of.

Miss D shot me a sly glance, her eyes sparkling with mischief. "Cliff checks all the boxes," she admitted with a nod, her voice light but earnest. "He's tall, kind, attractive…and he's Black," she added, her voice trailing off, as if acknowledging a sad loss.

"But Baby J still lingers in your thoughts, doesn't he?" I asked, my tone gentle, coaxing out a truth she hadn't fully confronted, even within herself.

Miss D nodded wistfully, her thoughts clearly elsewhere as she moved to stand on the spot marked with an *X* in front of the green screen.

"Cut!" Cliff's voice rang out before the session even began. His laughter followed, rich and warm, the kind of laughter that bubbled up uncontrollably and pulled everyone into its orbit.

"What?" Miss D asked, startled.

Cliff pointed to the monitor, his words barely squeezing past his laughter. "You can't wear green!" he choked out between breaths.

Miss D turned to the monitor and gasped. Against the green screen, her dress had disappeared, leaving only her floating head, hands, and that unforgettable wig.

Later that evening at Bottino's, Mary sat across from Miss D and me, her laughter bubbling over as tears streamed down her cheeks.

"I can't believe it. Your entire body vanished?" Mary gasped. She wiped a tear from the corner of her eye, finally catching her breath enough to add, "I just hope I'm half as funny as you in a few days."

I arched an eyebrow, intrigued. "What do you mean?"

Mary took a deep breath, leaning forward with a hint of nervous excitement. "I'm performing at Nancy Reagan's friend's club," she announced, her voice steady, though the way her hands fidgeted with her napkin betrayed the pounding of her heart.

Miss D and I erupted into jubilant cheers, the kind that drew a few curious glances from neighboring tables. "This is incredible news!" I exclaimed, my eyes sparkling with genuine excitement.

"Congratulations, Mary!" Miss D added, raising her glass. "I'll need to find a new comedy wig! When's the big day?"

"Friday," Mary replied, her voice tinged with a touch of panic.

"Mary, today's Wednesday!" I gasped, the realization hitting us all at once.

Miss D grinned mischievously. "I'd love to stay and help," she declared, her smirk pure mischief, "but I've got a date."

"With whom?" Mary asked, momentarily distracted from her looming performance.

Miss D's grin widened, her tone dripping with playful mystery. "Let's just say he has big hair and an even bigger package."

My jaw dropped, a mix of shock and amusement spreading across my face. "You're seeing Cliff?" I questioned, my words coming out in disbelief.

But before the sentence could fully escape my lips, Miss D had already vanished, slipping into the night like a green dress against a green screen.

In the hushed stillness that followed Miss D's departure, Mary's confidence began to waver. She turned to me, her voice barely above a whisper, as if scared to give shape to her doubts. "James, what if I'm not funny?"

"You've got this," I said, my tone steady and reassuring. "Stand up. Trust me, no one's paying attention."

I grabbed the fork from the table and held it up like a microphone. "Come on, let's practice."

Mary hesitated, her fingers twitching uncertainly, but then, with a deep, determined breath, she reached into her bag and pulled out her well-worn notebook. Flipping through the pages, she began to recite a series of shockingly cheesy, cringe-worthy jokes. Each punchline landed with less humor than the last.

My thoughts swirled in a chaotic dance. I wanted to be her unwavering support, but a voice in my head nudged me toward honesty. And in the quiet space between, a solution began to form.

"May I offer a suggestion?" I asked softly. "You tell the funniest true celebrity stories ever. Why not share those instead of trying to tell jokes?

Mary's shoulders sagged slightly, her worry palpable. "I don't have time to learn something new at this late stage," she replied, her voice tinged with panic.

"Exactly," I said, leaning in with quiet insistence. "You wouldn't have to. We've been rehearsing the 'Mary and James show' for years. Tell those stories—they're in your soul. Just be your magnificent self."

Mary's eyes flickered with a spark of realization, a faint smile tugging at her lips as my words began to sink in. "But they're your stories too," she said, her voice touched with the warmth of shared memories.

"I give them to you, my friend," I replied earnestly. Then, with a teasing lilt, I added, "And sprinkle in a few true stories about moving in with your boyfriend. People eat up relationship humor."

Mary's face lit up like a burst of sunshine, her eyes sparkling with amusement. "I have to admit," she said, laughter bubbling in her voice, "there's something undeniably hilarious about me having to leave my apartment and sprint across the street to Starbucks every time I need to use the bathroom."

I chuckled softly. "And don't forget your Charlie Sheen story."

Mary straightened in her chair, her confidence growing like a flame catching a gust of wind. "It won over Mabel Moses," she declared, her tone brimming with determination.

I smiled, knowing I'd done my part. Sometimes, all a friend needs is a reminder that they don't have to be anyone but their own magnificent self.

Chapter 23

In the heart of Los Angeles, where the boulevards twisted like ribbons dipped in sunlight and the skyline shimmered with the restless dreams of millions, Carol Ann stood on the precipice of what felt like destiny: her impending meeting with Nicholas Lee Shy.

"This is a *really* big deal for me," Producer snapped, his tone teetering between nerves and exasperation. "Replacing Keegan Kelly with Nicholas Lee Shy could change everything."

Carol Ann straightened, her resolve settling into her bones like freshly poured cement. "I won't let you down," she whispered. Then, with a self-assured smile, she added, "Even if he loathes me, he's sure as sugar gonna love the way I look."

Producer's eyes flicked over her. She wasn't wrong. "Focus on that," he replied. "With his fame and your looks, this could be huge."

She nodded, letting the words sink in. It wasn't the first time she'd been told to let her appearance do the talking, and it likely wouldn't be the last.

A rhythmic knock echoed through the suite—a sound imbued with confidence and star power. Producer's eyes widened as he turned to Carol Ann, his expression a cocktail of warning and plea. "Stay cool," he hissed.

Nicholas Lee Shy, once the golden boy of pop music, now stood before them. In his mid-forties, he exuded a tempered charisma that was still undeniably magnetic.

The boyish sparkle that had captured millions of hearts hadn't faded; it had merely shifted, carrying with it a tinge of nostalgia and reflection. His frame, once lean and athletic, had softened with the years, though it only added to his approachable air.

His gaze swept the room, landing briefly on Carol Ann.

Producer stepped forward, extending a hand with a practiced smile. "Nicholas, thank you for coming. I know your schedule is crazy."

Carol Ann's heart pounded as Nicholas turned his attention to her. "And you must be the woman who's supposed to make me look good," he said, his words teasing but not unkind.

Carol Ann held her ground, flashing him a dazzling smile that was as much armor as it was an introduction. "I think you've been doing a pretty fine job of that on your own," she said smoothly.

Nicholas chuckled, a sound that felt both genuine and rehearsed, as if he'd been complimented a million times before but still knew how to play along. "I like her," he said, turning back to Producer.

Producer exhaled, relief flickering across his face as he gestured toward the plush seating area. "Let's talk," he said, ushering them all toward the couches.

Producer pitched a few ideas—concepts he had, not-so-discreetly, lifted from me. To his relief, they landed well, especially the quirky notion of Nicholas singing the daily headlines, a nostalgic nod to his boyband days. Carol Ann observed quietly, taking it all in, just as Producer had hoped.

Feeling satisfied with what seemed like a successful first meeting, Producer pulled out his phone, already mapping out the next steps in his head, his fingers flying across the screen.

Nicholas turned to Carol Ann, his boyish charm still intact despite the years. "So, pretty lady," he began, his tone light but expectant. "I'd love to hear your thoughts."

Carol Ann hesitated, caught off guard. Her mind raced, searching for the right balance between the truth and what Nicholas Lee Shy wanted to hear. Then, taking Mary's advice to heart: *For once, tell the shocking truth!*

"I feel like the viewers want to hear gossip," she replied finally, her voice steady but cautious.

"I hate gossip," Nicholas shot back, his tone sharp and unwavering.

"Really?" Carol Ann tilted her head, genuinely intrigued. "Why?"

"Why?" Nicholas echoed, the word dripping with pent-up frustration. "Because they wrote that my ex-wife had to pay *me* $10 million when we got divorced," he snapped, the bitterness in his tone unmistakable. "It's humiliating."

Carol Ann, unflinching, leaned back slightly. "But it is the truth," she retorted, her tone sharper than she'd intended.

Producer's face paled, his discomfort almost tangible as his eyes darted nervously between the two.

"This is not cool," Nicholas declared as he rose to his feet. His glare was fixed squarely on Producer. "And this is not going to work."

His words landed like a gavel in a courtroom—final, indisputable. Without a second glance, Nicholas Lee Shy turned on his heel and walked out, the door closing behind him with a definitive thud.

The silence in the room was deafening. Producer sat frozen, his phone still clutched in his hand, his grand plans unraveling in an instant. Carol Ann stared at the door, her usual confidence replaced by a flicker of uncertainty.

For now, Keegan Kelly's job was safe, and Carol Ann's future was anything but.

The basement of Nancy Reagan's friend's comedy club in the East Village was already buzzing, the hum of conversations bouncing off the exposed brick walls. A chill hung in the air, prompting people to huddle closer together, drawing warmth from each other and from the flickering candles dotting the tables.

I leaned toward Miss D and Cliff, eager to share a bit of wisdom. "It's an old Joan Rivers trick," I said, my breath visible in the cool air. "People don't laugh or get excited when they're overheated."

Cliff raised an eyebrow, the thought visibly rolling around in his mind as he considered its comedic possibilities. "Makes sense," he said with a nod.

"Speaking of temperatures," I added, looking directly at Miss D with a playful grin. "You look *hot, hot, hot* tonight."

Miss D's smile widened, her hand instinctively smoothing the fabric of her red dress. "Thank you, James," she replied warmly, her voice carrying a hint of pride.

"I have to agree with James," Cliff added, his tone genuine as he gestured toward her. "You're positively radiant tonight."

Seizing the moment, I raised my glass with a wide grin. "To Miss D and Cliff," I declared, my voice brimming with enthusiasm. "I couldn't be happier that you two are dating."

He nearly choked on his drink. "Dating?" he repeated, his voice a mix of confusion and amusement. "I'm gay!"

Miss D's jaw dropped, her blush deepening as she turned to Cliff. "Well, no wonder I like you" she said with a grin, raising her glass in mock toast. "To fabulous gay friends."

Cliff laughed along, clinking his glass with hers. "I'll drink to that."

I shook my head, smiling as the unexpected turn of events only seemed to bring more warmth to the evening.

Before any of us could say another word, the spotlight swung to Mary as she stepped onto the stage, gripping the microphone like a lifeline. Her gaze drifted toward Nancy Reagan seated at the bar, sipping something amber and elegant. Just the sight of her seemed to smooth the jagged edges of Mary's nerves, grounding her in a way she hadn't anticipated.

Mary took a deep breath and closed her eyes for a brief moment. When she opened them again, something had shifted. It was as though a hidden switch had flipped inside her, unleashing a surge of energy that electrified her every movement.

Her stance firmed, her shoulders squared.

"Want to hear about the time I wore a wire to catch Mike Tyson with hookers and coke?" she began, her voice laced with a mischievous twinkle. The crowd leaned in, instantly hooked, their curiosity palpable.

With a sly smile, Mary launched into tale after tale. The audience roared, their laughter rolling over her like applause before she even reached the punchline.

Mary's words were magnetic, her timing flawless, weaving the crowd tighter into her narrative web. She paused, scanning their eager faces, and then went for the jugular. "You won't believe this, but I swear it's true," she began, letting the suspense build.

"Before Charlie Sheen would agree to an interview with me, he demanded I send him a picture."

The audience held their collective breath, already chuckling in anticipation.

"So, I sent him a photo of a bowl of cocaine," she finished, her tone a perfect blend of disbelief and amusement.

The crowd exploded, laughter cresting like waves on a sunlit shore. Mary basked in their energy, a smile dazzling under the glow of the spotlight. She took a deep bow, the applause swelling into cheers. From our corner of the room, Miss D, Nancy Reagan, and I added our voices to the crescendo.

As Mary stood there, soaking in the adoration, I caught the flicker of a tear at the corner of her eye. She wiped it away quickly, her grin unyielding, but I knew what it meant. She'd found her moment. Maybe even her calling.

The next morning, Mary woke up with a smile still lingering on her lips. Sunlight filtered through the curtains of her new apartment, casting a warm glow over Ben's peaceful, sleeping face. He'd come back late from a whirlwind business trip to Chicago, his exhaustion evident in the gentle rise and fall of his chest. She couldn't bring herself to disturb him. Instead, she slipped out of bed with the careful sharpness of a cat burglar, her every movement deliberate and quiet.

Her bare feet whispered against the cool wooden floor as she tiptoed across the room, savoring the sweetness of the moment. It felt like the first sip of coffee on a crisp fall morning—simple, perfect, fleeting.

A small pang of regret gnawed at her, though. If only Ben had been there to see her perform last night. She brushed the thought aside quickly, telling herself there would be a next time.

Pausing in the center of their new apartment, located next to the High Line in Chelsea, Mary let herself take it all in. The spotless surfaces gleamed in the morning light. The consistently hot water and the washer and dryer in-unit were luxuries she'd never take for granted. The friendly doorman downstairs greeted her no matter the hour, and the sixth-floor perch gave her a view of the city that felt just far enough away.

But it wasn't the physical luxuries that made the apartment feel like heaven. It was the man who shared it with her.

Feeling a surge of quiet bravery, Mary wandered into her bathroom—her very own bathroom—and sat down. It was such a small act, but it felt monumental, a declaration of belonging.

The cool tiles under her feet and the faint scent of Jo Malone grapefruit soap wrapped around her like a comforting embrace. In that still, private moment, Mary felt something shift. A readiness bloomed within her. She was finally ready to tell Ben that she loved him too.

Typically, Mary's mornings began with a quick dash to the bodega downstairs, where the rustle of newsprint and bold headlines grounded her in the day ahead. But today, she allowed herself a rare indulgence, sinking back into the warmth of her bed. Nestled between her two Bens—one purring, one snoring—she let the quiet moments stretch out, unaware that this fragile bubble of tranquility was about to burst.

A whisper that had started in her downtown conference room had exploded into a roar, splashed across the front page of Mary's newspaper.

The bold, screaming headline read: "Exclusive: Ann the Nanny Tells All!"

Chapter 24

I stood at the threshold of Carol Ann's apartment, momentarily disoriented, as though I'd stepped into an entirely different world. "The place looks…wow," I murmured, caught between genuine admiration and the unsettling realization that I might need a map to navigate this new terrain. The high-gloss crimson walls glistened under the soft glow of strategically placed Chinese lanterns, the light creating a hypnotic dance of shadows that made the room feel alive—almost as if it were breathing.

Carol Ann, glowing with satisfaction, waved a dismissive hand. "Had to shake things up before we start filmin' the new project, bless your heart," she drawled, the southern lilt in her voice adding a touch of honey to her words.

She glided through the newly decorated rooms with the air of a curator showing off her latest masterpiece, her fingers brushing over the impeccably chosen furniture.

Each piece was a statement of reinvention.

The coffee table, carved with delicate definition, seemed to whisper tales of distant lands, while vibrant tapestries on the walls sang songs of adventures yet to be had. The apartment wasn't just redecorated—it had been reborn, much like Carol Ann herself.

Settling gracefully beside Brett Bottom, who was draped in a kimono and looked more bewildered than elegant, Carol Ann flashed me a knowing smile. "We've been talkin' 'bout your idea for a show, darlin'," she began, her voice brimming with intrigue.

Brett leaned forward, his kimono shifting dramatically. "The kind of show where we're dropped into wild, exotic places and have to figure it all out—while looking absolutely fierce, of course," he added, his voice practically vibrating with excitement.

Carol Ann nodded, her eyes twinkling with mischief. "We're gonna push the boundaries, sugar. Take this to places people wouldn't dare dream of." Her words hung in the air, alive with a sense of adventure and ambition.

I couldn't hold back a chuckle, savoring the delicious absurdity of Brett and Carol Ann's banter. There was an undeniable spark between them, the kind of electric chemistry that could set any room—and hopefully any TV screen—on fire.

"It needs to be about relationships and weddings," I interjected, my tone firm but not unkind. The words rolled off my tongue with the ease of someone who had just cracked the code. "Not travel and games."

Brett's eyes lit up with sudden understanding. "Is that why Kim Kardashian keeps getting married…and divorced?" he asked, his tone equal parts awe and disbelief.

Carol Ann rolled her eyes but couldn't help smirking. "This advice is exactly why we need James," she said, her voice dripping with a mix of gratitude and mild irritation that Brett hadn't pieced it together sooner.

"Love is the ultimate adventure, after all," I added, injecting a bit of charm to smooth over the moment. "It's unpredictable, high-stakes, and it keeps everyone watching."

From that moment on, we were unstoppable. Ideas poured out like champagne from a newly popped bottle, each one fizzing with potential. Romantic settings that made you sigh, heartwarming moments that reignited your faith in love, and a wedding so lavish it would make every other TV wedding look like a backyard barbecue.

Their eyes glimmered with anticipation, their expressions a mixture of awe and delight, as if I were weaving a spell they were powerless to resist.

As the sun dipped below the horizon, the newly decorated space seemed to buzz with the energy of new ideas coalescing into a plan. Each piece was beginning to click into place, forming the framework for what could be a groundbreaking reality show.

However, one crucial element still lingered just out of reach—the pivotal moment that would define the entire project.

"We need to talk about the proposal," I said, my voice laced with a mix of hope and uncertainty. "It's where our story begins, so it has to be extraordinary. A moment that grabs the audience and refuses to let go."

They were teetering on the edge of something spectacular, but without the perfect proposal, the entire concept risked falling flat.

Brett Bottom, after a moment of contemplation, ventured cautiously, "What if I get down on one knee and give Carol Ann a red rose?"

Carol Ann stifled a yawn, her patience visibly wearing thin. "Or maybe James and I can put our heads together and come up with somethin' a tad more original," she shot back, her tone edged with sarcasm.

"Don't worry, old chap," I replied, my calm demeanor a sharp contrast to the tension simmering in the room. "We'll come up with something splendid. But there's one more thing we need to discuss," I continued, addressing the unspoken concern that had been hovering over the project. "We're talking about a significant production here. The venue, the decorations, the engagement ring—everything adds up."

Brett Bottom nodded in agreement, a trace of anxiety creeping into his expression. "The hair and makeup costs alone," he muttered under his breath.

I maintained my focus. "I've gone over the numbers, and we're looking at around $12,000 to produce a pilot that'll really dazzle."

"No problem," Carol Ann responded breezily, as if the sum were pocket change. "Darlin', there are boxes just brimming with cash in my closet."

A flicker of relief passed through me, though I had no desire to dive deeper into the murky origins of all that money.

"You are good on camera, aren't you?" I asked Brett, realizing a little too late that it was a question I should've addressed earlier.

"Brett?" Carol Ann interrupted, her enthusiasm brimming. "Why, he's simply a natural. Better than Nicholas Lee Shy!" she gushed, her Southern charm wrapping her words in sweet conviction.

But Brett's reaction didn't match her exuberance. A shadow of concern flickered across his face, his gaze darting away as though her confidence only deepened his uncertainty. The room fell silent for a moment, the weight of his hesitation hanging in the air.

It was clear: the cameras hadn't started rolling yet, but the real drama was already brewing.

In the heart of Chelsea, Mary and Ben's once-promising new apartment had devolved into a stark symbol of their unraveling. The new Pottery Barn coffee table, purchased with so much hope for fresh starts and bright tomorrows, now sat between them like a chasm. Its surface bore the newspaper, the weight of its presence echoing the things neither dared to say aloud.

The air was thick, suffused with a bittersweet tension, the scent of their shared future dissipating like smoke. Mary's hand trembled as she reached out, her fingers hesitating just shy of Ben's arm. She didn't touch him—he was a fortress now, unyielding, impenetrable. His gaze, once so full of warmth, was fixed on some far-off point past her shoulder, as if the answer to everything lay somewhere just beyond her reach.

"Are you ever going to talk to me again?" Mary asked, her voice barely audible, each word trembling on the brink of a plea.

Ben didn't look at her. His fingers drummed an uneven rhythm on the edge of the table, the only sign of the storm brewing beneath his carefully controlled exterior.

"I'm upset," he muttered, his voice taut, as though each word were a struggle to push past the tension coiling in his shoulders.

Even Ben Stiller had retreated to the pristine bathroom, hiding behind the toilet like a furry diplomat opting out of the tension-filled stalemate.

From his seat, Ben's gaze wandered into the bedroom. The sock drawer was slightly ajar, revealing the tiniest sliver of its contents. Inside, hidden away from even the nosiest prying eyes, rested an engagement ring. A secret he'd been guarding, waiting for a perfect moment—a moment that now seemed as elusive as the peace between them.

The silence stretched unbearably, only to be shattered by Mary's phone buzzing to life on the table. The sudden vibration sent it skittering across the surface, a stubborn, insistent reminder of the world beyond their apartment.

Mary glanced at the screen, her face lighting up briefly before darkening just as quickly. "Carol Ann just announced she's getting married," she gasped, her eyes flicking down to her own bare ring finger.

The words hung in the air, their weight settling on her like a leaden cloak. Her stomach twisted, emotions swirling—envy, sadness, resignation. It was an unspoken punch to the gut, one she tried desperately to conceal. But no matter how hard she fought, the bitter taste of jealousy clung stubbornly to her thoughts, tainting everything.

Ben didn't look up. His eyes remained fixed on the wooden floor, the slight tapping of his foot the only sign he'd even heard her.

The words burst out of Mary before she could stop them, fueled by the storm brewing inside her. "You hate me, don't you?" she said, her voice trembling. "And you hate my job too."

Ben blinked, genuinely taken aback. Confusion clouded his face, his brow furrowed as if trying to decode a language he didn't speak. "What does one thing have to do with the other?" he asked, clearly puzzled by her sudden outburst.

Mary's patience snapped, the dam holding back her emotions breaking in an instant. She stepped closer, her hands trembling, not with fear, but with the sheer weight of everything she'd kept bottled up.

"I wasn't born with a silver spoon in my mouth like you," she spat, her words sharp, each syllable cutting into the space between them. "There was no Wall Street job waiting for me! I had to take whatever job I could get."

Ben's frustration flared, shimmering in the air between them like the heatwaves rising from sun-scorched pavement. "That's not fair," he snapped, his voice tight as he struggled to keep control, his composure slipping.

Mary's eyes blazed, her anger burning hotter. "What's not fair," she countered, her voice a sharp, trembling edge, "is my mother kicking me out when I was sixteen. I had nothing. Not even a father."

Ben inhaled deeply, trying to steady himself against the tide of her pain. It was like trying to hold back a storm with his bare hands. The weight of the past hung between them, heavy and unrelenting, and for a moment, neither of them knew how to move forward.

"Why is it that people who've never faced a bad choice always think they've made a good one?" Mary's voice trembled, her anger now entwined with vulnerability.

Her eyes searched Ben's, seeking not just understanding but recognition—an acknowledgment of the battles she had fought, battles she had faced mostly alone.

Ben's gaze softened. For the first time, he truly saw Mary—the woman he loved, who had clawed her way up from nothing.

"I hear you," he said finally, his voice steady yet laced with emotion—a delicate mix of defiance and vulnerability. "But you need to hear me too. Being a Black man in America isn't easy—and pretending to be white is not an option for me."

Mary paused, her voice trembling. "I'm sorry," she added, her heart twisting in a clumsy dance of compassion and embarrassment.

"I'm sorry too," Ben replied, his voice steady, a poignant blend of love and pain.

Mary stood abruptly, grabbing her purse as if it were her armor. Her movements were sharp, a clear signal that she was ready to bolt. But just as she turned toward the door, Ben's voice cut through the tension, a tether pulling her back.

"Stop," he said, closing the distance between them with a few determined steps. His voice was gentle but firm, an anchor in the storm of her emotions. "The road ahead is uncertain, but I want us to face it together."

Memories of Mary's past swirled like a storm in her mind—a murky haze of mistakes, regrets, and the walls she'd built to survive. They clashed violently with the dazzling yet daunting prospect of what could be. She could almost see it—the future—shimmering just out of reach, promising everything she had ever dreamed of if only she had the courage to reach for it.

"You don't have to be afraid, Mary," Ben said, his tone steady and reassuring, like a hand offered to someone standing at the edge of a cliff. "Not with me."

Her heart pounded, her pulse echoing in her ears as the realization struck her with the force of a freight train. She couldn't keep running—not from Ben, not from herself, and certainly not from the possibility of love.

"I promise, I'll make this right," she whispered, her eyes flicking to the newspaper sprawled across the coffee table. Its bold headlines seemed almost mocking now, a silent witness to her quiet vow.

Ben's gaze shifted, his eyes landing on the slightly open sock drawer in the bedroom—the one where the engagement ring lay hidden, nestled among mismatched socks. "Me too," he murmured, his voice carrying a soft certainty that made it feel as though anything was possible.

A new kind of silence settled between them. Not the awkward, oppressive kind that had lingered before, but one dense with unspoken plans and fragile hope. They exchanged a look, one that spoke of possibility, of second chances, and a future they could build together.

As if sensing the shift, Ben Stiller emerged cautiously from the bathroom. Her reappearance felt symbolic, a quiet return to a happy haven.

Chapter 25

Mary didn't just walk into the office—she stormed in, a force of nature barreling through the glass doors with a fury that turned heads and silenced conversations. The once-familiar surroundings now felt alien, every corner of the newsroom tainted by the bitter aftertaste of betrayal.

Without hesitation, she flung her boss's door open, the wood slamming against the wall with a resounding thud. Her eyes locked onto him, the man she had once trusted, the man who had crossed an unforgivable line.

"You exposed my source," she said as if wielding a blade. The accusation hung in the air, heavy with the weight of betrayal. "She's just a kid." Her knuckles whitened as she gripped the doorframe. "You need to hire her right now, or I quit."

It wasn't a threat; it was a declaration, a line drawn in the sand, bold and immovable. Integrity mattered—to Mary, at least, even if it seemed to have slipped through the cracks of the office she once held sacred.

His gruff voice betrayed a flicker of something unspoken—guilt, perhaps, or the recognition that the specter of a lawsuit might loom even larger. "I don't respond well to threats," he moaned, his tone gravelly, though his hesitation was clear. He rubbed the bridge of his nose and let out a reluctant sigh. "But... let me think about it."

There it was. A reluctant acknowledgment, slight but undeniable. Mary wasn't just another reporter to him; she was the best, her talent indispensable. Losing her would leave a void that no amount of mediocre fluff pieces could fill.

Mary's lips pressed into a thin line, but she didn't wait for a final decision. The ultimatum was as much for herself as it was for him. Her mind had already begun solidifying the bold decision she'd made the moment she learned her source had been exposed.

As she began gathering her belongings, she felt the weight of every notebook, every mug, every memento she tucked into a cardboard box. They weren't just things—they were fragments of a life she had fought to build, a career she had poured herself into. And yet, they were also reminders of the world she was now choosing to leave behind.

Taking a deep breath, Mary exhaled the last remnants of doubt, and with a final push of resolve, stepped out into the unknown—a world beyond the confines of celebrity gossip, one that was waiting for her to write her next chapter.

The moment Mary stepped outside, doubts began to swirl around her like a brewing storm—dark, foreboding, and all too familiar. Just as the uncertainty threatened to pull her under, she caught sight of a familiar figure weaving purposefully through the sea of strangers on the sidewalk.

"Where are you going with that big box?" Nancy Reagan's unmistakable voice rang out, a melodic mix of curiosity and warmth.

Mary blinked, startled by the serendipity of the encounter. "I just quit my job," she confessed, her words tumbling out in a rush, filled with a mixture of relief and apprehension. "I'm done with silly gossip."

Nancy didn't miss a beat. "There is nothing silly about gossip," she said, her tone confident, as if stating a universal truth. "Gossip is just news running ahead of itself in a red satin dress."

Mary stopped in her tracks, the poetic elegance of Nancy's words catching her off guard. "That might be the most beautiful thing I've ever heard," she murmured.

Nancy chuckled softly. "Oh, I can't take credit for that one," she admitted, a twinkle of nostalgia lighting up her face. "That was my dear friend Liz Smith. God rest her soul."

Mary hesitated, her voice faltering as she asked the question that had been gnawing at her since the moment she walked outside. "Have I made a terrible mistake?"

Nancy smiled, the kind of look that carried the wisdom of decades. "The only mistake would be not trusting yourself enough to find out," she said, her words landing with quiet gravity.

Mary's grip on the box loosened as Nancy's words sank in.

"Running away never leads anyone to where they want to go," Nancy continued. "Start running toward what you want—and always wear red!"

With a flick of her imaginary wand, Nancy Reagan disappeared into the crowd, leaving behind the kind of magic only a fairy godmother could conjure.

Just then, Mary's phone rang, jolting her back into the real world. She glanced down, her editor's name flashing on the screen.

Taking another deep breath, she answered.

"I hired the nanny," the boss snapped, his tone brisk and unapologetic, as if conceding had physically pained him. "So, I expect you back in the office tomorrow morning. Bright and early."

Mary felt a rush of triumph, a warmth spreading through her chest. She had stood her ground, and for once, the universe—or maybe just her boss—had responded in kind.

"Thank you," she said simply, her voice steady but filled with quiet pride. "I'll be there."

As the call ended, Mary tucked her phone into her pocket, her steps feeling lighter as she started walking again. The doubts that had swirled around her earlier had faded, replaced by a clarity she hadn't known she needed. Nancy Reagan's words played in her mind like a mantra: *Start running toward what you want.*

And as Mary moved forward, she realized she wasn't just running toward what she wanted. She was finally ready to catch it.

Twenty minutes later, Mary flung open the door to her new apartment, her breath coming in short bursts, her entire body practically vibrating with exhilaration. The news she carried made her heart race, each beat a pulse of pure, unfiltered joy.

"Ben, are you here? I've got so much to tell you!" she called, her voice bubbling over with excitement. She darted around the corner into the living room, but then she froze.

There, on the sofa, sat Ben Stiller, purring contentedly, and a silent Ben, holding a small ring box in his shaking hands.

The sight knocked the wind out of her. The world around her seemed to tilt, narrowing until it was just the three of them—and the weight of what was about to happen.

"Mary," Ben said, his voice trembling, as if the words he was about to say carried the entirety of his soul, "will you marry me?"

Tears welled in her eyes, shimmering like tiny jewels as an overwhelming tide of emotion swelled within her.

"Yes," she exclaimed, the word bursting from her lips with electric, undeniable force. It wasn't just an answer—it was a leap of faith she had been too scared to make until now.

And then, as the tears spilled over and her voice softened to a trembling whisper, she let the words she had carried for so long finally escape. "I love you."

Carol Ann's upcoming wedding was the city's latest obsession, the kind of event that invited whispers at every café counter, subway car, and dinner table. The news moved fast, a wildfire of speculation and envy that even reached the corners of Miss D's well-worn uptown apartment.

"Well, it just goes to show, there's a lid for every pot," Miss D quipped, her voice lilting with bemusement.

Her gaze wandered to Baby J, sprawled naked on her bed, the youthful ease of his posture at odds with the weathered walls and cracked tiles of her little Harlem haven. Seeing him there, so relaxed and perfectly at home, made her heart swell unexpectedly. Within these walls, everything made sense. Everything felt perfectly right.

"I know we've only just gotten back together," she began, her tone light but deliberate, "but will you be my date to Carol Ann's wedding?"

Baby J's lips curved into that boyish grin she adored. "Are you sure you wouldn't rather take your mother?" he teased, the sparkle in his eyes betraying the seriousness underneath. He searched her face, his playful tone belying the question beneath the question: *Are you ready for this? For us?*

"You know," Miss D said softly, her fingers lightly tracing the worn edges of an old hardcover book resting on her lap. "When we're together, everything feels so right."

"Then stop reading and start feeling," Baby J teased, his hand gently guiding hers away from the book toward his chest, solid and steady beneath her touch. His voice softened, his eyes locking onto hers. "I never want to lose you again," he whispered.

Then a sudden shadow crossed her face, dimming the radiant light of the moment. "What are we going to do about my momma?" she asked, her voice trembling slightly, her joy tempered with the weight of reality.

Baby J didn't flinch. He remained calm, his hands steady as he took hers. "I think it's time your mother and I meet," he said, his voice carrying a quiet strength that felt like an anchor in the storm of her worries.

Slowly, she nodded, a glimmer of determination sparking in her eyes. "And sometimes," she said, her tone growing firm, "the most successful pairings are the ones that defy logic…and color too."

"Five…four…three…two…" I counted down, my voice dragging with the weariness of endless takes that had chipped away at my patience.

"Carol. Ann. Will. You. Marry. Me," Brett Bottom intoned yet again, each word landing with the mechanical precision of a well-practiced but completely soulless actor.

"Cut!" I exhaled, fighting the urge to bang my head against the nearest wall. Instead, I softened my tone, leaning in slightly. "Brett, what can I possibly do to assist you?" I asked, my voice warm with genuine concern, hoping to coax something—*anything*—real out of him.

Brett sighed, his shoulders slumping as he cast a nervous glance at the crew. "I think the problem is the crew staring at me," he whispered, his voice barely audible. "I don't feel comfortable," he added, his gaze dropping to the floor like a kid confessing to breaking a vase.

I clapped my hands decisively. "Alright, that's a wrap for today!" I announced, watching the crew exchange relieved glances as they began packing up their equipment. Then, I turned back to Brett with a smile that was equal parts sympathetic and cunning. "Except for you, Brett. I've got an idea."

An hour later, the front door creaked open, and in walked my secret weapon. Every inch of him was meticulously packaged in tight pants that left little to the imagination.

"Brett, meet Cliff," I said with a dramatic flourish, as if unveiling a prize on a game show.

Brett's eyes lit up, a spark of curiosity replacing the earlier hesitation. His posture straightened, and a faint smile curved his lips. "Pleased to meet you," he purred, the earlier stiffness melting away as he extended a hand.

"If Cliff can make Miss D and me look good in front of a green screen, he can certainly do the same for you," I declared, my voice infused with a renewed sense of determination.

Cliff, always the professional, surveyed the room with a critical eye before shaking his head. "First of all, it's way too hot in here," he said, his tone authoritative. Then, with a sly grin, he added, "Remember Joan Rivers's wise words: 'People don't laugh or get excited when they're overheated!'"

I chuckled and made a beeline for the thermostat. With the hum of the air conditioner kicking in, the room began to cool, and along with it, my nerves. "Alright," I said, clapping my hands. "Let's give this a try. Just the three of us. Five...four...three..."

But before I could reach two, Brett's voice cut through the countdown, trembling and raw. "I'm sorry," he said, his eyes darting nervously between Cliff and me. "I just can't do it with you both watching."

My heart sank, the high hopes I'd held onto now feeling like a cruel joke. "I'm running short on ideas here," I murmured to Cliff, my voice laced with desperation. "We need a miracle."

Cliff didn't miss a beat, his tone almost casual as he suggested, "Let's ditch the cameras altogether."

I blinked, trying to process the audacity of the suggestion. "Cliff, I can't sell a show we haven't recorded," I countered, my skepticism evident.

But Cliff's grin only widened, his confidence unwavering. "We're going to record *Big Brother*–style," he assured me. "Brett Bottom won't even know he's being filmed."

The sheer boldness of the plan made my pulse quicken. "Let me text Carol Ann and get her on board," I gasped, my voice tinged with sharp urgency.

Seconds later, my phone buzzed with her reply: *Well, sugar, it's a yes.*

"Obviously, the bedroom and bathrooms will be off-limits," I assured her, trying to keep my tone professional and calm.

"Don't be ridiculous," Carol Ann snapped, her drawl dripping with sass. "I do my best work in those two rooms."

Her assurance was bold, almost too bold, but I had learned long ago that when it came to Carol Ann, things tended to work out—if only by sheer force of her will.

This just might work too.

Two hours later, Brett Bottom pushed open the door to the freezing apartment, the sharp chill nipping at his skin as he stepped inside. Carol Ann lay sprawled on the couch, half-draped in a throw, her lips curving into a knowing, mischievous grin.

"Come keep me warm," she giggled, her tone dripping with playful suggestion.

Unbeknownst to Brett, Carol Ann had decided to keep the hidden cameras secret, at least until she had coaxed the performance I desperately needed from him.

"Follow me," she said, rising from the couch with an effortless air of command. With every step, she shed another layer of clothing—and inhibition—until the only thing left between her and her goals was a closed bedroom door.

"You've been a very naughty boy," Carol Ann murmured, her voice taking on a teasing, almost playful tone as she bent Brett over.

The mix of sensations overwhelmed him, each one blurring the lines between pleasure and pain until they coalesced into something indescribable. His breaths came faster, shallow, and urgent, as he teetered on the brink.

"Carol Ann, will you marry me?" he begged like a desperate prayer.

With a scream that could win her an Emmy, Carol Ann shouted, "Yes, yes, yes!"

It was a proposal like no other—sealed with a smile—and a strap-on.

Chapter 26

In a flash of what Carol Ann deemed sheer brilliance, she added her own address to her wedding invitation list. She wasn't about to deprive herself of the exquisite thrill of receiving a little piece of her own grandeur.

"Brett! Brett! It's here!"

Without waiting for his reaction, she nudged him aside with just enough force to make her point, her diamond ring catching the light in a dazzling display as she did so.

With the reverence of someone handling a priceless artifact, Carol Ann placed the cream-colored, custom-made linen box onto her new pristine Swedish Modern coffee table.

Lifting the lid with a delicate flourish, the *Gone With the Wind* theme swelled. Inside her and Brett's initials—CA and BB—intertwined in an elegant monogram, embroidered in gold thread atop silk-screened artwork depicting the couple in a cinematic, passionate kiss.

Nestled within the box, beneath a layer of artfully arranged tissue, was a fresh, warm peach pie from Maison Kayser, its tantalizing aroma filling the room. As if on cue, two delicate butterflies fluttered out of the box, their flight as graceful as a scene from a fairy tale.

Around them, hidden cameras captured every angle of the orchestrated spectacle.

"That's a lot of rules," Brett muttered as he picked up the embossed invitation. "Rule number seven," he read aloud. "Everyone, including men, must have professional makeup!"

"Trust me," she said. "You wouldn't believe what James looks like before Maria gets her hands on him."

He then flipped to Rule Eight, his puzzled expression deepening. "Use the hashtag #CarolAnnsWedding when posting all pictures," he read. Then, after a pause, he looked up. "Isn't it my wedding too?"

"Of course it is," she replied without hesitation. "But both our names would be too long to trend."

She reached for a slice of the peach pie, savoring her triumph like a taste of things to come. "I only wish I could hear what everyone else is saying right now as they open theirs."

Mary sprawled across the couch in the dressing room, her stomach aching after devouring every crumb of the peach pie. Miss D sat nearby, her expression a mix of confusion and mild horror as she scanned the list of wedding rules.

"Is this invitation for real?" she finally asked, breaking the silence.

I couldn't help but giggle. "It shall make for splendid telly," I said, leaning into the absurdity of it all.

We were all lost in the world of Carol Ann when she burst into the room, late as ever, struggling to balance a precarious tower of cream-colored boxes.

"Did y'all get the invite of the century?" she chirped.

Cliff trailed behind her, camera in hand, capturing every second as if he were her shadow.

Carol Ann's gaze landed squarely on me. "I know you're heading to the *Deadpool* junket after the show," she announced. "So, I brought you an extra invitation to personally deliver to Mr. Ryan Reynolds."

Miss D spoke up with a tone that hinted more at tradition than Tinseltown. "The whole point of a wedding is to invite people who are special to you, to witness your sacred moment."

Carol Ann waved her off, unfazed. "Nonsense. Do you think Harry and Meghan knew George Clooney when they got married at Windsor? And don't even get me started on Star Jones. I doubt she knew the groom!"

Miss D let out a sigh that spoke volumes. "Point taken," she conceded, shaking her head.

Carol Ann's eyes lit up as she revealed her pièce de résistance. "I've already locked in a Real Housewife," she said, her tone brimming with pride, "one of Tiger Woods's mistresses, and you three."

I rolled my eyes, unable to resist. "Together, the five of us almost add up to one real celebrity."

Miss D giggled, her mischievous grin growing wider. "Don't forget to invite Josh Ellis and his 'magic sauce,'" she added, barely stifling a laugh.

Carol Ann paused, the gears in her mind visibly turning as she made a mental note. "Not a bad idea," she said, nodding thoughtfully before turning her full attention back to me.

"Do you know which network has bought our show yet? Because if it's Bravo, I'm thinking about getting Andy Cohen instead of a priest!"

Mary, still feeling sick on the couch, finally sat up. "Are you actually serious about this dress code thing?" she asked as she gestured toward the list.

"Why, yes I am," Carol Ann replied sharply. "We're hiring security, so don't even think about showing up in one of your cat sweaters."

Mary gasped. "Joan Rivers is the only fashion police I acknowledge," she declared.

Carol Ann, unfazed as always, smirked. "Darlin', even Joan would agree—you better not cross me on this one."

After yet another successful show, I barely had a moment to catch my breath before rushing off to The Ritz Carlton for the *Deadpool* junket. Mary, by coincidence—or perhaps some divine intervention—was heading to The Essex House next door to meet a source. She offered me a ride. "I'll get you to Mr. Reynolds faster than Scarlett Johansson escaped his clutches."

Once inside the taxi, Mary couldn't contain herself. She practically buzzed with excitement. "With all the Carol Ann drama, I didn't have a chance to reveal my own little scoop," she said, her words tumbling out like a secret begging to be spilled.

"Do enlighten me," I replied, my curiosity igniting like a spark to kindling.

"Ben proposed!" Mary screamed, lifting her hand to reveal a diamond ring, simple yet breathtaking.

My eyes lit up with genuine excitement. "That's marvelous!" I exclaimed. "You have to tell me everything. How did he do it?"

"Oh, we had this huge argument," she began, shaking her head as if the memory itself still baffled her. "And then, the next time I saw him, there he was...with the cat and a ring."

"You know," I chuckled, barely holding back a laugh as the memory of Brett Bottom on all fours flashed through my mind, "that's not even the most peculiar proposal I've heard this week."

"Oh, and by the way—I quit my job at the paper," she added casually, as though dropping a grenade mid-conversation.

"What?" I exclaimed, my astonishment evident.

"Well," Mary continued, a sly grin playing at her lips, "I quit my job for about ten minutes." She leaned back in her seat, exhaling as if letting go of something heavy. "Let's just say the new Mary is running toward what she wants, not away from it."

I raised an eyebrow, intrigued. "What do you mean by that?"

She took a deep breath, her excitement bubbling just beneath the surface. "I signed up for a few open mics around town. Small, divey places where I can learn my craft."

My face broke into a wide smile. "Mary, that's extraordinary," I said. "You were amazing at Nancy Reagan's club."

"Beginner's luck," she replied with a modest shrug, though her eyes sparkled with pride. Then, with a mischievous grin, she asked the question of the hour. "Talking of comedy, are you really going to ask Ryan Reynolds if he wants to go to Carol Ann's wedding?"

"No," I replied, though my tone carried a faint thread of apprehension.

Mary picked up on it immediately. "Are you okay?" she asked, her voice softening with concern.

I hesitated. "It's just...I've never done a junket before, without a little extra help," I admitted, my words laced with unspoken struggles. "We've never talked about this, Mary, but..." My voice faltered, the words refusing to come.

"I know," Mary interrupted gently, her tone brimming with empathy. "Well, I suspected," she amended, reaching out to squeeze my hand. "Let them see the real you, James. You are enough," she affirmed, her words filled with the kind of quiet strength that could only come from a true friend.

As we stepped out of the car together, leaning on each other for support, fate had one last joke to play. A pigeon swooped in and deposited its unwelcome gift squarely on Mary's right shoulder.

For a moment, we stared at the offending mark in stunned silence before bursting into uncontrollable laughter.

"You know, they say it's good luck!" I teased, grinning as Mary shot me a playful glare.

"Then let's share it," she quipped, making a move as if to smear some of the mess on me.

"Noooo!" I protested, darting toward the hotel lobby. But just as I reached the door, I stopped and glanced back at her.

"I'm already lucky," I said softly, my voice tender. "I have you."

Later that evening, the cozy warmth of Delores's momma's home was filled with the mouthwatering aroma of a home-cooked meal, a comfort that seemed at odds with the tension simmering just beneath the surface.

Delores tried to fill the silence with a forced brightness that belied her own unease. "I'm so happy you two are finally meeting," she said as she glanced between her mother and the man she loved.

Finally, Momma broke the silence, her gaze lifting to lock onto Delores with a piercing clarity. "Why would you want to make your life more difficult?" she asked, her voice laden with worry and an edge of exasperation.

Delores inhaled sharply but didn't hesitate. "My life is easier with Baby J in it," she said, her tone steady even as her heart pounded in her chest.

Momma's expression didn't soften, her concern etched into every line on her face. "Everything is going so well for you right now," she said, her voice tinged with the kind of worry only a mother can feel. "You've worked so hard to get here. Why risk it?"

Delores turned to Baby J for a moment, her eyes seeking his before she faced her mother again. "What's the point of all this success if I don't have anyone to share it with? I've been alone for fifty-two years, Momma," she admitted, the words tumbling out like a confession she hadn't planned to make.

Baby J shifted in his seat, his own discomfort bubbling to the surface—not because of what Delores had said, but because of what he hadn't.

He took a deep breath, his hand tightening around hers as he leaned forward slightly. "I know I'm not the prince you imagined for your daughter," he began, his gaze fixed on Momma with quiet determination. "But I promise you, I will always treat her like a queen."

Delores felt her heart swell, emotion rising in her chest. No man had ever spoken so plainly, so black and white about his love for her before.

Momma's expression shifted, her sharpness softening slightly, though her practical tone remained. "Neither one of you can take care of yourselves," she said, her words firm but not unkind.

Delores sat up straighter. "Then we can take care of each other," she said simply, her voice laced with quiet defiance.

For a moment, the room seemed to hold its breath.

Momma's eyes drifted heavenward, as if seeking divine intervention to guide her through the tumultuous mix of emotions coursing through her. Finally, with a deep sigh, she brought her gaze back to Delores and the man who was about to become her son-in-law.

"God help us all," she murmured, her words carrying equal parts resignation and begrudging acceptance. "You have my blessing," she added. "Someone better make a toast quick before I change my mind."

Baby J didn't miss a beat. Raising his glass, he declared with a wide grin, "To my wife and my manager."

"Manager?" Delores echoed, a playful glint sparking in her eyes as she tilted her head, processing the unexpected title.

"That's if you'll take me on as a client as well as a husband," Baby J said.

Delores squealed with delight, her hands clapping together. "Yes to both!" she exclaimed.

But Momma wasn't done. "One more thing," she interjected firmly, raising a finger to ensure she had the floor. "No more of this 'Baby' nonsense," she declared. "Tonight, you proved you're a man. A skinny white man, sure, but a man nonetheless."

Baby J's face broke into a sheepish grin, but before he could reply, Delores chimed in, her eyes sparkling with affection. "Jay has a nice ring to it," she said, her words laced with pride and playfulness as she squeezed his hand.

"Almost as nice as husband," the newly christened Jay replied, savoring the word like it was the richest dish on Momma's table.

The next morning, with her momma's approval wrapped around her like a cozy blanket and her fiancé's love shining like a bright beacon ahead, Miss D practically floated into the gym.

"Congratulations!" Jess called out, sprinting across the room, still flushed from a grueling session with Bunny Deadline.

"Wow, news travels fast," Miss D replied, a shy smile creeping onto her face as a soft blush warmed her cheeks.

"Let's see the ring!" Jess demanded, her eyes sparkling with excitement as she held out her hand expectantly.

Miss D extended her left hand, feeling self-conscious despite herself. "I know it's not massive," she said, her voice tinged with a hint of apology.

Jess didn't hesitate. "It's perfect," she said firmly. "Big things come in small packages."

"Don't worry about size when it comes to my man," Miss D quipped, her confidence returning with a playful wink.

Jess laughed, her happiness for her friend shining through, even as a storm brewed in her own life. "When's the big day?" she asked.

Miss D's smile faltered slightly, uncertainty flickering in her eyes. "When we've saved up enough money to afford it," she admitted, her voice softening as the realities of life crept into her fairy tale.

Jess's expression softened. "Don't worry about that," she said. "With his talent, and more importantly, his new manager's talent, you two will be saying 'I do' in no time."

Miss D sighed wistfully. "You make it sound like money falls from the sky," she said, a skeptical edge to her voice.

Jess smiled slyly, her eyes glinting with excitement as she pulled a small, shiny disk from her pocket. It caught the gym's fluorescent lights, reflecting them like a tiny beacon. "Well, it fell from somewhere," Jess said with a smirk, handing the disk to Miss D. "Darby found this on the street."

Miss D's eyes widened as she took the disk in her hands. "Oh my god," she whispered, her voice trembling with awe. "I thought this was just an urban legend. Do you even know how much this is worth?"

"I'm hoping a lot," Jess replied. "Because we're going to need every penny of it to finally open our own gym together."

Chapter 27

Mary hovered at the back of the dimly lit comedy club, her posture deceptively casual, as if she weren't silently debating every life choice that had led her here. This wasn't just a room; it was a crucible, a place where fragile dreams went to either live or die.

It was a lottery of aspirations, a cruel game of chance where a name pulled from a hat could be the start of something extraordinary or the reason you cried into a soggy pizza slice at 2 a.m. Mary knew this. She also knew better than to believe success came wrapped in glitter and tied with a neat bow.

Even with a friend like Nancy Reagan, success was something you earned.

Her reverie was shattered by the host's voice. "Next up we have…"

And there it was. Her name, out in the open, leaving her no choice but to swallow her nerves and step into the blinding glare of the spotlight.

She stepped forward, gripping the mic with a confidence that felt as real as a knockoff Prada bag. "Well, folks," she began, her eyes catching the ugly smear of black ink spreading across her blouse—a cruel gift from a leaky pen. "Looks like we've got ourselves a little wardrobe malfunction."

Her gaze darted over the room, scanning faces until she caught the glimmer of amusement in the shadows. She latched onto it like a lifeline. "But don't worry," she added. "I'm not about to give you all a Janet Jackson moment. Let's be honest—no one here is dying to see my nipples."

The next three minutes unfolded in a whirlwind of groans, scattered laughter, and the relentless drumbeat of Mary's own heart in her ears. Her punchlines landed more often than not, each laugh a small victory that pushed her forward.

She saved her best for last—her story about Charlie Sheen that, as always, brought the house down—and tonight was no exception.

Backstage following her performance, Mary leaned against the chipped brick wall, her shoulders just starting to relax as the adrenaline ebbed away. She was suspended in that strange, weightless space between the stage and the rest of her life, her thoughts still echoing with punchlines and applause, when I burst through the door like a whirlwind that didn't quite know where it was going.

"You were brilliant!" I declared, one hand slicing the air as if trying to physically catch my feelings before they scattered.

"I knew you were out there somewhere," Mary said. "I could hear your English giggling."

"Does laughter have an accent?" I shot back, my words tumbling out as fast as the grin that tugged at my lips.

"Of course it does," she replied, her tone so certain it left no room for argument. "You can tell everything about a person by the way they laugh."

I hesitated for a moment, letting the weight of her observation hang in the air. Finally, I broke the silence. "I must say," I said, "I truly admire you for doing this."

Mary's smile widened. "I should be thanking you," she admitted. "I never would have done any of this if you hadn't convinced me to do the TV show."

"Rubbish," I shot back, the word tumbling out with all the conviction of someone brushing off a compliment. "This is all about your talent and hard work. I'm just here to watch you shine."

Night after night, week after week, month after month, Mary persisted. She dragged herself through the smoky corners of the city's comedy clubs, armed only with her wits and a borrowed blouse or two. Those early months were punishing—a ceaseless grind of late nights, lukewarm applause, and sets that barely held together.

The small, dimly lit clubs where Mary started, earning her stripes one shaky punchline at a time, began to lead to bigger venues. What once felt like dead ends became stepping stones.

As the audiences swelled, so did Mary's confidence. But no matter how full the room got, her ears always found one familiar sound: me, her steadfast cheerleader, laughter.

"Goodness, you have a proper dressing room," I marveled, my gaze sweeping the neatly arranged vanity and the couch that wasn't a repurposed lawn chair. It was a far cry from the dingy, fluorescent-lit storage closets where Mary had started.

She chuckled, her pride bubbling to the surface alongside a thrill of giddy excitement. "Just wait until next week," she teased.

"I think I'm getting a bathroom too. I've been invited to play the Comedy Cellar."

I froze. Surprise and pure joy collided on my face. "The Comedy Cellar?" I repeated, as if testing the words to make sure they were real. "Mary, that's *incredible!*" I burst out.

She nodded, warmth spreading through her chest as a wave of gratitude threatened to unsteady her. "Yeah," she said softly, the weight of her journey settling over her in the best possible way. "It's been quite the ride. And you've been there every step of the way."

A moment of silence passed, heavy with unspoken memories of nights spent celebrating small victories or commiserating over bitter defeats. Then Mary's grin returned, irrepressible and electric. "Guess who's coming to my next show?" she blurted, her words tinged with giddy excitement.

I tilted my head, a knowing smile already forming as I crossed his arms. "Ben?" I asked, my tone a playful celebration of the answer I knew was coming.

Mary beamed, her excitement practically spilling over. "Ben," she confirmed, her voice almost breathless.

My grin widened as I reached for her hand, squeezing it in a moment of shared triumph. "Well," I said, my voice rich with pride, "he'd better be ready, because you're about to leave him completely speechless."

For the first time, Mary truly believed it.

The following week, Mary stepped off the stage of the most prestigious venue she'd ever performed at. She didn't think—she just moved, launching herself right into my waiting arms.

"Did you spot Sandra Bernhard in the audience?" I gasped, carefully setting Mary back on her feet, though my own excitement threatened to lift us both off the ground.

Mary's grin widened, impossibly so, at the mention of the comedy legend. "Not only did I see her," she said, "but I could hear her. Sandra Bernhard was laughing at my material."

I arched an eyebrow, unable to resist. "You can tell everything about someone by the way they laugh," I reminded her with a knowing smile. "And in case you missed it, there was a queue outside the box office for standby tickets."

"No way," Mary gasped, her eyes wide with disbelief, though the flush of pride creeping up her neck betrayed her delight.

"The word is out about you," I declared. This wasn't just another milestone—it was *the* moment.

Mary waved off the praise with a modest smile. "That's because you keep raving about me on our show," she replied, trying to downplay her own triumph.

But I wasn't having it. I stepped closer, my tone firm and full of affection. "No. It's because you're funny," I said, locking eyes with her. Then, with a sly grin, I added, "And because you're wearing Joan Rivers's necklace."

Her eyes dropped to the turquoise QVC piece resting against her collarbone, a treasured relic that shimmered under the dressing room lights. "It's my secret weapon," she confessed softly, her fingers brushing over it as if it held the magic of every punchline that had ever landed. "Guess you could say it's my lucky charm."

"Speaking of lucky," I began, my tone shifting to something lighter, "where's Ben?"

Mary's smile faltered, just slightly, but it was enough for me to notice. "His flight got delayed," she said, the words dipping in disappointment, like the sudden drop at the end of a roller coaster.

Before either of us could say more, a sharp knock echoed through the room, making us both jump. Mary's wide eyes flicked to mine as the dressing room door swung open with the kind of theatrical flair that belonged in an old Hollywood movie.

"Nancy Reagan?" we exclaimed in unison, our voices landing somewhere between incredulous and giddy disbelief.

There she stood, immaculately composed, taking up space like she'd just walked into the Oval Office rather than Mary's modest dressing room. It was surreal, absurd—and somehow, perfectly fitting.

"I'd like you both to meet my dear friend Annette Rosenberg," Nancy announced, as though she were unveiling a masterpiece. "Annette was Joan Rivers's executive producer for years, and a friend of mine for even longer."

Despite her small stature, Annette Rosenberg commanded the room with a presence that could silence a crowd. Her wide mouth, hinting at a lifetime of sharp wit and sharper comebacks, curled into a knowing smile. Her perfectly styled blonde hair gleamed under the dressing room lights, rivaled only by the gold jewelry she wore—bold and unapologetic, each piece a testament to a life well-lived. She exuded sophistication in her sleek black ensemble, accented by a vibrant Hermès scarf that somehow managed to scream both boardroom power player and Parisian style icon.

Mary's eyes widened, disbelief flickering across her face as she breathed out the name, as if saying it aloud might shatter the moment. "Annette Rosenberg?" she repeated, as though she were in the presence of royalty.

Annette extended her hand, elegant but marked by years of navigating the fast-paced, high-stakes world of comedy and television. "It's a pleasure to meet you, Mary," she said warmly. "Nancy has told me so much about you and let me tell you—it's all true."

Mary felt her knees wobble slightly as the surrealness of the moment pressed down on her. "You worked with Joan?" she asked, barely able to keep the awe out of her voice.

Annette's eyes sparkled with a blend of nostalgia and pride, her smile softening. "Yes, I did," she said. "And she would have loved you, which is why I want to talk with you about a new scripted comedy show I'm developing. I need writers with fresh ideas."

Mary felt her heart skip, her brain scrambling to process what had been said. A show? Writers? Her? She opened her mouth, but no words came, just a small, incredulous sound that was halfway between a gasp and a laugh.

With a graceful flick of her wrist, Annette handed Mary an old-fashioned business card—thick, elegant, and far too sophisticated for this era of QR codes and digital contacts. It felt almost anachronistic, yet perfectly fitting for someone like Annette Rosenberg. "Call me," she said, her tone as decisive as a stage cue.

Mary's fingers closed tightly around the card, its weight grounding her in the moment. She wanted to say something—something witty, memorable, something worthy of Joan Rivers's inner circle. But before she could find the words, Annette and Nancy Reagan had already made their exit, leaving behind a wake of mystery and promise, as if they'd vanished into the pages of a particularly glamorous novel.

"Oh my God," I squealed. "I wish I could stay and celebrate, but I must dash," I added dramatically, already inching toward the door. "I have a fitting with Brett Bottom for a suit for the wedding…don't ask."

Mary's lips curled into a teasing grin. "A fitting with Brett Bottom?" she quipped. "You better go, then. Besides, I'm not drinking at the moment."

I froze mid-step. "Not drinking? Are you quite alright?"

Mary nodded. "Just taking a break," she said, her voice steady and thoughtful. "Trying something new."

I raised an eyebrow, impressed, and pulled her into a quick, tight hug. It was brief but loaded with the kind of affection only the closest of friends could exchange. "Good for you," I said with a grin. "Alright, I'm off. See you later!"

As I disappeared through the door, the room fell into a brief silence. Mary let out a long, steadying breath, the buzz of the evening still humming in her chest. But before she could get lost in her thoughts, another knock echoed through the room, pulling her back to the present.

"Forgot something?" she called, assuming it was me.

But it wasn't me.

It was Ben.

"What are you doing here?" Mary exclaimed, her voice a mix of surprise, delight, and just a hint of disbelief, as though he might disappear if she blinked.

He stepped forward, the door clicking shut behind him as he closed the distance between them in one easy, deliberate move. Without a word, he wrapped his arms around her, pulling her into a hug that felt like the perfect ending to a story she hadn't even realized she was writing. "I had a little trouble getting backstage, but I managed to get on a different flight," he said. "I couldn't miss seeing this incredible new comic everyone's been talking about. Did I mention she's also incredibly sexy?"

Mary tilted her head back to meet his eyes. "She sounds amazing. Who is she?" she teased, her voice light, her heart anything but.

Ben didn't miss a beat, leaning in as though her lips held the only answer he'd ever needed. "You," he said softly, a giggle slipping through his words. "Incredible you."

Mary smiled, her heart catching on the way his laughter sounded—soft, unguarded, and entirely sincere. She could tell everything she needed to know by the way Ben laughed.

An hour later, I found myself standing awkwardly in the middle of Carol Ann's impeccably redecorated living room, feeling like a misplaced statue among her carefully curated decor. Clad in nothing but my underwear, I shifted nervously from one foot to the other, acutely aware of the heat creeping up my neck and flushing my cheeks.

"Just a few more adjustments," Brett Bottom announced. "And we'll have you looking like a million bucks."

I tried to muster a smile, something to break the tension, but my lips quivered, betraying my unease. The silence that followed was louder than it had any right to be.

"Although," Brett added, his eyes locking onto mine, "you'd look great in anything."

His words hung in the air, and I struggled to find the right response. Before I could, Brett continued, the words tumbling out with surprising candor. "I've always liked you," he admitted, his voice quieter now, more measured. "You've always been kind to me, never asking for anything in return."

I froze, unsure of where this was going, as Brett took a deliberate breath, his hand slipping into the pocket of his tailored blazer. My heart pounded with a confusing mix of anticipation and anxiety. Finally, he pulled out a small, familiar object—the tape. The tape of Nancy Reagan's media training session. The one Carol Ann had stolen.

"Oh my god, Brett, are you serious?" My voice wavered, relief, disbelief, gratitude—it all bubbled up at once.

He nodded, his expression calm, though his eyes held a flicker of something harder to pin down. "Don't worry," he said. "There are no more copies. This is the only one."

"Thank you," I whispered. "You're a good man, Brett Bottom. A good man."

Brett's lips curved into a faint smile, but the warmth in his expression darkened as he took a step closer. "Actually," he murmured, his voice lowering to a near-whisper, "I'm a very bad man."

Before I could respond, he reached into his pocket again, this time pulling out a small vial of white powder. "Carol Ann won't be back for hours," he said as his free hand darted out, landing firmly on my bottom.

Chapter 28

As Mary and I stepped into Carol Ann and Brett Bottom's wedding venue, it felt like stepping into a dream—or a nightmare—one that would cling to you long after you woke.

The old bank, with its towering marble columns and echoes of a bygone era, had been transformed into a setting so otherworldly it bordered on surreal.

Mary turned to me, her borrowed pale pink tulle dress swishing softly as she spun. The fabric floated, but she couldn't help but feel the weight of the few extra pounds she'd gained. "What other surprises are you hiding?" she teased.

I shrugged, the movement casual, though the words that followed were anything but. "Oh, just the groom deciding to grab my privates and offer me a line of coke," I said flatly.

"What?" Mary replied. "Have you told Carol Ann?"

"Not yet," I admitted. "It's harder than you'd think to find the right moment to tell the bride that her fiancé plays for both teams."

Mary laughed, spinning around to take in the scene, her eyes wide with wonder. "I can't believe you pulled all this off," she said, her voice carrying a mix of amazement and admiration.

"I can't believe *we* pulled it off," I corrected, the emphasis deliberate. "I'm producing my first reality show, and you're writing your first comedy show."

"It's not a done deal yet," Mary cautioned. "But my manager is very confident."

My eyebrows shot up. "You have a manager now?"

Mary's smile grew wider. "The best in the business," she said, her excitement bubbling over. "Her name is Miss D!"

"No way!" I exclaimed.

Mary tilted her head. "Please tell me Brett Bottom got down on one knee?"

I chuckled. "Even better," I said, grinning mischievously. "Brett Bottom got down on all fours."

Before Mary could press me for more details, the door swung open with the force of a gale, and Lori Letmein breezed in.

"Attention, everyone!" Lori's voice sliced through the room, crisp and unyielding. "You all need to sign release forms consenting to being on camera," she declared. "And I'll be assigning spots—uh, seats!"

Mary and I exchanged a quick glance before sinking into our assigned gold chairs near the front of the venue. Nestled between Miss D and Jay—both of whom radiated the kind of bliss that came from knowing *they* were next in line to say "I do"—we settled in for the inevitable wait.

And wait we did.

"Where on earth is she?" I muttered.

Mary leaned in. "Maybe she's still trying to convince Ryan Reynolds to make an appearance."

Miss D's gaze drifted toward Brett Bottom, who was pacing nervously at the end of the aisle, his eyes flickering in our direction once before darting away, deliberately avoiding mine.

Brett, in a striking tan-grey shell jacket with green and yellow trim, was a spectacle that teetered between bold fashion and historical reenactment. His sky-blue trousers added a daring contrast, giving him the air of someone who might command attention at both a runway and the Civil War.

"Is it just me, or does that outfit scream Confederacy chic?" Miss D quipped. "And wasn't he designing something for you too, James?"

I chuckled, throwing an exaggerated wink in Mary's direction. "Let's save that story for Bottino's," I replied.

Then the crowd erupted into a cacophony of excited murmurs. The opening strains of the theme from *Gone With the Wind* reached our ears.

There she was in a dress that had to be seen to be believed.

Layers of cascading tulle, sequins, and crystals formed a shimmering mountain of excess.

Mary didn't respond, her attention snapping to the person standing behind Carol Ann. "Oh my god," she breathed. "Bunny Deadline is giving her away."

Miss D and I craned our necks, the sea of heads parting just enough for us to see Bunny Deadline striding down the aisle in a dazzling white pantsuit tuxedo, complete with a top hat and a cane.

"Wait," Mary wheezed, clutching my arm for balance. "Keegan Kelly and Johnny Futura are her bridesmaids!"

As Carol Ann and her entourage finally reached Brett Bottom at the end of the aisle, the room fell into a reverent stillness. The weight of the moment pressed down like a heavy velvet curtain, every eye fixed on her.

She took a deep breath, steadying herself as the anticipation crackled in the air. Then, with all the poise of someone who knew exactly how to command a room, she began her self-written vows.

"If I should stay," she started. "I would only be in your way. So I'll go, but I know I'll think of you every step of the way."

My left hand shot up before I could stop myself. "That's Whitney!" I exclaimed.

Ari, seated next to me, leaned forward. "Actually, it's Dolly," he corrected gently, ensuring the original songwriter received her due recognition.

Finally, when Carol Ann was finished, the priest, who looked suspiciously like an actor from a *Law & Order*, raised his head to ask the most important question. "If anyone here today has any objection to this couple getting married," he intoned, "speak now or forever hold your peace."

For a moment, the room held its breath, the tension stretching so taut it seemed ready to snap. And then, just as the silence reached its breaking point, a voice shattered it like a clap of thunder.

"I've got to take this!" Producer declared. All heads turned in unison as he leapt from his seat, phone pressed tightly to his ear. "Big star on the line from Hollywood," he muttered, barely glancing at the stunned faces around him as he strode down the aisle.

"I've changed my mind," Nicholas Lee Shy admitted on the other end of the line. "I want to host the show."

"You do?" Producer gasped, now standing outside.

"I do!" Nicholas declared, unwittingly stealing Carol Ann's moment inside. "My ex-wife's money ran out," he explained.

"You'd think ten million would last a little longer. Expect a call from my manager tomorrow."

Producer's pulse quickened. This was it—the kind of name that could resurrect his career.

But Nicholas had one more demand to deliver. "My contract must include a clause to keep that Southern girl far away from me," he said. And just like that, the line went dead.

By the time Producer marched back into the venue, Carol Ann and Brett were officially Mr. and Mrs. Bottom.

He scanned the scene, his mind already racing ahead. But reality, as it so often does, came crashing in. This time, it arrived in the form of Keegan Kelly.

"I've got some big ideas for next season," Keegan snapped as she cornered him.

His expression shifted. "I'm afraid there won't be a next season for you," he replied.

Keegan's face fell, her carefully constructed bravado crumbling as confusion clouded her features. "What are you saying?" she asked, as though the answer might knock the wind out of her.

"Nicholas Lee Shy will be replacing you," Producer declared, his tone cool and final. It was a clean break, delivered with the precision of a man who'd done this before.

Before she could respond, Producer was already walking away, his "goodbye" tossed carelessly across the bustling room like an afterthought.

On the other side of the venue, where the energy hummed free of Keegan's unraveling, Mary lit up as she spotted Jay standing at the bar. "I'm so thrilled you're here!" she exclaimed, rushing forward with a bright smile.

Nearby, I leaned closer to Miss D. "I'm so happy the bride let you bring a plus-one," I said. "She's so weird about that. Mary had to *beg* to bring Ben."

Miss D chuckled softly. "Oh, Carol Ann didn't," she said. "Her wedding singer bailed at the last minute, and she called me in a full-blown panic. Carol Ann thinks I know every gospel choir in New York."

She shot a fond glance at Jay, who was nodding politely as Mary peppered him with questions. "Instead, I convinced her to book Jay."

I smiled, a flicker of pride warming me. But the moment was short-lived. Across from me, Mary's expression shifted, her bright eyes narrowing as she stiffened like she'd spotted an approaching storm.

"Red alert," Mary hissed at Miss D and me, her voice low and urgent. "Bunny Deadline is heading over."

Years of navigating New York's crowded venues had trained Mary for moments like this. Her instincts kicked in like clockwork, the kind of polished finesse only survival in this city could teach.

"Follow me," she declared with a confidence that left no room for debate.

Without hesitation, we moved.

"It's creepy down here," Miss D remarked as we descended a narrow, spiral staircase, her fingers trailing along the damp, stone wall.

"And dirty too," Mary added, her wide eyes darting around as the dim light revealed tattered furniture and suspicious stains. "Can you imagine what's gone down on those old sofas?"

I squinted into the darkness ahead, my pulse quickening as I caught the faintest movement. "I think something's going on right now," I muttered.

"Let's get out of here," Miss D urged.

"Good idea," I agreed, my steps quickening as I trailed after her.

Mary turned to follow, but a sudden tug at her dress brought her to an abrupt stop. Her heart sank as she glanced down and saw the soft pink tulle of her borrowed dress snagged on something sharp protruding from the wall. She gave it a gentle pull, but the fabric held fast, refusing to budge.

Finally, with a heart-stopping sound of tearing fabric, the delicate tulle gave way, sending Mary stumbling backward.

She squinted through her glasses, her eyes adjusting to the dim light as she took in the disheveled pair.

Recognition hit her like a freight train.

It was none other than Producer and a naked chef.

Not Jamie Oliver, but rather Gilda Green.

Running upstairs Mary shoved open the ballroom doors.

She moved with purpose, weaving through the guests, barely noticing the polite nods she passed. There was only one thing on her mind, one person she needed to find: me.

Across the ballroom, Ari and Miss D were lost in Jay's rich, soulful voice, holding the crowd spellbound with a performance so magnetic it seemed to suspend time.

"He's incredible," Ari murmured, his words more to himself than to Miss D. "I think I may have just found the singer I've been searching for."

Miss D leaned in closer, her lips curving into a playful smile that hinted at a secret waiting to be revealed. "Well, you're in luck," she said softly. "You're talking to his manager."

While Ari and Miss D dreamed about the warm glow of tomorrow, Mary remained firmly anchored in the sharp, unyielding reality of today.

"Mary!" I called as I spotted her approaching. Her face was flushed, her breathing quick. "Are you okay?"

She stopped in front of me, her hands gripping her torn dress. "We need to talk. Now."

But before Mary could get the words out, a distressed Keegan Kelly materialized at our side. She huffed, crossing her arms so tightly over her chest it seemed like she might crush her own ribs. "I'm getting replaced by Nicholas Lee Shy," she spat.

My mind raced, trying to untangle the mess forming in real-time. "Wait a minute," I interjected. "Nicholas Lee Shy? Isn't that who Carol Ann met with in Los Angeles? I thought Nicholas passed on the job."

Keegan's gaze shifted to Mary. "I might not be the Queen of Gossip like you," she hissed. "But I do know two things: First, Nicholas Lee Shy is replacing me. And second—" she paused, as she jabbed a boney finger toward Mary's torn dress, "you've gotten so fat again that dress is ripping at the seams."

Mary's face froze as her hand instinctively brushed the large tear.

"Keegan, that's enough," I said, but my attempt to intervene seemed to only pour fuel on the fire.

With a sudden burst of force, Keegan Kelly's hands gripped Mary's dress and yanked it away.

Mary was left standing in nothing but her underwear.

Her heart pounded in her chest, each beat matching the frantic rhythm of her hurried footsteps as she fled through the crowd. She couldn't stop. Not until she found a place to hide.

Mary dashed into a small, secluded office tucked behind the stairs. She collapsed into a wobbly chair. Tears of humiliation welled up as she looked down at the tattered remains of the pristine pink dress, now lying in ruins across her lap—a cruel mirror of the shattered pieces of her heart.

A knock at the door jolted her from her deep thoughts.

"Mary?" said a worried Ben as he stepped into the cramped room. "Are you okay?"

"I will be," she whispered.

He knelt beside her, taking her trembling hands in his own. "James told us what happened," he said softly. "We've all been looking for you."

Without a word, he slipped off his tuxedo jacket and extended it toward her.

"For better or for worse," Ben began.

"For richer, for poorer. In sickness and in health," Mary continued.

"To love and to cherish," Ben affirmed.

"Till death do us part," they whispered together, a shared promise sealed with a tender, heartfelt kiss.

"How did I find you?" Mary asked. "It must be luck."

Ben smiled. "It's not luck, it's right," he said. "And you have excellent taste!"

She laughed. "Thank you," she said, the warmth of his presence knitting her confidence back together.

"For what?" Ben asked, gently tilting her chin up so their eyes could meet.

"For looking at me the way you do," Mary replied, her voice soft and sincere.

In that moment, she began to confront the truth of who she really was, flaws and strengths intertwined. The tears that finally fell weren't just of sorrow; now they were the bittersweet release of painful, yet liberating, acceptance.

"Come on, let's go back to the party," he gently suggested.

"Wearing this?" Mary mused aloud. "I look like Judy Garland."

Ben gently shook his head, his confusion deepening. "I don't know who that is. But there is no way she looks as good as you in that."

Mary smiled. "This might be the best piece of clothing I've ever borrowed."

"Maybe you ought to keep it," Ben teased, as he gestured to the oversized jacket like a cloak of triumph.

Mary giggled, pulling the jacket a little tighter. "Well, I'm *definitely* not borrowing anything ever again," she admitted.

As the music swelled, she found herself at the edge of the dance floor. She glanced up and caught her reflection in a gilded mirror mounted on the far wall. She studied it.

The reflection wasn't just an image. It was a promise. A promise of self-love, a promise of acceptance and a promise of many more nights like this one—where the past didn't haunt her, and the future no longer frightened her.

Mary took Ben's hand and placed it on her belly.

"Ben," she whispered, her voice carrying the weight of everything this moment meant. "We're going to have a baby."

Chapter 29

At the head of the table, the network's pint-sized boss lounged back in his seat, his grin the kind that could convince even the most hardened cynic that Cinderella's fairy godmother had a LinkedIn profile.

"This footage is *gold,*" he declared.

"And that *theme song*?" someone chimed in. "Who's behind that brilliance?"

I sat a little straighter, pride swelling in my chest. "My husband, Ari, wrote it. And the singer? That's Jay."

A ripple of impressed murmurs swept through the room.

"It's the best pilot I've seen since *Jersey Shore,*" another executive said with a kind of reverence usually reserved for a Vatican blessing.

The pint-sized boss didn't waste a breath. "It's a *yes* from me," he said, his words like a gavel strike. Final.

Carol Ann let out a bloodcurdling scream and hit the floor in a chaos of limbs and hair. "*Oh my God!*" she gasped, scrambling back to her Louboutin-clad feet. "Trust me, it's only going to get *better.* I'm still settling into the role of 'wife.'"

"Don't worry," one of the executives said. "You'll have *plenty* of time to work it out. This show's going to run longer than *Grey's Anatomy.*"

Then, with a frown that could've slashed Andy Cohen's confidence—the pint-sized boss leaned in. "There's just one thing missing."

The room collapsed into silence. The executives, who had been high kicking with enthusiasm seconds earlier, suddenly looked like kindergarteners who'd wet their pants.

"We need a *killer ending,*" the boss said. "Something that leaves the audience starving for more."

All eyes turned to me. A beat passed—too long.

Without waiting, I snatched Carol Ann's wrist like I was pulling her off the stage of a disastrous talent show. "We'll get back to you shortly," I added with a quick nod to the room before practically dragging her out.

The hallway passed in a blur. Ahead, the dressing room beckoned—our *safe harbor.*

"We *did it*! We *did it*!" Carol Ann shrieked, collapsing into the makeup chair with the grace of a fallen pageant queen.

Mary shot to her feet, heart pounding and eyes wide with delight. "Congratulations!" she cried, flinging herself at me. "You're officially a *producer!*"

"*Hold on,*" I warned, raising my left hand like I was about to deliver a sermon in the church of brutal reality. "The boss wants a *killer ending* before he commits."

Mary straightened, a slow grin crawling across her face like it had just been given a second wind.

"What if…" she started. "What if Carol Ann and Brett get *divorced* at the end of season one?"

Carol Ann's lips twitched. "It's not the worst idea," she purred, her voice a velvet ribbon wrapping around just enough mischief to keep me guessing.

Before I could even consider it, Miss D burst in like a hurricane. Her presence was a force, all motion and intent, the kind of entrance that demanded answers before anyone even asked the question.

"What's wrong?" I asked, my stomach already lurching, the way it does just before the ground drops out from under you.

Miss D turned to us, her eyes blazing with the kind of fury that could ignite a room. "Producer left Jess for *Gilda Green.* He took the Emmys. And Darby," she added, her voice as sharp as shattering glass.

"The dog?" I croaked.

"The *Emmys*?" Carol Ann squealed.

"The bastard," Mary muttered.

"I should never have removed that file on Johnny Futura," Mary continued, her words heavy with regret.

I blinked, thrown off by her cryptic confession. "What does *that* have to do with *this*?" I asked.

"Johnny Futura, that's what," Mary said, turning to face me. "He's a total *fraud,* and I'm certain he's behind all of this."

Disbelief flashed across my face. "Johnny Futura *already* has what he wants. Producer's developing his show."

"And that new program he's cooking up with Gilda Green," Miss D added.

"You *don't get it,*" Mary snapped. "Gilda Green is *Johnny Futura's sister.*"

I turned to Mary, my vision tunneling in on her like she was the only thing holding the world upright. "*What?*"

Mary didn't flinch. "Together, they've got a long history of defrauding people. And Producer? He's just their latest mark."

Miss D stepped forward, her eyes narrowing into a fine line of suspicion. "If Johnny Futura is a fraud," she began, "then how did he get so much right about you and Ben? And me…and Jay?"

Carol Ann, perched nervously in the makeup chair, glanced at me, a plea in her eyes. I gave her the smallest of nods.

"Well, I *reckon* I might have somethin' to do with that," Carol Ann confessed. "A tape just happened to fall right into my hands…," She trailed off, the word *fall* landing a little too softly.

"*Fall?*" I corrected.

Carol Ann swallowed hard and started again. "I took the tape of your media trainin' sessions with Nancy Reagan…and I *played* it for Johnny Futura."

"You did *what?*" Mary snapped. "You gave that clown our most *intimate secrets?*"

"No," Carol Ann shot back. "I didn't *give* him anything. I *showed* him. We watched it together. On my phone."

Carol Ann staggered under the weight of our anger and disappointment. Her lips parted, desperate to spin a web of lies, but this time…the words wouldn't come.

All she could muster was a fragile, breathless, "I'm so sorry."

I stepped forward, placing a hand on Carol Ann's trembling shoulder—a gesture steady enough to remind everyone there was still work to be done.

"What Carol Ann did was *awful,*" I said. "But we can't rewrite the past. What matters now is how we fix this."

Miss D inhaled, her strong belief in second chances momentarily tested but still intact. "James is right," she said. "We need to focus on what comes next."

I turned to Mary. She was still bristling, arms crossed like a shield.

"Do you still have the file?" I asked, the urgency in my voice slicing through the tension like a letter opener through expensive stationery.

Mary hesitated for half a second—before nodding. She reached into her bag. From its depths she pulled a folder, dog-eared and frayed.

I took it without hesitation. This wasn't just a folder. It was *everything.*

My grip tightened as I approached Producer's office door.

I didn't knock.

Inside, Producer sat slumped over his desk, a tableau of crumpled defeat. His four Emmys were scattered around him like witnesses to a crime. At his feet Darby sat miserably, his bloodshot eyes blinking in eerie sync with Producer's as I strode in.

Before I could speak, he shot upright. "My father told me to do it," he snapped.

I stopped cold, disbelief spreading through me like an uninvited chill. "*No,*" I said. "He did not." I stepped closer. "Johnny Futura told you to do it."

"Johnny is *merely* a messenger," Producer fired back.

I blinked at him, stunned. "Let me get this straight—you betrayed your *wife and stole* her dog because your father told a psychic you should *do it?*"

For a split second, something flickered across Producer's face—shame, regret, maybe just the weight of his absurdity—but it passed. Like a fortress repairing itself, his walls went up. "To be honest with you, James," he said, "*I'm* the one who's been betrayed here."

I froze mid-breath. "What on earth do *I* have to do with this disaster?"

Producer pushed himself to his feet. Anger, hurt, and some twisted sense of nostalgia darkened his face.

"I thought we were a *team,* James," he said. "Don't you remember? That first cold, snowy night at Bottino's?" He paused. "And now...now you're the one who sold Carol Ann's show. Behind my back."

My patience snapped, years of frustration bubbling to the surface.

"First of all, you *declined* Carol Ann's show," I shot back. "And let's be clear about one thing—we were *never* a team." I steadied my breath. "You stole my ideas and paraded them as your own. You don't *collaborate.* You *consume.*"

Producer's face flushed. "That's not true," he said, though his voice wavered, each syllable betraying him. "Just ask Johnny Futura."

I stepped forward, closing the space between us. "You need to see this."

With a satisfying *thud,* I placed Mary's folder on the desk between us.

Producer's eyes flickered to the file. "I've seen this folder before," he murmured.

I nodded once. "Yes, you have. But this time, you're going to *read* it."

Silence descended—thick and absolute—as the revelations bled from the paper into his consciousness. His eyes darted across words, across dates, across buried truths that had been hiding in plain sight.

"I blamed myself for my dad's death," he finally confessed. "That's why I trusted Johnny. I just...I just wanted one more conversation with my dad." He paused, his chest sinking under the invisible weight. "To say I'm sorry."

My gaze flicked briefly to the floor, searching for courage, before locking back at Producer.

"You've been sabotaging yourself ever since your dad died. The drinking, the women..." I hesitated, my tone dropping with the weight of an unspoken truth. "The *phone sex.* Yes, I know about that too."

Silence settled over the moment, thick and suffocating, the weight of the truth pressing down on both of us.

For a moment, all he could do was stare—at the folder, at me, at the Emmys scattered like broken dreams around the room.

Then a bitter taste curled at the edges of his mouth as denial and anger turned into realization. The trust he'd given Johnny and Gilda, the power he'd handed over so easily, was now poison in his veins. He blinked hard, his mind spinning through the implications, the betrayal gnawing at him like moths through expensive cashmere.

"I've invested *everything* I have in their pilots," he croaked. "James, you've got to help me."

"I won't assist those two," I replied.

"You wouldn't be helping *them.* You'd be helping *me,*" Producer pleaded. "If I don't sell these two pilots, Jess and I will lose *everything.*"

Silence stretched between us, taut as a wire, until finally, I exhaled.

"Alright," I said, leaving no room for misinterpretation. "I'll find a way to salvage both shows. But once you've got your investment back..."

I leaned in, each word deliberate. "We're going to expose Johnny and Gilda for the frauds they really are."

I let the silence settle for a beat before continuing.

"And," I added, my gaze locking onto his, "I have one *non-negotiable* condition."

"Anything," Producer replied, his voice tinged with desperation.

"You can keep the Emmys," I said, each word precise, unyielding. "But the dog goes *home*."

Producer swallowed hard, his Adam's apple bobbing as the words hit.

He didn't hesitate. He nodded, the flicker of something close to gratitude softening the hard edges of his face.

And just like that, Darby let out a howl—a small, joyful sound that pierced the tension and filled the room like sunlight breaking through storm clouds.

Chapter 30

Johnny Futura and Gilda Green's two disastrous pilots swirled in my brain, a toxic cocktail of bad lighting, worse scripts, and a vacuum of charm so vast it could swallow the Chrysler Building whole.

Behind me, Ari floated into view, his energy light and buoyant, a perfect counterpoint to my stormy mood. Still riding the high of another brilliant rehearsal with Jay, he handed me a glass of wine without a word.

I turned, collapsing onto the couch in our apartment with a sigh so heavy it felt like it might leave a dent in the cushions. I grabbed the remote, clutching it like it owed me answers.

"Can you believe they're actually brother and sister?" I muttered, half to Ari, half to the universe. My voice carried an edge sharper than I'd intended as I added, "A lack of talent clearly runs in the family."

Ari chuckled. "Can you imagine Thanksgiving at *their* house? Gilda making dinner, Johnny cooking up their dead friends."

I froze, my mind stalling. "What did you just say?"

Ari blinked. "You know—ghost stories and lots of food sounds fun to me."

Like a flicker of light bursting through a blackout, the idea struck me. *Hard.*

I shot up from the couch so fast I nearly knocked over my glass. It was the kind of sudden, delicious inspiration that made you feel like you'd just stumbled upon a Keith Haring piece in a flea market.

"That's *it!*" I gasped, grinning wide as if the room had turned golden.

Ari stared at me, eyes narrowing in confusion. "What's *it*? Should I be scared?"

I was already pacing, my mind spinning at warp speed as the ideas began colliding. I turned back to Ari, giddy with excitement.

"We merge the two shows into *one,*" I said.

Ari's brow furrowed.

"Think about it!" I rushed on. "Gilda cooks an elaborate dinner while Johnny cooks up—metaphorically speaking—dead relatives, friends, *ghosts* of the past."

Ari blinked again, a slow smile pulling at the corner of his lips as realization set in. "Dinner With *Dead Guests.*"

I pointed at him, triumphant. "A little true crime, a little *Top Chef,* and just enough family dysfunction to keep viewers on the edge of their seats."

Miss D, Jess, and Darby eased into their seats at an outdoor table at Fresco by Scotto, the kind of place where the scent of perfectly cooked pasta danced with the soft croon of a Sinatra classic. The early evening air was perfection, a golden hour glow casting the world in a haze of warmth and endless possibility.

But for Jess, no light could soften the tight knot in her chest, the one that refused to loosen no matter how hard she tried to will it away.

Determined not to dwell on her husband leaving—or the chaos it had left in its wake—Jess exhaled slowly, pasting on her best *everything's-fine* smile. It was the kind of smile that fooled just enough people to keep the questions at bay.

"Did you watch the tape?" she asked, her voice light, casual, though the flicker of urgency in her eyes gave her away.

Miss D's nod came slow and heavy. "I did," she said. "And did you see who was lurking in the shadows, egging Trevor Twinkle on to say those awful things?"

Jess frowned. "Who?"

Miss D leaned back in her chair. "Johnny Futura."

The name landed like a pebble in a still pond, sending ripples through Jess's carefully constructed calm. Her eyes widened, a flicker of something darker dancing behind them—recognition, dread, maybe both.

"What do you mean?" she pressed.

Miss D tilted her head slightly, as if deciding just how much of the truth Jess could handle. "Johnny Futura is a *fraud.* A total fake. And it's worse than you think—he and his sister, Gilda Green, yes, *that* Gilda, have been stirring up trouble for *years.*"

Jess froze, her breath catching like a silk blouse snagged on a thorn. The words hit her square in the chest—unexpected, unwanted. "Wait…" she stammered. "My *husband* left me for *Johnny Futura's sister?*"

Suddenly the golden hour light felt too bright, too cruel as Jess's world tilted sideways. Her voice trembled, fragile as fine china. "How do you *know* all this?"

Miss D leaned in. "Mary, the best reporter in this city, dug deep," she began. "Turns out, Johnny Futura and Gilda…they prey on people's weaknesses. They *exploit grief for profit.*"

"I've been such a fool," Jess whispered. "I thought Johnny Futura was trying to *save* my marriage, not *destroy* it."

Miss D paused, as if testing the weight of what she was about to say. "There's more," she said finally, her voice thick with the burden of truth. "You need to know *everything.* Really, *everything.*"

Jess's eyes darted to Miss D's face, searching for answers. "What is it?" she whispered, her voice trembling like a house of cards in a stiff breeze.

Miss D exhaled—a deep, steadying breath that sounded like the release of years of secrets kept locked away. "I told you I once worked as a phone sex operator," she began, her voice calm but distant, as though the words belonged to someone else.

Jess nodded slowly.

"Well…one of my clients was your husband," she whispered like a confession made in a cathedral.

Miss D's eyes dropped to the floor, guilt carving itself into the fine lines of her face.

"I didn't know it was him at the time," she admitted, her tone heavy with remorse. "I only found out later, thanks to James." She paused, searching Jess's face for some flicker of understanding, but it wasn't there. "Jess, I'm so sorry. Please…please give me a second chance."

Jess's breath hitched, her carefully constructed restraint threatening to crumble under the weight of the revelation. Finally, she looked at Miss D, her voice trembling, the pain bleeding through her measured calm.

"I…I don't know what to say," she whispered, her words raw, unsteady. Her eyes narrowed, not in anger, but in disbelief, her mind grappling with the betrayal that had just been laid bare. "How could you keep something like this from me?"

Miss D's shoulders sagged. "I was scared, Jess. Scared of what it would do to *us.* To the business we were planning, to our friendship."

Jess bent down, scooping up Darby like a shield. Without another word, she turned and walked away.

Each step carried her further from the table, further from her dreams of opening her own gym, and further from the friend she thought she knew—*forever.*

Alone now, Miss D sat motionless as the world around her continued its unrelenting swirl—plates clinking, laughter drifting from other tables, the hum of life carrying on as if nothing had happened.

But for Miss D, everything had.

One question looped relentlessly in her mind, circling like a restless predator: *Did she deserve a second chance?*

Did Producer? Did anyone?

The questions hung there, heavy and unforgiving, demanding an answer she wasn't sure she had. Her eyes narrowed, the weight of it pressing down as she considered.

Finally, when she decided her answer, Miss D reached into her bag, fingers brushing past the smooth leather lining to retrieve her phone. She hesitated, ready to call Jess, to say *something*—but instead, her fingers landed on something cold and familiar.

The Trevor Twinkle disk.

Her breath hitched. Trevor Twinkle.

Did he deserve a second chance too?

Slowly, deliberately, she pulled the disk from her bag and slipped her high-heeled shoe from her foot.

Then, with a sudden, decisive motion, she brought the heel down hard.

CRACK.

The disk shattered into a thousand jagged pieces, scattering across the table like tiny shards of a long-buried past.

Miss D stared at the fragments, her reflection fractured across their sharp edges. In their destruction, something within her cracked open too. The weight she had carried for so long—the guilt, the regret, the pain—finally began to lift, piece by shattered piece.

Redemption, she realized, wasn't about holding onto someone else's darkness. It was about letting go of your own.

Carol Ann stood in front of her bathroom mirror, her gaze fixed on the reflection staring back at her. The dark circles beneath her eyes were a reminder of the pressure weighing her down. She must come up with a killer ending to save her show.

Her lips pursed as she thought of me—buried under the avalanche of Johnny Futura and Gilda Green's disastrous pilots. She felt the full weight of it now: if this was going to happen, *she* would have to make it happen. Alone.

From the far end of the room, Brett Bottom piped up, his tone teetering between hopeful and hopeless. "Should I get on all fours again?"

Carol Ann barely spared him a glance. "Been there, done that," she said curtly. "We need somethin' fresh. Somethin' *outta the box.*"

Collapsing onto her sofa, she grabbed her phone and began scrolling, her search for inspiration turning frantic. And then—

There it was.

The new Armie Hammer interview.

An idea began to take shape, reckless and audacious, the kind of idea that made lesser people hesitate. But Carol Ann? She *thrived* on audacity.

"This is it," she murmured. "Erotic asphyxiation is the *new thing.*"

Brett froze, his mouth opening just slightly as his brain tried—and failed—to catch up. "You want to...suffocate me?"

"*Absolutely,*" Carol Ann shot back, her enthusiasm unshakeable. "It's edgy. It's controversial. And it's going to be the *killer ending* we need to wrap this season."

Carol Ann didn't wait for approval. She didn't *ask* for it. She *took it.*

"I'll get the props," she called over her shoulder as she disappeared down the hallway.

Brett stared after her, stunned.

But Carol Ann didn't see him. Didn't care. The idea had already taken hold, her mind racing through the details.

This wasn't just audacious. It wasn't just wild. It was *genius.*

"Now, we just need a little inspiration," Carol Ann drawled upon her return. "Tell me somethin' that's gonna make me want to *punish* you," she challenged. "Come on now, sugar. You must've done *somethin'* I can use."

Brett's lips curled into a half-smile—wicked, self-satisfied, the kind of smile that was equal parts charming and foolish.

"Well..." he began, his eyes glinting with mischief as though he was holding the juiciest secret in his palm. "Do you remember that tape...?"

Carol Ann's pulse quickened, a spark of relief flickering in her chest. "Oh, thank God. You found the Trevor Twinkle tape?"

Brett's smirk faltered. "Not...exactly," he admitted, his voice softening. Suddenly, the mischief was gone, replaced by the faintest whiff of regret, like he'd just realized the bomb he was about to drop. "But I *did* find a tape of James, Mary, and Miss D…with this old lady. I might've given it to James," he added quickly, as though saying it fast would make it sting less.

Carol Ann's reaction was immediate, her voice slicing through the room like a knife. "Pass me the plastic bag," she snapped, fury radiating from her like heat off pavement in August.

Half an hour later, the room had fallen eerily still. The deed was done.

Carol Ann lay stretched across her side of the bed, the sheets rumpled, her perfectly coiffed hair slightly askew.

She wasn't just a wife anymore.

No, darling. She was now a *widow.*

Brett Bottom was dead.

Chapter 31

Ben's heart pounded in sync with his footsteps as he hurried down the apartment hallway. Nearing the bathroom door, his foot caught—*hard*—on something. Mary's hairdryer. Its cord stretched across the floor like a perfectly laid trap, poised to take him down.

"Mary?" he called out, trying to steady his voice. "Everything okay in there?"

Her reply came too fast, words tumbling over each other in a rush—like someone desperately trying to stack up excuses before they crumbled. "Yes! Fine. Everything's *fine.* I just, um, dropped the hairdryer."

Ben froze, his instincts flaring like a red warning light.

"Are you *sure?*" he pressed, his voice laced with concern.

"Yes!" she snapped from behind the door. "Stop fussing and give me some privacy!"

He hesitated. Privacy. It was always *her* thing when it came to the bathroom. And right now, stepping back felt like the only move left.

"Okay," he murmured, retreating a few steps as doubt clung to him like a shadow.

But then he heard it—

The *scream.*

The kind of sound that strikes you somewhere deep.

Ben didn't think. His body moved before his brain could catch up, adrenaline surging as he crashed through the locked door.

The scene on the other side stopped him cold.

Mary lay sprawled across the cold, black-and-white tiles, a pool of crimson spreading between her legs.

Her hands fumbled, desperate to cover herself. "I'm so sorry," she whispered. "I'm so sorry…I've lost the baby."

Ben dropped to his knees beside her.

His own tears welled, clouding his vision as he pulled her close—*gently,* like she might break apart in his arms. "Honey, it's going to be okay," he replied. "We're going to be okay."

But even as he said it, he knew—their world had been shattered.

"We're out of paper towels," Mary said, desperate for something—*anything*—familiar to anchor her against the storm raging inside.

Ben was already on his feet, a man trying to *do something* when there was nothing left to be done. "I'll go and get some," he said, the urgency betrayed by his need to stay. "But I don't want to leave you alone right now."

"You won't be," Mary whispered. She pointed a trembling finger across the room.

Ben Stiller stood there—slightly disheveled, a knight in… well, furry armor.

"I know I don't have the words you need right now," he said—words chosen like stepping stones across dangerous water. "But know that I *love you.*"

In that moment, Ben was completely unaware that those words were *exactly* what Mary needed.

She nodded. "I love you too," she managed to say aloud.

Seconds after Ben left, Mary reached for her phone, her fingers trembling as she dialed.

When I answered, my voice faltered, cracking under the weight of the news.

"Oh, Mary," I said, the sorrow in my tone unmistakable. "I'm terribly sorry. I'll be there in a minute."

"No," she replied. "It's funny...I've spent my whole life fearing being alone, and now it's all I want."

I inhaled, my words careful, the kind of softness reserved only for those you love most. "Whatever you need, just ask."

Mary swallowed hard. "There is one thing you could do," she said. "I was supposed to give the eulogy at Brett Bottom's funeral tomorrow. Tell Carol Ann I can't do it. I need to say goodbye...to someone else."

The next morning, Brett funeral arrived with the kind of *surreal disbelief* that clings to you like a bad perfume.

The church, normally a quiet refuge for whispered prayers and murmured reassurances, had been consumed by chaos. Reporters pressed against one another, turning sacred ground into something closer to a red carpet.

Police loomed at the edges of the crowd, their presence less about control and more about untangling the knots of a story that refused to sit still.

Carol Ann arrived early—*early*—for the first time in her life, a detail so jarring it might've required its own headline. She was draped in sultry black that clung to her curves like it had been tailored from shadow and secrets.

She latched onto my arm, her grip tight enough to keep us both upright in the whirlwind.

"Can y'all believe how many news crews are here?" she declared. "I've been on the cover of the *New York Post* this week more times than Hunter Biden."

I froze, her words settling like ice against the unease in my chest.

"Are you sure you want to *film* this?" I asked, as my gaze drifted to Cliff. Ever present. Ever filming.

Carol Ann's response was swift and sharp, her Southern drawl cutting through the tension like a blade. "Brett Bottom would *want* this, bless his heart."

Across the church, Lori Letmein—clipboard in hand, headset firmly in place—moved through the scene with the rigor of a seasoned director orchestrating a live telethon. Her enthusiasm was palpable, as though every detail of Brett's funeral was another line item on a star-studded production. With a brisk nod and a quick gesture, she was assigning Jay and Miss D their seats.

Miss D leaned in toward Jay. "Don't worry about all the cameras," she murmured. "Just remember, you're singing for *God.*"

Her gaze drifted to the front of the church, where the choir master, Nancy Reagan, stood by the organ, framed by the light streaming through the stained-glass windows.

"Where on *earth* is Mary?" Carol Ann snapped, glancing at her Tiffany watch.

"Oh my *God!*" I blurted out, momentarily forgetting where I was. "I completely forgot to inform you. Mary shan't be coming."

Carol Ann's wide eyes burned into me, like a heat that refused to dissipate.

"What in *tarnation* are you talkin' about?" she hissed.

I took a deep breath, as the tension between us thickened. "Mary's dealing with something very personal and deeply private," I said, my tone protective.

"*Unacceptable!*" Carol Ann snapped. "Being late is one thing, but not showin' up at all? That's beyond unprofessional."

"Stop," I said firmly. "You *know* Mary. She wouldn't miss this unless it was truly important."

The sharpness in Carol Ann's expression softened—just slightly—as her eyes flicked from me, calculating her next move.

"Then *y'all* are going to have to do the eulogy," she declared, her voice unyielding.

"Wait, *what?*" I replied, my eyes widening, a cocktail of surprise and panic swirling within them. "I barely knew Brett Bottom!"

Her demand didn't waver for a second. "Then talk about somethin' you *do* know. Like me," she asserted.

"Carol Ann," I began, my voice balancing protest and disbelief. "This is a *funeral,* not a television show."

Her smile flashed, quick and defiant, as though she were daring me to challenge her again.

"Don't you get all high and mighty with *me!*" Carol Ann shot back. "Remember, this was *all* your idea."

"What are you talking about?" I asked, my voice tinged with bewilderment as I searched her face for answers.

"You said we needed a killer ending," Carol Ann replied, her voice dipping into a low whisper, heavy with implication. "Don't worry, your secret is safe with me."

"Wait a second," I said, taking a step back. "What are you trying to say?"

She opened her mouth to respond, but before the words could escape, a figure emerged from the shadows—ethereal, almost unreal, like a vision conjured from another world.

Mary stood there.

My jaw dropped as I rushed over. "What are you doing here?" I asked.

"I want to do this," she said. "No, I *need* to do this."

"Are you absolutely certain?" I asked, though the answer was already etched into the lines of her determined face.

"Yes," Mary affirmed with a small, deliberate nod as she stepped up to the microphone.

Her eyes drifted to Brett Bottom's open casket. The delicate craftsmanship of Maria's work glimmered softly in the dim light—a quiet last testament to the care poured into preparing him for this final farewell.

Mary inhaled deeply, steadying herself.

"If anyone was expecting a Charlie Sheen story or a funny joke, I'm afraid you'll be disappointed," she began, her tone direct yet tinged with vulnerability. "I'll admit, I didn't know Brett Bottom very well. But unfortunately, I now know grief better than I ever wanted to."

She paused, drawing in a deep breath, grounding herself before continuing.

"Grief isn't a disorder, or a disease, or a sign of weakness," she explained. "Grief is the price we pay for love."

In that moment, Mary wasn't just speaking for Brett Bottom. She was speaking for herself and for anyone else in the room carrying the unspoken burden of loss.

"You don't get over grief," she continued. "You learn to walk alongside it. Because when someone you love becomes a memory, that memory becomes a treasure."

Her eyes lifted, as though searching the heavens for answers. The divine frescos painted across the ceiling offered none—only silent beauty, still and eternal.

"I lost my baby yesterday," she confessed, her gaze unwavering despite the tears threatening to spill. "I had a miscarriage."

The room collectively seemed to inhale, the silence that followed so profound it was almost deafening.

Mary's eyes drifted over familiar faces in the crowd—Miss D, Carol Ann, and me. She paused, letting the warmth of our presence wash over her like a quiet embrace.

"Tell your friends and loved ones how much you love them," she urged. "And never waste an opportunity to tell yourself the same thing, too."

The atmosphere shifted, a subtle yet profound transformation. Strangers glanced at one another, tentative smiles spreading like ripples across still, cold water.

Mary felt the energy shift and seized the moment.

"Kiss that boy in the rain," she said, her gaze locking onto Ben in the crowd. "Eat that piece of cake. And most importantly…" She paused, her lips curving into a small, knowing smile as her gaze swept to Nancy Reagan, who stood gracefully in front of Jay and the choir.

"Run toward whatever you want—preferably in a red satin dress!"

And then Mary made her move.

With a flourish, she shrugged off Brett Bottom's black cape, letting it fall to the floor like the weight of the past she was shedding.

Beneath it, she revealed a gown in a blazing, unapologetic shade of crimson.

It wasn't just a red satin dress; it was a declaration.

A bold, unmissable beacon in the darkness.

Much like Mary herself.

Applause erupted, lifting her as if she were floating above the crowd.

She strode toward Miss D, Carol Ann, and me, her crimson gown flowing behind her like a fiery trail. But just before she reached us, Mary paused.

Her movements slowed, deliberate, as she turned her head slightly, casting a sly grin over her shoulder.

And then, she tucked the hem of her dress into her panties.

A ripple of laughter burst through the crowd, as Mary revealed a crack—*instead of cracking a joke.*

Thirty minutes later, Mary, Carol Ann, Miss D, and I found ourselves seated together at a cozy table at Bottino's. A moment that felt oddly sacred.

"My goodness," I said, shaking my head with a mix of disbelief and affection. "Is there anything we don't know about each other at this point?"

The words hung in the air, half-joking, half-serious, until Miss D broke the silence.

She took a deep breath, her resolve hardening. "I once worked as a phone sex operator," she said, letting the words land without a hint of apology.

We barely had time to process before Miss D reached up, her fingers brushing the edge of her wig. With one decisive motion, she removed it.

"And I'm bald," she added, her voice carrying the weight of someone reclaiming a piece of herself that had been hidden for far too long.

For a moment, there was only silence—not of judgment, but of reverence.

Inspired by her boldness, I felt a surge of courage. "I've been struggling with a substance abuse problem for a while," I confessed as the shame I had carried for so long seemed to lift, replaced by a lightness that came from finally being seen for who I truly was.

Mary leaned forward slightly, drawing in a deep breath. "Well, here goes," she began, her voice carrying a note of liberation. "I have an eating problem."

The admission hung heavy in the air, yet it felt freeing, too. She hesitated for just a beat before adding, "And my dad is Black."

This time, her words weren't laced with fear—they carried a newfound excitement, as though she were finally stepping into the fullness of her own identity.

Slowly, almost instinctively, we all turned to Carol Ann, like an invisible conductor had waved a baton to signal this exact moment.

Would she do it? Would Carol Ann finally unravel the tangled thread of what happened that night with Brett Bottom?

She took her time, letting the moment stretch impossibly thin.

"I used to be a high-end stripper," she confessed.

Mary, Miss D, and I exchanged glances, a shared moment of disbelief quickly unraveling into laughter. The kind of laughter that bubbles up not because of what was said, but because of what wasn't. A slow, creeping understanding settled over us—perhaps we would never know the truth about that tragic night.

"Wait," Carol Ann teased, her smirk curling into something mischievous. "There's *one more thing* I need to tell you...."

This was it. She was going to finally spill the truth she had been dancing around for weeks.

But before another word could slip from her lips, the door crashed open.

Two police officers stormed in.

"Carol Ann, you're under arrest," one of them announced, "on suspicion of murder."

She sat back slowly, her smirk fading as she reached for her glass once more.

"Well," she said, lifting her glass with a cool defiance, a glint of mischief in her eye, "now *that's* a killer ending."

THE END—ALMOST....

Chapter 32

Nine months later, the studio buzzed with the kind of electricity that lingers after a storm—the air a little crisper, the colors a little sharper, as if the world itself had been rinsed clean and was now holding its breath, waiting to see what would happen next.

The show's freshly minted producer—me—moved through the space with a practiced ease.

"Alright, everyone!" I called out. "Drinks at Bottino's tonight. My treat."

The cast and crew erupted into cheers, the kind that felt like music to my ears.

At the table, Eve—once the eager intern tucked into a corner of Bunny Deadline's office—sat comfortably in Carol Ann's old chair. She glanced up from her phone.

"I might be late," Eve said. "Gotta stop by The Tipsy Teapot—meeting some old morning show host who insists on wearing sunglasses indoors."

I chuckled, a strange blend of amusement and mild horror bubbling up inside me as I watched history repeat itself in real time.

Ann—former nanny and little sister of Ben's friend Peter—slid out of her seat next to Eve. "I'll be early," she declared.

The studio chair she now claimed had once belonged to Mary, but Ann had transformed it into something entirely her own, much like she had with her name at the top of Mary's former column.

"Will there be food, or should I eat before?" Ann asked.

"Don't worry," I said, still pinching myself at the reality that I had become the producer I'd always dreamed of having. "There will be plenty of everything."

"Yummy," Ann replied as she slid on her oversized glasses with a practiced flick, grabbing her beloved bag—a fixture that never seemed to leave her side.

"Wait!" I called out, catching her just as she turned toward the door.

Ann paused mid-step.

"Wear them on camera?" I declared, wanting to make sure she felt seen—not just for the glasses, but for the reporting star she was becoming.

I stepped into Bottino's with Ari by my side, his steady presence anchoring me as the door swung open. The second I crossed the threshold, a wave of cheers crashed over me. A sprawling banner stretched across the bar, proudly declaring the milestone: *James's 100th Episodes as Executive Producer!*

"I told you this little show would be a huge hit," a familiar, golden voice chimed from behind me.

I turned, my smile exploding at the sight of Miss D with the latest and greatest new phone in her hand. Her wig? Gone.

"Miss D!" I exclaimed, pulling her into a tight embrace. "I see your fitness business advertised on every bus in New York," I said stepping back enough to take her in. "But seeing you in person is *so* much better."

Her chuckle was like the first sip of hot cocoa on a chilly day. "That was Jess's idea," she confessed, her eyes shining with the thrill of a successful partnership and the sweetness of second chances. "Business is booming thanks to those ads."

"Not at all," I replied. "Business is flourishing thanks to *you.*"

Miss D beamed, her joy radiant and unrestrained. Delores, the little girl from way uptown, had become a force of nature—working twice as hard to carve her path, revolutionizing the fitness industry while managing a growing stable of future singing stars.

"You always believed in me," she said, her voice steady and strong, her feet rooted like a beautiful tree firmly planted in its purpose.

"And I always will," I replied, my words carrying the weight of unwavering faith and pride.

Miss D paused. "You know, if I hadn't crushed that Trevor Twinkle disk, I would never have come up with the idea of over-the-phone workouts," she confessed.

I nodded. "I'm just delighted that you're still employing that golden voice of yours to get people hot and sweaty."

"Shhhhhh," Miss D giggled. "I'm a *respectable* married lady now."

"Speaking of which," I replied, "where is your talented husband?"

"Jay is in London," Miss D said. "Two nights from now, he's opening for Michael Bublé. It was the easiest deal I ever negotiated, and it includes business flights for his manager to join her client tomorrow."

My expression turned thoughtful as I reached into my wallet. Slowly, I pulled out a worn twenty-pound note. I held it between us, the moment heavy with unspoken meaning.

"Here," I said. "I want you to have this. I don't need it anymore."

Miss D took the note, her fingers brushing against mine, her eyes widening with a mixture of relief and understanding.

"Cheers," Miss D giggled. "It's not the $2,000 a week you promised when we first met. But it's a start."

I chuckled. Our friendship had grown to mean more than I could ever have imagined.

"I hate to do this," she said reluctantly, her gaze flicking to the time on her phone. "But I've got to go. I'm meeting Jess and Cliff to brainstorm some new business ideas before I leave for England."

I let out a groan, rolling my eyes for dramatic effect. "Just make sure you don't wear green," I teased. Then, with a sudden spark of inspiration, I added, "Or better yet, ask Jess and Cliff to come here instead?"

Miss D's eyes lit up at the suggestion. "Another great idea," Miss D admitted, her voice softening as the weight of her words lingered between us.

And then, as if the universe itself had a flair for timing, conversations froze mid-sentence as every gaze swiveled toward the entrance.

Standing there, commanding the room without saying a word, was America's brightest new reality sensation: Carol Ann—still letting her appearance do all the talking.

She had reinvented herself—completely. A new name. A new brand. A new empire. Her show, now titled *The Widow,* was a runaway success, cementing her place as the queen of reinvention.

Carol Ann hadn't been found legally guilty of Brett Bottom's mysterious death, but in the court of public opinion, she had been tried, convicted, and somehow—bizarrely—celebrated.

Her sentence? A life filled with everything she'd always craved: whispered rumors, scandalous headlines, and a shocking kind of success that she wore like an invisible crown.

"James, darlin'," Carol Ann drawled. She was dressed head-to-toe in black, the color of mourning turned into the ultimate statement of power.

"We *simply* must discuss the next season of my reality show," she continued. "I've got a new beau lined up. You might've heard of him—Nicholas Lee Shy!"

She twirled theatrically around a pole in the bar, her movements as unapologetically bold as her reputation.

"And," she added with a wicked smile, "I'm opening my own *ultra-exclusive* adult club."

I took a deep breath, bracing myself for the conversation I'd been avoiding since her arrest. "I think it's time you find a new executive producer for the reality show," I began. "Someone who thinks like you."

I couldn't quite bring myself to believe Carol Ann was guilty, but I also couldn't be sure she was innocent either. That uncertainty was why this was the only way forward—for the sake of the show, and perhaps more importantly, for the sake of myself.

She huffed, but couldn't resist falling back on an old trick, even if she doubted it would work this time. "How does li'l old Meghan handle Harry's British uncircumcised penis?" she asked.

I started to howl with laughter. "You are still the most *fascinating* person I've ever met," I said.

Then, cutting through the air like a splash of cold water, a voice from behind us broke the moment.

"Now *that's* a headline," gasped Bunny Deadline.

Carol Ann and I spun around, our expressions twin masks of shock and disbelief.

"What on earth are you doing here?" I exclaimed. "I thought you were still incarcerated!"

Bunny Deadline shrugged, a knowing smile playing on her lips. "Good behavior," she explained. "Plus, it doesn't hurt to have a few secrets on the judge."

Carol Ann's eyes lit up with that peculiar mix of desperation and excitement that always meant one thing: she had a plan.

"Miss Deadline," she began. "I'm in the market for a new executive producer for my reality show," she added as though she'd just orchestrated the deal of the century. "Someone who thinks like me."

I felt a mix of fear and relief flood through me. "It's a match made in tabloid heaven!" I surrendered.

Just as the three of us raised our glasses to toast, a voice—one I hadn't realized I'd missed so deeply—echoed across the room, carrying that unmistakable mix of wit and wisdom.

"Just imagine," it said, "if Whitney had just taken a shower, she might still be with us today."

There she was—Mary.

Beside her stood Ben, his arm draped protectively around her, and in her own arms, she cradled her most cherished possession: Chloé Joan River, her daughter.

"You're here!" I exclaimed, my voice bursting with warmth and the depth of years of friendship. "You're *all* here."

Mary, dressed in old jeans and a well-worn cat sweater that only she could make look effortlessly charming, replied with a radiant smile. "Of course. We wouldn't miss this for the world. You let them see the real you, James. You are enough."

Her words, so simple yet so profound, settled over me like a soft blanket of reassurance.

I reached out gently, my hand coming to rest on Chloé's delicate little head. The silky strands of her red, curly hair glinted like spun sunlight under my fingers. "She's a little miracle," I breathed, my voice filled with quiet wonder.

Mary's eyes shimmered with gratitude as she effortlessly plucked an hors d'oeuvre from a passing tray, popping it into her mouth with zero guilt or shame.

"*You're* the miracle that brought us all together," she said.

Seeing a happy and healthy Mary filled me with a warm sense of joy, though I couldn't help but wonder about another member of her family. "How's Ben Stiller adjusting to the newest addition?" I asked, a playful glint in my eye.

"Puuurrfect," Mary replied with a grin, just as Chloé Joan River let out a tiny, unexpected toot.

"Oh my," I gasped, holding my nose in an exaggerated gesture of mock horror.

Mary chuckled. "Just wait until she discovers tacos," she quipped, her treasure trove of comedic gold safely cradled in her arms.

"She's getting big," I remarked, the words slipping out before I could stop them. Immediately, I cringed, wishing I could take them back.

"It's okay," Mary reassured me. "I want Chloé to learn that beauty comes in all sizes, colors, and shapes. And who better to teach her than her fairy godmother?"

The question shimmered between us, a reminder of the incredible journey we'd all been on together—and the beautiful, unpredictable chapters still to come.

"Me, a godparent?" I exclaimed. "Hand me my wand!"

Mary laughed, her joy bubbling over like champagne. "Still practically perfect in every way," she teased, mixing up her godmothers with her nannies in a way that made me feel both *bibbidi bobbidi boo* and *supercalifragilisticexpialidocious.*

"I can't wait until she's old enough to hear the story about Charlie Sheen and her mummy," I teased, my eyes sparkling with mischief.

Mary chuckled. "I'm counting on you to remember every detail," she replied.

I opened my mouth to respond, but the words caught in my throat as my eyes landed on someone I hadn't seen in what felt like a lifetime.

Producer.

"The place where it all began on a snowy night," he said as though no time had passed at all.

He still carried that signature Ben Affleck swagger, but there was something different now—a softness that hadn't been there before. It was as if the sharp edges had finally been sanded down. He looked…lighter somehow, like the weight of old regrets and the shadow of his father had finally been lifted.

"Let me tell you both a little secret," Producer said, stepping closer. "You two never needed me. The 'Mary and James's show was great long before I showed up."

I glanced at him. "Maybe," I said softly. "But you sure made the ride more interesting."

With a quiet reverence, he reached into his large Jack Spade bag.

Mary and I both froze, our eyes widening in disbelief as we saw what he held.

"This is for you," Producer said as he handed me one of his Emmys.

I could only stare, my mouth slightly agape, as the weight of the gesture—literal and metaphorical—settled over me.

Producer's gaze shifted to Mary. "And this one's for you," he said, revealing another Emmy.

Mary's hands trembled as she reached out, her fingertips brushing against the smooth, cool surface of the golden statue.

"And these are for you two!" Producer called out to Miss D and Carol Ann.

"What are you doing?" I finally asked, my voice tinged with confusion and disbelief. "These are your everything."

"Not anymore," Producer replied. He nodded politely to a passing waiter—who was also an actor—asking for a glass of water on the rocks.

He turned back to us.

"When you start worshipping gold statues instead of real people with hearts of gold, you end up listening to shady folks like Johnny Futura," he added.

But he wasn't done.

"I'm working on making things right," Producer continued. "Netflix is interested in my documentary pitch delving into the murky world of psychics and drugs."

"We can help with that," I volunteered immediately, shooting Mary a glance.

She nodded in agreement.

Producer's eyes shimmered with relief. "And this time," he said, "all three of us will share the title of Executive Producer."

Before Mary or I could respond, a rich, velvety voice cut through the moment like silk.

"That sounds like the perfect reason to celebrate to me."

Our heads turned as they stepped forward, commanding the room with effortless grace.

"Nancy Reagan?" we blurted out in unison, our voices a perfect harmony of disbelief.

"Hello, Mommy," Producer greeted her with a casual familiarity that hit like a lightning bolt.

I nearly choked on my drink.

Mary dropped an hors d'oeuvre.

A gleam of nostalgia twinkled in Nancy Reagan's eyes. "After watching you and Mary perform the best show in town each night from that sofa over there, I called Ron immediately."

Mary's mouth fell open. "Your name is Ronald Reagan?"

Producer—*Ron*—grinned. "Now you know why I just go by Producer," he quipped.

Laughter erupted, spilling into the room and filling the space with a warmth that felt almost magical.

But, as always, it slipped away too soon.

And honestly? We wouldn't have wanted it any other way.

"Have you seen this?" I gasped, my eyes widening as I scrolled through a string of explosive texts from Eve and Ann.

Mary, Miss D, and Carol Ann leaned in closer, their curiosity instantly piqued, the glow of the screen casting soft shadows on their faces.

And just like that, all over again—it started with a whisper.

About the Author

Rob Shuter is a British-American celebrity journalist, author, and TV personality known for his witty take on Hollywood's biggest stars. With a sharp instinct for scandal and strategy, he helped shape the public images of some of the biggest names in entertainment.

In 2007, Shuter became Executive Editor of *OK! Magazine*. He later expanded his media presence with the launch of *Naughty But Nice with Rob* on Mark Cuban's HDNet and as co-host of VH1's hit morning show, *The Gossip Table*. His signature style—cheeky, bold, but never mean—earned him fans across TV, print, and digital platforms. He's a regular contributor to outlets like *Good Day New York*, CNN, and *The Wendy Williams Show*.

Printed in Dunstable, United Kingdom

82305008R00170